MARINES DON'T RUN

Baronne saw men spinning, dying, others running, moving out of range, but not soon enough. He aimed his M-16 into a pocket of V.C., squeezed off rounds methodically. There were more than one hundred of them, and more were coming.

"We got to *move*, Colonel—or they'll be on top of us!"

Baronne saw that only the river offered a way out. "We get into the water," he said, "and we're goners."

Bertram peered down the midnight riverbank. "We could try that way."

"No," Baronne said in his smallest voice, as he shook his head. He understood now. He accepted that their only answer was to stand, there, and fight. To stay, do their heroic best, and die, probably. "No, damn it!" Baronne fired into the Cong repeatedly. "We win this one, gentlemen, or we lose it. But here we stay, and here we're going to fight it out!"

A FEW GOOD MEN

"For my money, the author, the men he served with and commanded, and the composite figures about whom he writes with understated but clear affection in his first novel—well, the word for any of them is 'hero.' "

—J. N. Williamson
author of *The Longest Night*

A FEW GOOD MEN

Donald A. Gazzaniga

A SIGNET BOOK

NEW AMERICAN LIBRARY

PUBLISHER'S NOTE

This is a work of fiction. Names, characters, places, and incidents either are the product of the author's imagination or are used fictitiously, and any resemblance to actual persons, living or dead, events, or locales is entirely coincidental.

Copyright © 1988 by Donald A. Gazzaniga

SIGNET, SIGNET CLASSIC, MENTOR, ONYX, PLUME, MERIDIAN and NAL BOOKS are published by NAL PENGUIN INC., 1633 Broadway, New York, New York 10019

First Signet Printing, May, 1989

1 2 3 4 5 6 7 8 9

PRINTED IN THE UNITED STATES OF AMERICA

for the Marines,
without whom there would be
few freedoms remaining

ACKNOWLEDGMENTS

I am indebted to many friends, but especially to Tony DiMarco and Mark Hammond—both of whom kept me going with their continuing encouragement and appreciation for the story.

And to hundreds and thousands of Marines whom you've never seen or heard, but who were nonetheless there—protecting, waiting—admirable, highly trained vanguards.

And to "Scoop" Adams.

Here's health to you and to our Corps
Which we are proud to serve;
In many a strife we've fought for life
And never lost our nerve;
If the Army and Navy
Ever look on Heaven's scenes;
They will find the streets are guarded by
United States Marines.

PART ONE

1

The Score

To prevent this morning's disaster from overwhelming him, Lieutenant Colonel William Baronne prodded his soul-weary Marines through the thick, overgrown jungle down to the river. There had to be a way out of the morass of shit and bungie sticks and mosquitoes and God-knew-what-but-wasn't-telling.

All of Baronne's officers and hundreds of men in his battalion had died in fewer than six hours of intense, early morning fighting. Their faces insisted upon coming to his mind, and when that happened, Baronne's mental bridge was down and all the haunts came swarming across it. "God's own hell couldn't be that bad," he muttered to freshly promoted Master Sergeant John Scales. Soon enough Scales'd be an office poge—ride out the balance of war pushing pencils.

"Yes, sir!" The brisk agreement was automatic, because they were closer than that. Scales was clearly preoccupied. Perhaps he was thinking about the fact that, like Baronne himself, this was his third tour in Vietnam. His last, if he got out alive.

When they'd reached the river, Baronne reminded the sergeant of his one reason for hope. Glancing questioningly toward corporals Spuzetti and Washington, the point men with whom they'd caught up, Baronne added sardonically, "Come to think of it, Scales, this'll be our last tour even if we don't make it."

It was quiet here, aside from the rushing roar of water and the arch protest of bizarre birds that rose squawking into the steel-blue sky like blobs of raucous color. Quiet, except that a gentle breeze moved too many leaves and branches. Helmeted heads looked up, spooked again, expecting the worst.

Two hundred Marines, roughly—it was awful, approximating human lives, but always there was an urgent clock in the belly insisting on telling time in a timeless land—had survived the morning. They'd had just enough strength to drag with them another fifty survivors, roughly; they'd hauled them along on sheer guts, carrying them on makeshift stretchers or Indian-style on toboggans cinched together from ponchos, bamboo sticks, and boot laces. They were all a unit, or they were nothing. From time to time they'd had to be nothing.

"Hold it up!" Gunny Sergeant Trop yelled. Nam-experienced enough to never ask questions, Trop did his job with such dogmatic sureness that no one questioned him either. Baronne watched Trop from his position near an outgrowth of jungle, heard the gunny sergeant grumble about "what a bitch this is to cut through." Trop's combat had been learned in these same killing jungles "back in '66 and '67," as he put it, "when I took one in the ass."

Baronne, smiling tightly, glanced at his once proud battalion. They'd started out innocently enough, he thought. *Damn, what happened?* We were so strong together, the whole Ninth Regiment. He knew the answer, didn't like it. When the VC counterattacked it had split them apart from the 2nd Battalion. T.C.'s men. He hoped that they'd fared better, because his was decimated beyond recognition, and he yearned desperately to say something, do something, that might inject the necessary feeling of strength and pride—something, anything, to help save lives.

But nothing came. Baronne too was exhausted beyond human endurance. Then he jumped. Bird sounds began, or ended, for no reason. Here, movement rushing through the sardined trees was nothing, period, or seemed to turn out so—if your luck held. He blinked away a new dead face, thought of how they weren't running away now. Hell, no! It had cost a great deal, but when they'd found themselves encircled by more Cong than any of them had ever seen before—they'd fought back, to a man. And "beat the shit out of 'em, killed every last mother-loving son of a bitch,"—as grinning little Corporal Spuzzetti had put it—"who even looked Oriental."

The breeze was changing direction slowly, decidedly. Baronne tilted his bearded, sunburnt face toward the rolling river and squinted his eyes tightly together. Was anything remotely out of order? His helmet had become unbuckled long ago; it was dirty, barren of the silver oak leaf he'd long ago earned, waiting, he thought, for the full colonel's eagle, he had coming. Looking steadily down the river, he finally glanced at the chart in his hands.

Scales came alongside. "Can I break 'em?"

They needed rest badly, Baronne knew. Doggedly he jabbed a finger to a spot on the map. "I think we'll be better off here."

Master Sergeant Scales had known Baronne since his first days as a second lieutenant at Camp Fuji in Japan. He'd been one of Baronne's teachers, that being Baronne's first tour. He followed the colonel's long index finger with a growing frown. "Jesus, Colonel," he began, "it'll kill 'em to move that far right now. I dunno."

Baronne's broad shoulders moved in a slight shrug. "It may kill 'em if we don't," he answered. Seeing Scale's homely face, he managed a feeble smile, tugged his canteen from his hip, and offered it. "Here, take a swig of Vat 69, Sergeant. On the house."

Scales shook his head but not with denial. Chuckling, he drank some of the smooth-tasting scotch without saying a word. Returning the canteen, he sighed heavily and immediately walked briskly over to Trop.

William Baronne read Trop's eyes before Scales got there. The spidery Trop had in turn already read Scales's answer. The dark-thunder flash of hatred that seared Trop's brain quickly registered in Baronne's mind. Of course, Trop yearned for a break. They all did.

Like a finely tuned road-racing car that had been entered once too often at too great a distance, the damaged battalion maundered slowly along the river, following its torturously twisting path southward, dragging rifles and backpacks and their wounded.

Corporals Spuzzetti and Washington again provided the point. Washington was a dark, expressionless loner who showed flashes of a keen wit. The two men continually searched for mines or trip wires or snakes, bungie sticks or grid traps, even while being alert to the slightest sign of ambush. All of them walked with nerves twitching, memories from the recent battles indelible in their minds.

Spuzzetti hesitated at each step, looked to his left and right, and up and down, before stepping forward again. Corporal Washington gripped a fifteen-foot bamboo pole in front—"carrot with a stick, 'cept the mule's invisible"—with a bayonet lashed to the probing, distant end. Washington'd step, push the bayonet into the mulch-covered earth, as if he meant to pole-vault with it. When his nerves permitted it, he'd jab firmly, searching for hidden death in the form of buried explosives.

Each advancing step was like that. Spuzzetti hacked away at the brush with his left arm swinging, his right hand clutching his M-16—bullet in the chamber, safety off. The black Washington accompanied Spuzzetti on his pole-and-bayonet instrument.

"Oh, Jesus H. Christ!" Washington gasped.

"Whazzat?" Spuzzetti was immediately frozen in place.

"A fucking wire." Washington hissed the words, "My goddamn pole is tangled on a mother-fucking trip wire!" but Baronne, well back, read his lips and similarly froze.

"Ahhhh-h for chrissakes!" Spuzzetti whispered. He edged closer, keeping the other corporal between the wire and himself, and looked over Washington's shoulder. "Aw, shit. Aw shit."

"Get somebody, Spuzzetti," Washington pleaded. Now his face was alive with expression. "Quick! Get the sergeant."

Saying, "Yeah, yeah," Spuzzetti spun around to run back to the main body.

"Get your ass back there," Trop commanded, already moving forward.

"Sarge, Washington's tangled up with—"

But Trop was brushing past him and the expression on his face confirmed what had happened for every man present. Baronne saw exhaustion become an alertness that could be felt, packaged, and mailed. All the Marines within earshot were braced. Bolts shot forward on M-16s as men jumped to the brooding lip of the jungle which overlooked the river, unable to measure the scope of the danger, informed by their surge of terror to set themselves for the worst.

Colonel Baronne had loped forward to intercept Trop and Spuzzetti yards from where Washington was as rigid as some great Ethiopian sculpture. Baronne maintained his calm demeanor; he even felt calm. Long ago he'd learned that the men could not afford watching their senior officers becoming overly excited.

"Take whoever you need, Sergeant," Baronne ordered. He didn't insult Trop by telling him to be careful. Both men understood that since the wire hadn't exploded any device yet, it must either be hooked to a friction fuse—or nothing at all.

Trop nodded, then pointed to the three men nearby. Together with Spuzzetti, they headed for the sweating, frozen Washington.

Baronne stood stock-still, watching as they merged with the greenery, and then glancing around at his men who had, without requiring the orders, built a quick defensive perimeter of sorts. To protect themselves and their helpless comrade.

Perhaps it will be all right, the tall colonel reflected, *this time.* Smiling tightly in admiration for his remnant of troops, unwilling to think of what could happen to Washington or the others, Baronne trudged through the thick underbrush and vines toward Sergeant Scales. He had to lift his long legs over fallen trees; he wasn't surprised to find Scales staring out at the noisy, deceptive river.

"See anything?"

Scales grunted. "No." He turned from the water, looked off at the tableau of Washington, wary amidst Trop, Spuzzetti, and the others.

"Ka-boom!" Chunks of ancient Vietnamese earth and

American men rose into the sky simultaneously with the explosion. After the instant of booming thunder, debris appeared at once to rise and drop. Then silence.

Baronne and Scales, along with two other Marines who had stationed themselves with the river to their backs, were on the site within seconds.

The scene was hideous in part because it was redundant. Corporal Washington was dead, a piece of the bamboo still tightly clutched in his hand. So were Spuzzetti, Trop, the others. There would be no more hatred anymore, no way for Trop to reflect on his distaste for this war, these people, and how, more than murdering his men, the enemy seemed to be murdering their spirit.

The bayonet Washington had held before him in his strong hands was twisted, the handle ashes.

"My God," Scales said.

"It's always—so fucking sudden," said Private Davis, the stubby, rosy-cheeked radio operator. "Jesus, they—they—"

Davis stepped back as if executing an about-face and vomited into the brush with sounds like strangling.

William Baronne stood straight, motionless, looking as much inside as at the stricken men. He was afraid of what would happen to him if he moved. A tear rolled down his cheek, making him glad. Because he knew that it was solely not for these men who had just perished, but for all the good men who perished before them. He'd seen so many really fine men die—disappearing from Mother Earth in ways that no deity pure or evil could have or would have invented. One second later, this latest horror seemed already distant.

He was a tough son of a bitch, but was sensitive too. He started to speak to Scales.

"Sir?" Before Baronne had quite succeeded in speaking.

Bill Baronne shook his head slowly, his eyes closing. He inhaled deeply from the direction of the uncritical river. "We must bury what we can."

2

Marines Don't Run

Night closed around them like a clam.

But in Nam, night scooped up a lot of other things—including the enemy—and sealed them in together.

Long ago, drugs to kill the pain of the wounded, or camouflage it, had run out. The stillness of twelve night hours stitched together without any glimmer of light burning awakened nerve endings only the witching hour could arouse. Unwanted, terrifying memories were born anew in Nam by night, and lent clear meaning to the wailing, agonized cries for help.

Those who were physically whole were pushed to the ragged edge. Here sanity mingled with insanity and didn't always go home with the Marine who brought it. Added to this was the sound of strange creatures that hissed as they moved through the razorlike grass. Gate-crashing shadows swung through the trees or popped out in a flash from dangling, dark vines. All of it blended into a night music only lunatics or the native Vietnamese could find restful.

"I thought the jungle'd be like, you know, Tarzan's jungles," Davis whispered. The whites of his eyes flashed in the blackness. "They're not, they're fucking eerie. It ain't the same, Sarge."

"Sh-h!" Scales was sitting on the ground, leaning against his backpack, which in turn was pushed between him and an inky tree.

Private Davis sighed, continued his complaint: "It's just that—"

"Davis," Scales rumbled, close to the boy's ear, "you know what sh-h means? Huh?"

The private, shifting in a mixture of annoyance at being yelled at and ongoing fear, didn't answer. *Edgar Rice Burroughs and Tarzan'd puke at this hole,* he thought. Still afraid he'd looked chicken when he threw up, he turned the squelch knob on his radio till it hissed back at the shushing Scales. Immediately he cut off the sound and leaned back against his tree, shaking his head.

He died from a bullet that penetrated his forehead. Entering just above his stubby nose, it freely dispersed his brains as it came out the side of his obliterated head and lodged itself in the tree.

Scales had rolled over and flattened to the ground, M-16 pulled with him and properly pointed straight ahead, before Davis could have been legally pronounced dead. The rifle poked into the black night like a needle point into a giant-sized bowl of black raspberry Jello. All around him he heard others diving for cover and milling around, but it wasn't possible to be certain all of them were Marines. Scales shouted, "Night scope! Who's got the fuckin' Starlight?"

"Over here, Sarge," said Corporal Brannigan, sometimes called Tubs.

"Come on over here, man—quick."

Brannigan crawled on the ground as flat as the brush, vines, and the body of Private Davis would permit. Once, a thousand nights ago, Brannigan had called his residue of babyfat his "cushion against Cong luck," claiming no Nam slug would "reach anything vital." He'd seen the truth when Fats Levin got it. "Here," he whispered, handing the special rifle to Scales.

Scales lifted the weapon and night scope up, clicking it into place, and peered off into the direction from which Davis's bullet had come. "Horseshit." The scope had come up bright, green, and full of jungle. Scales guided it slowly right, then left. "Nothing. Just jungle."

"What did ya expect?" Tubs asked.

"Charleys. Slopes. V.C. Gooks. Bastards! What the mother-hump you think I was expecting, Santa fucking Claus?" He looked back intently into the scope. "Hold it." Scales shifted his elbows on the hard ground, adjusting the weapon additionally. He didn't even glance at Tubs Brannigan. "Get the colonel."

Brannigan stared at him from wide eyes. "Me?"

"For chrissakes, Tubs, move your fat ass before we're both statistics."

Galvanized by Scales's suggestion, Brannigan disappeared on his formerly protuberant belly. Scales stayed motionless, keeping a fix with his scope on the identified target, scarcely breathing for fear of giving away his position. It felt like an eternity until he sensed Baronne crawling up behind him. The master sergeant had gotten to the point where he could name most of his men just from the way they crawled. Colonel Baronne always crawled too low to be spotted by an enemy at ground level. He had learned to slither like a serpent.

"What you got?"

"Charley," Scales replied without glancing up from the scope. "Colonel, he's looking right back at me."

"A scope? Him too?"

"That's right, Colonel, a Starlight. And unless I'm mistaken, one of ours."

"Is he certain what he's looking at?"

"Don't know. Can't tell for sure. Shall I plunk him in the ass?"

There was barely a pause. "No. No, not yet."

"Why? Why not?" Scales neither quite understood nor could accept the negative response.

"Scales, he could be the point for a much larger unit." Baronne silently inclined his head to other Marines to the rear. "I want to get the wounded moved first."

"Uh-h," Scales swallowed, "he's not gone stay there forever. He's not setting up house and picking out the furniture, Colonel."

"Hmm-m." Baronne started to move off. "Just give us five."

"Five? The fucker could shoot me first."

"Yes, that's true." Baronne began edging away. "Thing is, Scales, he's got his own problem figuring out what his scope is telling him!"

"He figured out Davis," Scales whispered as loudly as he dared.

"But Davis,"—Baronne came back, smiling—"Davis was white." He slid backward, then moved off toward the wounded.

Scales itched and didn't know if it was sweat, a bug that looked like it came from Neptune, or nerves. Swallowing hard, he stayed motionless, thought of deer hunting, and duck hunting, and fishing for cat—remembered holding his pole uttering steady. Despite himself, he saw Charley, Charley-at-the-other-end of this military expo, deadly as a cobra on the toes of his boots. *That ain't no deer out there,* he thought, wishing that he could scratch.

"He still there?" Baronne had returned more quietly even than usual.

Scales started to jerk in fear, narrowly kept control. "Jesus, Lieutenant," he began, then chuckled softly. "Colonel, I mean."

"I'll get you for that someday," Baronne told his old friend. "Lock you to a desk."

"Maybe not." Scales felt his fingers begin to pain him from the enduring grip. "Charley's still out there."

"It's okay. The men are formed along a line to our right; there are none to our left, Sergeant. Wounded are back about a hundred yards, down in a ditch."

Scales's voice was a tight fist starting to open up. "Kill him now, then?"

"When you are ready."

Scales's rifle fired.

But Charley didn't budge. And neither did his scope.

Scales gaped through his own scope, knowing he'd hit his target. He fired again anyway, in case the other man could return his shot.

Still nothing.

Scales dropped down low, his head beside Baronne's. He breathed like an asthmatic. "Gawd, Colonel—he was already dead."

"Or a dummy."

"No, uh-uh." Scales shook his head. "No way. That man killed Davis."

Bill Baronne thought hard. "You remember back in '57? Recall what happened to T.C. on that first tour?"

"Yeah . . . but those were our guys."

Baronne couldn't help but wonder how far away T.C. and his battalion were now, and if there was any chance of his close friend's troops meeting up with his decimated unit. He responded quietly to Scales. "They were Vietnamese. This is the same country, Sergeant. Same tactics, same lunatic games."

"Then that means . . ." Scales's eyes opened wide. "God damn it!"

They jumped up, began running back, yelling for the other Marines to face in the opposite direction, to pick up and run to the wounded, to help them—be ready for anything, now. Yet the wounded remained in the ditch where Colonel Baronne had put them for safety.

For a moment no one could time, uniformed men tripped, bumped, searched for a safe route, wondered if they'd ever see daylight again. Then they fell silent except for labored breathing and frightened gasps.

"Nothing," Scales said, scarcely a whisper. But there was no need for silence now. "Nobody coming for us, and we're out here—"

"Damn it!" Baronne swore. "Goddamn it, the wounded are back there."

Scales blinked, mumbled something, and added, "It's not your fault."

"The hell." Baronne snapped. "Check out the area with the scope—fast." Then he left his master sergeant, darted up and down the ragged line, checking on his remaining troops. They had to be prepared; none of them could possibly figure out what was happening. Then Baronne took what was left of the Baker Company, moved them back to face off the rear, and returned to Scales. "Anything?"

"Yes sir," Scales said hoarsely in low tones. His hand was again steady on his scope. "There's a bunch of 'em out there, Colonel, and they look loaded for bear."

Baronne bit his lower lip, choked it out: "And the wounded?"

"I don't think, sir, that they've found 'em yet. I don't think." It was still darker than Scale's hand by many shades.

"We gotta get them out of that ditch."

"Colonel," Scales said evenly, "we gonna have to wait. If we move to that ditch now, we're all dead."

Baronne's head jerked to face the muscular shadow before him. "You saying there's too many of 'em for us to attack?"

Scales handed Baronne the rifle with the night scope.

Bill, taking it promptly, eagerly, scanned the area ahead of them. For a few moments he saw nothing. Not until he'd looked past the brush, and the jungle—

And pinpointed the enemy. Baronne inhaled sharply.

There were hundreds of V.C. heads bobbing up and down, all but beyond counting. Apparently they were passing supplies along a line, shifting them from right to left and back again for more. Baronne carefully moved the light-giving rifle in the direction of the ditch, but failed to see any of his wounded, in sight.

"I'm going up to the ditch," Baronne said.

"Ah, Colonel," Scales began, "didn't you tell me once that it isn't good leadership for the commanding officer to be the designated hero?"

"Right, I did. So—you come with me."

"Colonel Baronne, sir! Pardon, please, but if we're killed, who's going to get the rest of the battalion out of this mess?"

"All right, I read you." Baronne turned. "You can stay."

"Aw, Colonel," Scales sighed. Baronne had done it to him again. "I'll go."

"Look, Scales." The colonel smiled and clapped Scales's shoulder. "I merely want to know that they're okay. And, well, that they understand we know what's happening,—that we're still here." He sobered. "I don't want you to play hero, either."

Scales, crawling efficiently, vanished into the night. Watching through the scope, Baronne held his breath until he saw the master sergeant drop into the ditch. Then he lowered the rifle and momentarily buried his face in his hands, eyes tightly shut, trying to shake away his weariness.

"Colonel?" It was Private Adams's somewhat nasal voice.

Bill looked up and around, but could only hear Adams's breath, stentorous in the pitch-black night. "Yes?"

"Sergeant Bravo says we got company—moving around behind us."

Would it never stop? Didn't the Cong ever sleep, like human beings? Baronne whirled to raise the scope to the rear and squinted into it for all he was worth.

Nothing. He saw nothing. "Lead me to Bravo," he told the enlisted man, dropping to his knees and motioning.

They crawled off together, Adams slithering just ahead. It was hard to put Scales and the wounded out of his mind. How long until daylight now?

Within approximately fifteen feet the two of them had reached Sergeant Bravo. Only a couple of feet away could Baronne even discern the bulky outline where Bravo knelt, raising his arm to point.

"Over there," Bravo reported emotionlessly.

The colonel raised the rifle with the scope, scanned his search, and then froze. "Jesus," he said aloud, sagging in on himself. "We have ourselves a bunch of damned V.C. all around us."

Bravo only grunted as if he'd expected it.

Private Adams was breathing heavily through his nose. They seemed like a trio of drawfs where they knelt, almost in an attitude of prayer. "Are we surrounded, Colonel?"

3

The Ditch

William Baronne had always considered the sun his friend.

When he'd been Big Bill Baronne for the University of Southern California, he'd preferred day games, watching the mounted Trojan gallop past with golden rays rebounding from his glittering armor. When he'd skied or swam or hiked, Baronne had always preferred early morning—growing into the new day.

But in Vietnam, Baronne had found that at least one memory from his Southern California boyhood had been turned upside down. Nighttime could be as friendly as daytime, he had learned, and because he valued his life and those lives of his men, he was convinced that darkness was a helluva lot more comforting now than he could ever remember it being at home.

He had come to appreciate it mostly, though, because he could sneak up on the enemy. The top brass had another term for it, "Covert strategical operation," and "Surprise the GD hell out of 'em."

It was the night scope that had often provided Baronne with the edge he sought and capitalized on. But when the enemy also had recourse to night scopes—almost unfailingly acquired by capturing the unique weapon from fallen American soldiers—it made his life tougher. The protective shadows of night yielded as before the spying equipment of the K.G.B.

Now, trapped so suddenly along the inky river, Baronne was faced with the choice of moving his men from this silent circle of enclosing terror or waiting until daylight, obliged to fight their way out through what appeared to be overwhelming odds.

A three-stripe sergeant, an Indian named Sequoya, older than Baronne or even Scales, spoke in his long-time smoker's rasp. "Colonel, the slopes know we're here."

Baronne's eyes glazed as he tried to make out the massive Sequoya's features. The man had put into words what the colonel himself had known inside, but had not wished to express. "Yeah, Sarge, I think you're right. They've tracked us all the way." He knelt at the center of a rough circle of noncommissioned officers. He knew that they had come to him as much to see if they might help as to seek his reassurance. Sighing heavily, he looked into each of their shadow-etched, exhausted faces. He could not lie to them. "And there's no help coming, Sequoya. I'm afraid it's our hour, our battle."

"You mean, there won't be any cavalry?" Sequoya chuckled hoarsely and smothered a rising cough.

A corporal named Bertram, whom Baronne knew had been a sergeant knocked back down the chain of command for some infraction, wiped his perspiring face. "Be getting light shortly," he said. The message was implicit and Baronne nodded. An experienced career Marine, Bertram was telling him to make a decision before it was taken from his hands.

Sergeant Scales, panting slightly, seemed to materialize in their midst, and Baronne resisted the impulse to hug him. Scales brought one piece of heartening news. "The wounded are undetected," he told them wonderingly.

Sequoya scowled. "But Charley still has the scope," he rasped. "Bastard won't leave 'em alone for long."

"Their courage," Scales said, "man, it's astronomical. Most of 'em are in one helluva lot of pain and they know what the enemy will do if he catches 'em, but they're holding it down. Not a peep out of them."

Baronne seized Scales's hard bicep and squeezed it. "Let's go get 'em out. And move south—down the water from here."

"That's a big gamble."

Baronne's jaw was set. "You want to wait till daylight and chance that?"

Scales, at first hesitating, nodded. Judging from the glimmer of illumination making an already ghostly scene eerier, they had thirty minutes tops if they meant to retrieve their wounded and pick their way out of the enemy trap.

"The ditch isn't deep. Everybody's got to stay low." Scales, who was accustomed to Nam nights if any American was, scanned the perimeter for his most trusted men—the ones who remained alive. "Bertram, get your ass into the ditch. Recon to the end, follow? Make sure it leads to the river."

The war-tested ex-sergeant headed down the ditch, bent double, and was swallowed by the darkness. Baronne knew those wounded who were able were scooping up those who were not. Already they were slowly trailing down the cut-out, hoping they might follow it around the bend of the river.

Other men, weapons at the ready, stayed flat at the crest of the shallow ravine, prepared to hold back any attack that came. Then Bertram, more gray ghost than man now, was back. His white teeth caught the moonlight like a vampire's fangs. "It leads right into the water."

Baronne motioned the men to continue, and they slipped through the darkling morning southward toward the safe side of the river. His other men guarded the route, lying on the crest, then rolling over the edge and dropping into the ditch as the column passed.

Seconds later, Bill moved to the head of his shabby column, alert to the enemy's presence and the threat of daylight. He was so tired his mind tried to fall into sleep with his sagging body. *It really hasn't been that long since Quantico and basic training,* he pondered, thinking of T.C., Greene, and the others. Of those peaceful years at U.S.C.

Scales broke into his reverie. "Point's at the river."

"Keep 'em moving."

"Yes sir."

"Tell 'em—" He paused. When he looked at his column of troops, he was reminded of some zombie march in a silly old late-movie flick. "Tell 'em to keep their goddamned eyes open." The command sounded hollow, useless.

But Scales's head bobbed and, bent at the waist, he trotted back to the point. For a moment Baronne watched him as his men trudged by, slow and still because of exhaustion as well as fear. They trusted him to lead them from the disaster they were gradually leaving in the past. A disaster planned by those who were waiting for the sun, eager to advance the glory of Ho.

"We gonna make it, Colonel?"

The face was young but aging by the minute. The voice and the loyal face belonged to seventeen-year-old Brian Johnson, and Bill had recognized the high-pitched, whispered whine. What surprised him was the look of gnarled maturity that he saw behind Johnson's watchful eyes. The kid's M-16 was straddled over his left arm, his right hand ready on the trigger housing guard, his index finger ever readier at the trigger. Macho cool, that'd been young Brian Johnson's way to keep going. It'd kept him taut with tension but ready as hell.

"We gonna make it, Private," Baronne assured him. Johnson's face, barely visible beneath a helmet that seemed grotesquely large, was absorbing grease and dirt for his zits.

Bill smiled. "We gonna make it!"

"But we ain't running away from them. Are we, Colonel?"

Baronne was startled by the question. The lessons he'd learned a hundred years ago spun into his troubled brain. Colonel McNeil had joked, "Marines never retreat, men. Never bug out or cop out. We may advance to the rear—an aggressive retrograde . . ."

God knows where McNeil was now. Dead maybe. If he'd been fortunate, passed away in an easy chair while he was watching Huntley and Brinkley. For all Baronne knew, McNeil was somewhere else on this godforsaken—

"No," he whispered to young Johnson, abruptly aware of how long he'd taken to answer. "When we've returned the wounded, we'll be back." Then he leaned down slightly to whisper the words officers were not allowed to let enlisted men hear them utter. "And we'll kick the mother-fucking piss out of the bastards."

Blinking, Johnson grinned and walked along with the tail of the column just passing their position. He even lifted his hand to the colonel, thumb and index finger linked and the other three fingers raised in an A-OK.

At the head of the column, Master Sergeant Scales was pushing his men along the river bank. Maximum distance from their previous position was mandatory. Again his antennae were out, his sense honed to register even shifts in the air. He knew the sun was coming up fast because the sky had developed a grayish-blue hue which poked fingers of light down to the floor of the thinning jungle. They were, Scales saw, approaching an open area flanking a wide spot in the river. Exiting one threat, entering another again.

He motioned the column to stop, his command ricocheting back to Colonel Baronne the way dominoes are evenly toppled.

"See something?" Corporal Dobbins rasped.

Shaking his head, Scales raised his index finger to his lips. He slipped his helmet off, separated the pith cover, and dropped it to the earth. Holding the helmet top to his right ear, Scales slowly oscillated his head, using the helmet as a concave radar disk that would accentuate any noises beyond the commonplace. His eyes informed the men near him that they'd better be watching while he was listening. Each man responded by swiveling their heads in every direction.

"Nothing," Scales said at last. Satisfied, he lowered his helmet and smiled tightly at Dobbins. "That Indian make it this far?"

"Sequoya? Yeah, he's carrying Sergeant Timmons."

"Get him. Replace him. Send him here." Dobbins took off promptly and a few moments later, Scales recognized the tall, dark-skinned Cherokee who always wore two feathers in his helmet and a mean scowl on his face. "Sequoya, you see that clearing ahead?"

"I see it." His lower jaw masticated the plan distastefully. "You want me to be a target?"

"Shit, Chief, we've had enough targets." Scales sighed. "I want you to search the perimeter of the clearing. To move all the way around it."

"Across the river too?"

"Across the river too."

"Take awhile. Got to move through a lot of bush."

Scales looked at his watch. "You got ten minutes, Chief."

"Christ, Sarge, I—"

"Now."

The Indian, accepting the order, turned his hatchet-faced profile to look at a fate he halfway anticipated. "What if I run into something? We ain't got no radios, Sergeant."

Scales shook his head. Why couldn't these men figure things out for themselves now and then? "You don't run into something, big Chief. If something is there, spot it and come back. Crap, I don't want this column moving through that area just to be wiped out."

Sequoya had nothing else to say. Wordlessly, noiselessly, he seemed to disappear from the spot as if he had never existed.

Corporal Roberts, not as tall as Scales and not nearly as tall as Bill Baronne, was as wide as the two of them put together. Sometimes he complained that he should get extra combat pay for being too generous a target. "Sarge, what happens next—if the Indian don't come back?"

Scales spat. "For chrissakes, Roberts," he retorted, "for a brother, you are sure dumb. That goddamned redskin's probably the only one of us who will survive."

Baronne appeared at the head of the column, concerned about the halt. To his amazement he felt his customary mental sharpness click back into place. He felt nearly as good as he had three days before, the last time he remembered sleeping. "What's the score, Scales?"

"Chief's out checking," Scales reported. As he turned to look at his colonel, he recalled their first days back in Japan when Lieutenant William Baronne was just a young Marine. He had been an officer who'd had sound ideas, an innate grasp of battle tactics, which Scales had at first doubted, then admired.

"Slopes are gonna find we launched an aggressive retrograde in a few minutes."

"Yes sir, imagine so."

"And they'll be coming down that ditch like floodwater out of a drain."

Scales paused. He glanced at the men around him, then back to Baronne. "Clearing's a real setup, Colonel."

"What about crossing the river?"

"Might not fucking make it with the wounded."

Baronne's smile at Scales's peremptory obedience in front of the men was a flicker. The air was still, hot. Wasn't like hot air other places, civilized places. The sun wasn't even full in the sky and this goddamned stinking Nam air made a man feel he was waking up in a casket, six feet under. Annoyed, Baronne looked up in the direction of the sun.

But what he saw put him flat on the ground as everyone else followed suit. An F-4 jet was streaking overhead no more than fifty feet above the tops of the queer, alien trees. And as Baronne and the others stared, it released a napalm bomb.

Bill closed his eyes. Seconds passed before the bomb smacked into the ground, safely behind the column and near—prayerfully near!—the entrenched Cong.

"Jesus H. Christ," Baronne automatically shouted.

"How'd they know the V.C. was there?"

Baronne shook his head at Scales. "Dunno."

"Davis, maybe. Maybe Davis got through on the radio."

Baronne closed his eyes briefly. He knew it was hard to remember who was alive and who wasn't. "Davis is dead."

Scales did not reply at once. The jet, passing overhead

again, waggled its wings, then disappeared. Scales said into the silence. "I meant, before he died."

Bill, still stretched flat on the earth, turned his head sideways to look steadily at Scales. Over the years, Scales had been loyal, dependable, and fearless—without taking dumb chances. He pushed himself to his feet and offered his sergeant a hand.

Sequoya rose from the brush like the dead. "Clear." He showed no surprise at seeing Baronne at the head of the column. "Clear all the way around." He pointed along the river past the open area. "And there's a way to ford the river right where the woods begin again."

Baronne felt full of life. He jerked his head in that way Scales knew so well. "Move 'em out, Sergeant," he ordered.

The column passed safely through the open area, as Sequoya had predicted, and found that the Indian had referred to a sandbar. Carefully, one by one, they began moving across the river.

Baronne took a position beside the river as the men stepped out ahead of him, some carrying the wounded, others toting their packs, weapons, and the heavy burden of death that they all felt by now awaited them. All of them, even the youngest, seemed so old. Had others, jealous of youth, magically wished it on them?

His three tours in Nam had forced him to take a new view of the Nam oldsters. They had become a collection of lunatics. Wasn't it they who had invented the cruel traps and weapons so damned peculiar to the place, the same horrible implements that killed so many of his young men? *Damn them,* he cursed to himself. *Why should they be allowed to continue walking here?* Living? Such small, crusted men, like last week's dinner rolls. His mind had collated the images now, everything was suddenly so clear. These old men had poppyseed eyes imbedded in wrinkled faces that never moved except for the gaping mouths which barked meaningless retorts with all the belligerent authority these grandfathers could muster. Nothing was true but what they said was true. They claimed the life of a private, knowing only the delusions of the institutionalized mad. *And if I am not careful, I may become one of them.*

When all the rest of the Marines had already stepped onto the bar, Baronne saw a corporal named Luke Williams. Bent at the waist, his knees were nearly buckling beneath the additional weight of a Marine who'd been worse wounded. The grimy, scared Williams had just entered the open area and could hardly walk or stand.

Bill looked across the river to Scales. He pointed in Williams's direction, motioning that he himself would run back to help.

Scales nodded and pulled his M-16 from his shoulder. Enlisting two men, he ran up the riverbank to take a position from which they could protect the colonel and the men.

William Baronne let his guard down. Running into the opening, right along the bank, he remembered, fleetingly, all the times he'd run in a similarly carefree way, as a boy. Puffing, he reached Corporal Williams and motioned the Marine to lower his wounded comrade so that Baronne could scoop him up. Williams smiled gratefully. He eased the injured man down from his shoulders.

A shot was fired from virtually nowhere and Williams dropped, startled, to his knees. He looked once at Baronne, then fell forward on his face.

Baronne stooped behind Williams's dead body at once, pulling the wounded but still living Marine toward him, struggling to save one of these two young lives. Glancing down, he looked into the wounded man's eyes—and saw how dead he was. Luke Williams had been carrying a dead man. Probably all night.

Bill became aware that across the river Scales and his men were pouring heavy fire into the area from which the single shot had come. "Colonel!" The master sergeant's aged voice carried incredibly well, galvanizing Baronne. "Get the hell out of there!"

Immediately Baronne ran for the bar on the river. A massive target, he ducked, swerved, and twisted as Scales's party continued the barrage. Baronne leaped out on the bank, confident now.

That's when another single shot blazed from the jungle behind him, piercing his flack jacket and striking him in the back. Out of reach of his men on the opposite side of the river, the colonel fell just short of the water.

Sergeant Scales wasted no time. Whirling, he threw down his rifle and, casting his helmet aside as well, ran to the river and jumped in. He was wading at first, then able to swim with long, desperate strokes. Additional Marines joined the raging battle, firing round after round into the jungle across the water.

Small, vicious geysers spouted around Scales: enemy gunfire. Several of his men fell back, wounded from the return barrage. Sequoya screamed: "Scales! Come back, man. You can't do anything to help him!"

Roberts called: "The colonel's dead, Sarge!"

The Indian's tone surprised Scales, stopped him. Roberts crying out added impact. He dove under the water and returned to the shoreline near the place he had vacated. While Marines covered his return with heavy fire, two jumped down to assist Scales up and over the brushy, protective parapet. Exhausted, nearly in shock, Scales lay gasping for a moment.

"Nice try, Sergeant," Roberts said, his broad bulk blocking out the sun.

"He hasn't moved since he went down," Sequoya told Scales.

"You can't save the dead," Bertram, his eyes on the colonel, put in.

"But he isn't!" Scales exclaimed. He got to his knees, twisting around until water sprayed from him as from a shaking German shepard. "So fuck that, Jack." Scales stood, staring across the river to where Baronne lay unmoving. "Nobody gonna kill my man, you hear? Nobody!" He looked around wildly until he found his M-16. "He's our main man, you got that? Nobody's killing him!"

Before any of the others could move, Scales fired furiously across the river as he rushed down the bank. "Follow me, Gyrenes!" he yelled. "We gonna bring our main man back!"

The fusillade of bullets ripped through Scales's powerful body, and sent shrapnel and vital body parts spinning like skyrockets. His blood splashed out in geysers of crimson while he went on shouting. Scales walked forward like that for another five feet, as if he might cross the river alone and fulfill his self-appointed mission. He went on firing his weapon through the rising water and unbroken hail of bullets and his own torrent of blood.

Then he bent at the waist, as if to pick something up, fell over, and began floating face down in the river. At once, his body moved southward with the flow as if he might somehow be swimming.

But it was just another dead body in a country where dead bodies clad in green were commonplace, and crusted grandfathers with poppyseed eyes thought they could win a war by counting bodies.

4

Genesis

The heat was intense, the air stifling, and the dust choking. The river moved slowly, shifting twigs and dead leaves—and a few bodies—southward.

In the open meadow, scores of V.C. moved in the same direction, stepping over Corporal Williams and his deceased companion, booting their bodies, sometimes prodding them with bayonets or long, cruel sticks. The camouflage and footwear had already been stripped and were now worn by one of the enemy. The Marines' M-16s had gone to war against their comrades who lived.

Earlier in the day, avid men clad in the familiar, mundane clothing of the North Vietnamese Army had rolled William Baronne's body over the bank, down to the water. Now his legs and arms were beginning to burn black from the throbbing sun; he was actually *tanning*.

Bill Baronne was not dead.

He'd wished—prayed—they'd shove him into the water so that he'd float away like so many of the others. Instead he'd been left to rot—stripped of his uniform and boots, his canteen belt and helmet, his pistol, of course.

He was barely aware of the enemy around. He passed out and regained consciousness, then passed out again. His face was pressed into the dry dirt, his nose breathing shallowly, his gut and lungs trying desperately to stay motionless. He wanted to survive, to live through this, to fight again. His power was centered in the brain and Baronne knew it; mind over matter, brain over pain.

His wounded shoulder ached like hell. His broken rib stabbed something—probably pushing against his lung, piercing his whole nerve center. Yet Baronne disciplined the urge to yell out for aid, to cry out in pain. He waited for the enemy to go away or his friend, the darkness of night, to arrive.

In order to banish the intensity of the pain, Baronne scanned the inside of his eyelids for pictures of happier times. There, at least, he could escape, detach himself from the sound of the marching feet a few feet away along the Mekong River.

He could slow the movement of time, relive pleasant experiences. *Oh God, why didn't I go to law school or medical school or become a vet or something?*

"Because," the man standing before him in his mind said directly, "You wanted to be a gung-ho, foot-stomping, crisply uniformed, macho son of a bitch, that's why!"

"I'm not that gung-ho."

"Yes. Yes, you are." T.C. was definite.

"Besides, you can be a son of a bitch at times," Greene added cheerfully as, in memory, they debarked from the C-141, arriving for their second tour in Vietnam.

"I'm a perfectionist," Bill answered them, smiling.

"That's why you're a major, now."

"What about you?" he was addressing Don Greene.

"I'm getting out after this tour."

"That's nuts." Bill was hesitant, sorry. "Put in a lot of years already."

"But I don't like it the way you do."

The remembering Baronne paused, then responded, "I want things to work. And I work hard to make 'em work."

"Ease up," T.C. chided, "sometimes you're too intense."

He wanted to turn his head, to stretch his neck muscles in the other direction, to switch nostrils for breathing. "You can't do that, dummy," he shouted, only inside his shell. "Those smelly gooks will carve you into flotsam."

He stopped thinking for an instant. He concentrated instead on the neat magic trick of breathing. He felt the hot air scorching his lungs, his bare skin burning, dust plugging his nose—almost choking him with each cautious inhalation.

He'd long ago learned to ignore the voracious, man-eating flies that crawled stubbornly over his body and buzzed menacingly from time to time around his ears and eyes.

"I sat in that goddamned Jap hole for three days, watching them, trying to hide while all those golf-ball-sized flies swarmed around me. One slap, that's all I wanted, just one slap and I'd be happy. But no, I couldn't do that. They would have heard me and I'd be dead."

Baronne asked the speaker, an Army colonel, "How in hell could anyone possibly sit in a swarm of flies like that, pretending to be dead among other dead soldiers, and not give himself away?"

The Army colonel looked down from the basic-school stage. He chuckled loudly and boasted, "It wasn't easy. But it kept me alive."

White spots floated around the darkness of Baronne's eyelids, darting here and there, trailing black squiggly lines, falling and then climbing, shooting left and right—could he be going blind? Baronne took a chance and squinted them tightly, then loosened the lids. Incredibly, they made a noise that was sudden and seemed outrageously loud. Terrified, he waited for the long V.C. bayonet to pierce his back, but it didn't come. He experimented with squinting again and the white dots were gone. Privately he smiled. He'd pulled a fast one on Charley. He might even live.

He found himself standing on an asphalt path outside Bovard Field, next to the gymnasium this time, shouting for T.C. to hurry. It was good, it felt free, this memory. He could certainly handle being with T.C., back on campus in Los Angeles—graduating.

But when T.C. dashed from the N.R.O.T.C. doorway to join Bill in their run to the Doheny Library where ceremonies were about to begin, a sharp bayonet poked his buttocks, startling him with the yawning awfulness of disorientation and nearly giving him away. Snapped to the present, he heard the foreign chatter of the Vietnamese. Then they laughed and walked away, satisfied by the trail of crimson from one buttock that Bill was dead.

Before his newest pain could matter much, Baronne was stunned by a sporadic burst of gunfire. His men were moving farther and farther away. A burst was always followed by a stillness until the Cong continued the chase. It pissed him off knowing that Charley would definitely slaughter his wounded men if they were caught.

He counted, more or less, to ten. Nothing happened. His skin burned and the flies' activity intensified. The pain came back. He had to escape into his thoughts again, his past . . .

The grass was nearly dead no matter what the grounds keepers did to it. Water and fertilizer and seed couldn't fight off the penetrative cleats. USC had a powerhouse team and Tom Chapman was a key to the offense. He ran the ball and ran it well, often behind the blocking of tight end William Baronne.

Every day. Bovard Field. Run and pass and block and bruise their bodies. And on Thursdays, march on the same field in their Navy R.O.T.C. uniforms.

God! he thought in wonder, drifting almost to a hovering position above his own wrecked body, those were such simple years. His wounded shoulder filled with acute pain. His mind blanked for a moment until the white dots floated back and became one with gold buttons. He was graduating with T.C. They were wearing their Marine Corps dress whites for the first time and listening to graduation speeches that confidently promised a safer, cleaner, warless world. The speakers supported the Eisenhower administration policies, spoke ringingly of their splendid education, America and its strength and purpose, the future.

"Bullshit!"

T.C. looked at him, surprised. "What?"

"I said, it's all bullshit."

"How can you be so cynical?" Chapman laughed at his friend's curt analysis while they walked quickly to their swearing-in ceremony.

"Not cynical, just realistic. How can they know all

that? They've been wrong before and they're full of crap now."

"Whew! Bear, you're so damned absolute."

Bill smiled and rolled his eyes to move the pus that had been forming during the heat of the day. He listened intently to gunfire that again broke the silence.

"You hear that, T.C? I was right, damn it." He spoke the words in his head but nearly coughed. He kept the Cong at bay by exhaling slowly, purposefully. Shadows began to cover his eyes. The sun was easing down upon the horizon. Night would arrive soon.

"Sweet Jesus, do I need you now, Tom. Where the hell are you?"

"Over here, Bear." His voice was soft, at once close and so distant. "Goddamn, Bear, look—a snake!"

Baronne's crusted eye snapped open painfully in the direction of the longest cobra he'd seen yet in Vietnam. For a moment Bill and the glittering, bronze-eyed serpent regarded each other. It wasn't coming directly for his face, Baronne realized. Instead it was angling, moving parallel with his body—but near it. When it vanished from view, Baronne rolled his pus-filled eye to see if V.C. were still in the area. Almost simultaneously he felt the slithering touch of the cobra and saw a Cong soldier snapping his handgun into a dead aim.

The cobra jerked up, its hood flaring—and two shots rang out in close succession. Charley, grinning, stepped idly over Baronne's body to grab the dead snake, wave it in the air, and, shouting exultantly in Vietnamese, move away with the main course of that evening's meal.

"Only the really immoral girls go to bed with you," T.C. explained during one of the nightly—and mandatory—fraternity dinners. Brother Kazinski had given T.C. and the others a doorway they enjoyed walking through.

"And only the most godless men would drag them there in the unmarried state." Bear Baronne always tried to help T.C. explain their seemingly terminal virginity. "I've always wondered which state that is?"

"Pit the godless men!" Kazinski said, and laughed.

"You speaketh truth, Kazz," brother Farr put in

pompously. "Man dare not sleep for long without sexual outlet."

"Right. What about the dreaded semen backup?" brother Jenkins inquired with a wink at Baronne.

"Only sailors have seaman backup," T.C. chuckled.

Night came on blessedly and he knew that the Vietnamese had passed through. There were no fires, no inexplicable new sounds. Soon he could leave. But he'd wait a little longer, guarding against the chance of another trap. Wait until he was sure. *Lord, I probably can't move now anyway,* he thought. He tried to figure out the exact location of the bullet wound he'd suffered. Had it healed at all?

Baronne moved his right arm slowly across the dry ground as he searched the night for any lights. His ears were tuned to any sound other than the running river water. Nothing. Slowly, carefully he rolled his right foot over, allowing it to stretch his ankle and ligaments in the other direction. That done, he moved his left foot the same way. Gingerly he bent his knees a few degrees, stretching, testing, hoping and praying that he was indeed alone.

He opened his other eye. He was in danger. The only thing that mattered was to escape. The night was pitch-black and incredibly quiet. He experimented with moving his other arm, stretched his fingers, unknotted his elbow. When he did, he put stress on the wounded shoulder for the first time, and severe pain shot to his brain like machine-gun fire.

Gasping, Baronne pushed his right knee up and worked at shoving his buttocks into the air. His arms supported him when he brought the other knee up, and he remained that way for a moment, letting the pain shift and regaining his balance. His sunburnt skin cracked with each move, his joints screaming from inactivity. His mind wavered . . .

"Pogey-assed bastards!"

"Who?"

"Supply officers. Cowards mostly, just sit here at Barstow and chew on their cuds and steal heavy equipment and fuck the natives and never go to war.''

"You're bitter." Baronne was in the officers' club talking with Captain Barnes. *"I'm* forced to get out of here, to put in for a transfer to the FMF, probably back to Vietnam, and you're bitter."

"No way! I know. Look at me. I spent twenty years as an enlisted FMF type. Some son of a bitch makes me a lieutenant in Korea, and before you know it I'm back at Quantico going to supply school, and here I am. Looking down at this fucking dime martini and playing putssy-putssy with a Univac computer that breaks down every day and a bunch of sluts who wear Marine Corps uniforms.''

"You're gonna get our asses kicked out of here," Bear cautioned Barnes.

"No way. They don't know what to do with me. I'm the only sonofabitchin' supply officer among 'em who's ever been to war. Remember that, Baronne, you ain't nothing in this Corps until you've been to war.''

"Barnes, you ol' asshole!''

Somewhere in a corner of his agonized brain, Baronne realized he'd spoken aloud, knew he should be frightened for having done it. Instead he raised his head and tried peering into the night. He couldn't see anything, and didn't know how much of that problem was the ferocious Nam night and how much might be his vision. "Jesus," he said aloud, chuckling, "I'll bet I'm a heck of a sight."

His humor drained away as Baronne slipped. With a sickening sense of falling forty floors he reached out for a vine hanging from a nearby tree . . .

"Attention!" The familiar face and form floated sternly before Baronne's eyes. It was Major Pohl! "I'm your commanding office. For the next eight months—"

Bill's head jerked around, responding to a sudden snapping sound. Somebody afoot, maybe—walking not far off. He lowered his bulk against the crackling of his popping knees and ligaments. Then nothing was moving. It was still—yet he heard it. With his senses attentuated by fear and pain, it was loud, near, and definite. He turned his head with microscopic slowness and stealth, ears tuned to the night.

He dropped to his knees and edged backward toward the river, slipping into the water gently, easily, quietly. The water flowed over his body, cooling the hot, sunburned skin. He continued to search the air for the sound he knew was that of another man.

"Psss-sst, Colonel. You alive?"

Baronne cast around frantically, with bursting hope. One of his men, returned for him. Or, was it? He stayed still, listening.

The man took another step. He was close now. "Psst, Colonel. The gooks have boogied—they're gone."

Baronne closed his eyes, praying this really was a Marine, trying to identify the rasping voice from his jumbled memory bank.

The man moved even closer, dropping to his knees and reaching ahead of himself, groping for Bill in the dark. "It's me, Sequoya."

Baronne smiled his relief. No goddamned Charley would make up *that* name. "Chief?"

Sequoya's head spun around in the dark. "Colonel? Where are you?"

"Here. In the water."

Sequoya moved toward the voice and reached for Baronne's hand. He found it and pulled on it slowly with his great strength. "I got voted to come back. We didn't think they could kill you."

"Bullet's in my shoulder blade. One rib's busted."

"Much pain?"

"Yeah. Where's the unit?"

" 'Bout three miles west. No way we gonna find it in the dark."

"We're gonna have to move out of here."

"Yes sir." Sequoya stood, a towering figure, put his rifle sling over his shoulder, and helped Baronne to his feet. "There's a trail back the way we came. We can hide in the brush there and head out first thing in the morning."

He led the colonel through the friendlier night, up a trail he felt with his instincts, finally reaching the spot he liked. He stopped and helped Baronne stretch out on the poncho he pulled from his pack.

"I'll keep watch."

Baronne's nod was undetected in the night. He put his head on his right arm, pulled his knees up toward his chest, and closed his eyes, comfortable in the knowledge that Sequoya, a Cherokee Indian, was going to protect this son of a son of an Italian immigrant.

This was an interesting Marine Corps.

5

Give Me Your Boy

"Colonel. Colonel Baronne. Get up, sir." Sequoya shook Bill, fearing for a moment his colonel might have died during the night. "It's getting light enough to travel, sir."

Baronne rolled over and jerked with agony as his shoulder touched the ground. His skivvy-covered pink body crinkled with pain.

"Here." Sequoya handed Baronne his own boots and green jacket top. "I can make it on bare feet, sir."

Baronne pulled the boots on and then allowed Sequoya to help him slip the jacket over his shoulders. He stretched his legs and arms, and reached up for Sequoya to help him stand. He probably couldn't make it without the boots.

"How's the shoulder?"

"Hurts. Pretty bad."

"Colonel?"

"Yeah!"

"Scales, he was killed, sir."

Baronne stared at the big man with the rasping voice, unable to grasp it. Somehow, stupidly, it seemed impossible. Baronne tightly squeezed his eyes shut. He tried to summon Scales's homely, dutiful face, and when it wouldn't come, Baronne said, "Damn, damn, *damn.*" Then he fell to the ground, striking it, fighting back tears.

Sequoya maintained his perspective. "We better go, sir." Reaching down, gently locking Baronne's arm, he hauled the big officer to his feet. He steadied him, his colonel and his dizziness, sickness, and grief. "You gonna be all right?"

Baronne nodded, moved. Winced.

"You've lost a lot of blood."

"I'll be fine," he said, took a step, and nearly passed out. "Sequoya . . . ? Aw, Jesus, Chief."

Sequoya slung his M-16 over his shoulder and grabbed Baronne. "Here, put your arm over my shoulders."

"Yeah." Bill put his left arm over Sequoya's back and leaned into his Marine comrade. "Let's go."

They had walked about ten yards when Baronne buckled at the knees and fell to the ground, unconscious.

"Get up, Colonel. Come on!" Sequoya, seeing Baronne's eyes open, yanked his arm. Then he peered around nervously as Baronne climbed laboriously to his feet.

"Yeah, sorry. Dizzy."

"Yes sir. But if we don't move, we're gonna be more than dizzy."

They walked into the tangled brush and sought to disappear into the gray morning mist, Sequoya in bare feet, Baronne with a jacket but no pants—plus boots a size too small and a hole in his shoulder. "Best equipped military in the world," he grunted to Sequoya.

"Yessir," Sequoya answered, exhausted from the effort required to save his colonel and himself. He didn't much care right now about the kind of equipment they had or didn't have, only that they would eventually be able to hook up with the remainder of their men and then, *God help us all*, he prayed to himself, *we'll find Colonel Chapman's battalion, and get the hell out of this war.*

Baronne was the first to see the open patch of land ahead of them. He flung out his large hand, catching Sequoya's shoulder and pulling him down next to him as they neared the clearing. He was more exhausted than he'd thought humanly possible. The wound was taking its toll, the infection spreading, and the loss of blood was weakening him even more than earlier. He sat on the ground and tugged the boots off.

"Too small?"

The colonel nodded while rubbing his toes. He fell back against a stump and breathed heavily, closed his eyes, and tried to regain his equilibrium. "How much farther?"

Sequoya looked around, then back to Baronne. "At least two miles." He reached into his backpack and pulled a small green can of greasy potatoes and meat out, pulled the can opener from the chain around his neck, and cut the lid off. He reached into a small pouch hooked to his belt, pulled out his metal spoon, handed the food to Bill. "Here, Colonel. 'Bout time you got on the outside of something."

Baronne didn't argue. He took the can and spoon, smiled gratefully at Sequoya in a signal of thanks, then ate ravenously. Sequoya found another can in his pack and began preparing his own food. Half-filled, Baronne looked dreamily in Sequoya's direction.

"You two boys get in here!" Little Bear's mother was yelling at both T.C. and her son. They had been across the street in the vacant lot, playing football with other boys. Now, at ten in the evening, they still had to be ordered into the house. T.C. stayed over at Bill's often. His father had died in the war. His mother worked afternoons and evenings at the local drugstore.

"We're just playing football, Mom," Bill called back.

"It's ten at night. You should be in bed."

"Tomorrow's Saturday, Mrs. Baronne." Young T.C. sought to help.

"I don't need a calendar that talks. You two can play football all day tomorrow." From across the street, Bill saw her shake her head. Her hair was up in curlers and they glittered like jewels in the porch light. Her son thought she looked like royalty, like a queen. "You two get in here, brush your teeth, and get into those beds." Her look was full of love. "I swear, I believe you two would stay out all night if I let you."

"We gotta get back Colonel."

Baronne, wearing a half smile of dreaminess, looked at Sequoya. "We gotta go, Colonel," Sequoya repeated.

He'd buried the cans from which they'd eaten survival rations and was helping Bill to his feet.

"That's right," Bill said hazily, as if Sequoya had said something profound.

Together they stood anew and staggered around the perimeter of the open area. When they moved into the bush, passed through some rubbery vines, four fully-armed Viet Cong troops stepped into the clearing ahead of them. They were trudging ahead, chattering with animation, and none was aware of other people in the vicinity.

Immediately Sequoya and Baronne fell to the earth and hugged it, motionless as stones.

"Where'd they come from?" Sequoya whispered. "Jesus, they're like shadows."

"I dunno, but that's the direction for us."

They stared while the quartet of Cong moved closer but toward a segment to their left. Sequoya worked his M-16 around himself carefully, quietly. He loaded the chamber and took aim. "Just in case."

Bill nodded as if hearing something profound. He needed to close and open his eyes and close them again to stay focused. Abruptly an F-4 screamed overhead about a hundred feet and disappeared to the north.

Sequoya met Baronne's eyes as both men shook their heads. "Not for us." Bill whispered it.

The four V.C. stopped in the middle of the clearing and began pointing in different directions, seemingly lost. They debated until one of them raised both his arms, shouting at the others—yelling something that instantly quieted them.

The first man—the leader of the pack—turned to point directly to Baronne and Sequoya. They replied with a few fast, indecipherable sounds.

Then the whole quartet shifted the weight of their weapons and packs and began trodding straight toward the pair of almost helpless Marines.

"Get ready to squeeze the round, Chief," Baronne ordered. Only half clad and decidedly out of uniform, even more decidedly continuing to float off on mental clouds, the big man saw the V.C. pause ahead of them. It was as if Charley half expected an ambush, because the two Marines, out-manned, stood squarely in their path. "Sequoya, did I ever tell you how ugly you are?"

"No sir," Sequoya snapped. He didn't turn his head to peer at his wobbly legged colonel. "But shit, I knew about that already."

Bill Baronne smiled almost sweetly. The pain in his shoulder had nearly become a part of him now, and while he didn't like it, something innate as well as taught by experience was helping Baronne make the adjustment. Clutching two grenades against his belly, where they were half concealed, he was remotely aware that his partly bent-over posture gave him a rudimentary Oriental look of obeisance. It occurred to him that he knew little about the other man with whom he was probably about to die.

"Funny thing about ugly," Sequoya muttered. He'd raised his M-16, was looking down the sights while he tried to decide which of the four V.C. to fire at. "Some of it's scars. You know, from fights with drunks in Enid and women who didn't cotton to my style. Another part of it's being what I am."

"What's that, Sergeant?" Bill's hand hurt from clutching the grenades so hard in wait. Was it possible the Cong was looking past them, had not really seen them? "What are you that makes you so ugly?"

"Well, I suppose, being a half-breed—" Sequoya waggled the M-16 barrel just faintly. "Come closer, you mothers."

Baronne glanced at Sequoya, surprised. He saw that the big man seemed to be enjoying this waiting. He also saw that Sequoya had confided in him because he doubted that either of them would be alive long enough for anyone else to learn the truth.

In blinding motions, the quartet of V.C. began pulling their weapons from their shoulders and inserting clips into the rifles. Whatever they'd shot at most recently—snakes like the one that almost got Baronne, maybe—they hadn't reloaded. "Close enough, Sequoya," Baronne shouted.

The colonel lofted the first of his two grenades and was so accurate that it killed two of the enemy. Their shattered bodies crumpled to the ground. As Sequoya fired, the dirt kicked up by the grenade gave the other two V.C. time to dive for cover. One, whether from accident or sacrifice, landed almost directly on top of the second grenade, which exploded at once and ripped his screaming body open.

The fourth man disappeared into the brush and ceased moving. As the noise stilled and the air cleared, Sequoya and Baronne squinted at the open area, then to the left, where the last V.C. had run. The sergeant, aware that Baronne was in no shape for it, pointed and then fell to his hands and knees. He began to move noiselessly through the bush. Baronne marveled at the deftness and courage of the man who'd found and saved him. What kind of world made a good man feel he had to hide from danger, or his responsibilities. Looking with ragged nerves and newly raging pain toward the nondescript ground cover into which the Indian had disappeared.

"Tough son of a bitch, Sergeant."

"You ain't supposed to talk that way, Lieutenant." The sergeant scowled but held his position.

"All sergeants like you?"

"Could be."

"I mean, you really love combat that much?" Baronne slung his M-1 rifle over his shoulder.

"Yeah, I guess." Sergeant Gaines paused. "You'll find out."

Bill narrowed his gaze. "Maybe."

"You stay in this outfit and you will."

"What was the worst?"

Gaines rubbed his late-afternoon stubble, wrinkled his aging eyelids, and smiled tightly. "Korea. At the Yalu. Hordes and hordes of gooks. Wave after waves of human flesh. Sometimes I didn't think we'd have enough ammo."

"Jesus."

"He didn't help." Amusement rumbled from deep inside Gaines. "In the end, we used their carved skulls for ashtrays and their fibulas for swagger sticks."

Baronne looked incredulously at Gaines. "That's sick!"

"That's right, Lieutenant. But we were too stoked to know it. There was just too much of it, everything was too quick. Like that's what life was. That, and being scared shitless all the time."

Shots, piercing, sudden, unrealistically loud. Then quiet.

Baronne sat up, gripping his last hand grenade, prepared for anything. The moments seemed to stretch to hours before he finally heard the brush move and saw Sequoya limping, pulling on his right leg, blood soaking his pants. Baronne, grabbing a vine for balance, stood and lumbered toward Sequoya.

"Down! Get down!" Sequoya was closing quickly. When he arrived next to Baronne he fell prone beside him and pointed his rifle in the direction from which he had come. "I hit him twice, but he didn't die."

Bill began wrapping Sequoya's leg with cloth sliced off from his borrowed jacket with the K-BAR.

Sequoya looked down at the leg. "It's bleeding more than it hurts. Just tore away some meat. I've had worse, riding bulls."

"Charley follow you?"

"Couldn't tell. It's the guy who was in charge out there."

They waited that way for a while, listening and looking, prepared. After half an hour the colonel spoke softly. "Maybe you finished him."

Sequoya shook his head. "No, he's not dead. Probably waiting like we are." He turned and looked at Baronne's hand holding the grenade and wondered if his colonel were in shock. "We can't stay here. The battalion is packing up and leaving tonight if we aren't back. Do ya remember?"

Baronne nodded. "Let's go."

They moved quickly, quietly through the vine-crowded

jungle, but only as their wounds would allow. They felt someone following them, knew Charley was there. He was persistent, and, in his own way, courageous.

"Colonel, you keep going." Sequoya stopped, lowered himself to one knee, and brought the rifle up. He motioned in the direction Charley must come, pointed to his own rifle, and shook his head to the right. "Make a lot of noise."

Bill hesitated at first. Then dimly seeing the Indian's reasoning, he responded by moving as noisily but as safely as he could. He stepped over fallen trees, pushed through dangling vines, leaves, and branches, occasionally maintaining his wandering balance by grabbing at everything in sight. Yanking hard, he snapped limbs and let them fall noisily to the ground.

Behind Bill, Sequoya waited, listening intently. For the moment, the intensity of the pain in his leg was oddly invigorating. He felt alert and incisive, much the way he had when, during his drinking bouts, he had felt himself magically poised on the "edge." As the colonel ranged farther and farther away, Sequoya clearly detected the presence of a new jungle sound: Charley, also wounded, coming for him. Setting himself low, raising the M-16 to his shoulder, the big Indian muttered softly through his teeth, "Okay, you mammy-jammer,—I'm ready for you this time."

"I am," Baronne said loudly, declaiming the words, sounding for all the world like a man standing at a podium to make a speech, "for all purposes, your adversary."

"What the fucking hell?" Sequoya wondered, looking in his colonel's direction.

"Christ, what kind of guy *is* he?" T.C. inquired, looking sideways at Bill Baronne.

"My name is Captain Forbes. This is the third platoon and, over the next eight months you will learn something of the Marine Corps." He paused and looked each man in the eye before continuing. They were standing on the macadam parade street in front of the evenly lined Quonset huts which made up the barracks for basic school.

"You will be trained by combat-experienced officers. The only time you will be subject to enlisted personnel will be the rifle range and during field exercises." He began to strut from his right, then to his left in front of the new lieutenants. "At no other time will you be under the supervision of enlisted. At no other time, now or in the future, will you ever subject yourself to enlisted, or become familiar with them . . ."

The noise had stopped. Charley knew Sequoya was there. *Smart son of a bitch,* Sequoya thought. He rolled quietly to his right about ten yards and came up with his rifle pointed in the direction where he suspected his enemy was hiding. He wanted to fire the weapon, or blast the bushes and trees. To blow the shit out of the little gook. But his Indian instincts were sharp. He waited, understanding patience must win out.

Baronne plummeted to his knees, gasping, pulled himself next to a tree, hugged it. He sat right there, weak and dizzy, breathless, waiting. One hundred yards from Sergeant Sequoya, he was in dire trouble. He knew that he was completely dependent now, because he was in need of medical attention.

"Kill the bastard, Sequoya!" he rooted. He sighed and allowed his head to drop against the tree. He closed his eyes and listened as hard as he was able. The sound of the river was gone and the wind had died and there weren't any birds.

Suddenly there was gunfire.

Sequoya rolled again and fired, came up to his feet, and ran directly at Charley. "Mother fucker!" He continued to fire his M-16 at his enemy.

As the soldier dropped, he bent over. He pulled a cord stretching from his belt. His whole body exploded with a force that disintegrated him and knocked Sequoya thirty feet through the air. He smashed to the ground against a fallen tree, limp, injured, conscious—in excruciating pain.

Baronne sat up straight, listened, stood at last, and began limping the hard walk back.

* * *

"Over here, Colonel." Sequoya was hurting. He was bleeding, his right arm was broken. His good leg, the left one, showed lacerations along the calf, just below the knee.

Baronne took it all in at a glance. "Christ, the other wound has reopened." He moved next to Sequoya and went to work promptly on the bleeding wounds.

"Looks like you're really in charge now, Colonel."

Baronne hesitated a beat, looked at Sequoya, and smiled. It was true. He had lost control. Although he hadn't given up, neither had he shown the strength to command. "I have no idea where the battalion is, Sequoya. You gonna be able to help me with that?"

Sequoya nodded. His eyes were shut tightly and his mouth curled in pain. Marines in pain, ever proud.

Concentrating hard, Baronne managed to wrap Sequoya's leg. He also made a splint for his arm and wrapped the sergeant's massive head. "You know, Chief?" he prompted. He badly wanted to keep this man awake; it would keep them both alive. "We get out of this, you're gonna get the biggest, shiniest medal a colonel can recommend."

"How about an honorable—discharge—instead?" He bit the words off, spat them out, in his torment.

"Sequoya? You telling me the fun has all gone out of this?"

Sequoya worked hard at coming up with a tight smile and a quip. "Indians never laugh." He squinted his eyes hard. "Not even half-breeds."

"Why didn't you tell me about that, Sergeant?" Baronne eased up. "What are the two breeds?"

"Choctaw . . ." Sequoya mumbled, but passed out. He wanted to explain his family's heritage—and his blood mix . . .

For a long moment Colonel Baronne stared at him and then looked around, frustrated. Somehow, some way, he had to carry Sequoya away from that spot. Action had occurred there; the sound of shots carried. They needed to escape possible detection, at least until Sequoya had time to recover.

Bill hauled himself to his feet. He took in a deep breath and held it. On the ground, mighty, raspy-voiced Sequoya looked ridiculously young and vulnerable. "Give me your boy," Baronne growled, mocking the poster boards they had lining Main Street, U.S.A., "and we'll give you back a dead man."

Baronne lowered Sequoya to the ground and fell next to him, more exhausted than he could recall. The sun had moved across the sky. It was late afternoon, too late to find his battalion. They would leave, thinking them both dead.

He pulled the M-16 to his chest and lowered his back against the tree, darting his eyes from right to left and tuning his ears to the area. He glanced at Sequoya, shook his head a little, and closed his eyes.

With his eyes still closed, he pulled the bolt back on the M-16 and allowed a cartridge to enter the breech, snap forward into the chamber. The rifle was ready now for anything. It had been a long time since he handled a long weapon. Since basic school his only contact with weapons had been a pistol and his only rifle contact his annual qualification firing.

"Spread those legs, Lieutenant Baronne. We ain't hunting any gee-dee deer around here!" Forbes kicked Bill's right foot away from his left. Baronne, directing his rifle to the target area while lying on his stomach, nearly fell through his propped elbows. "Got that, Baronne? Huh?"

"Jesus," the young second lieutenant muttered after Forbes had walked off to the others. He glanced back to the sergeant questioningly; the training noncom loomed overhead from Bill's prone position. "He always like that?"

The sergeant's scowl was undisguised. "You was in the wrong position, Lieutenant . . ."

Bill's eyes popped open and he sat up straight, stiffly. "What was that?" he asked anyone at all.

Sequoya, the sergeant, stirred. He moaned a little, then stopped.

"Sh-h." Baronne gently placed his hand on Sequoya's leg to communicate with him. The sun had fallen below the horizon, but the Indian gave off a terrible, unnatural warmth. They'd been passed out, Sequoya and the colonel, for at least four hours.

"We're in deep shit." Sequoya's eyes did not open. He was racked by a tremulous, partly terrified and wholly terrifying sigh. "I think maybe we've bought it."

You're probably right. Baronne said aloud, "Don't be an asshole. You, me, we're both gonna make it, Chief."

A noise ahead of them: a rushing motion. Baronne willed himself to take Sequoya's M-16, but his body would not respond. Shifting slightly to hide the sergeant with his own body, he braced himself—and saw a Marine private, one of his own men, burst through the brush and stand directly in front of them.

Baronne almost cried. But as his eyes filled with tears of relief, he slapped Sequoya on his good leg, anxious to share the good news. "Wake up, Sergeant."

Sequoya's eyes opened in a slit of agony. He moaned, tried to focus on Baronne, again passed out. He'd tried to shake his head and it'd gone limp.

"Colonel Baronne, hang on, okay? I got three Gyrenes on my tail." And as swiftly as the private had come, he was gone. Feeling both relief and pride, Bill struggled upright, hearing the private wade into the jungle and call for the others to help.

"God, what men!" Baronne said aloud, glancing down. They had maintained the pride in themselves and their outfit to search for their wounded. "Your buddies have learned their lessons well, Sequoya."

Reaching to pat Sequoya on the leg again, Bill stopped short.

Sequoya looked funny, different. Cold.

Baronne fell down beside the sergeant, looked into Sequoya's clouding, pain-filled eyes.

But the pain was merely an overt memory trace and Sequoya was dead.

"Damn it, Sequoya! Goddamn it, Sequoya, don't die now!"

The young private had reappeared in company with three other Marines, and they all leaned down, trying to pull Baronne away. But Bill, his two strong hands locked to the Indian's broad shoulders, was trying to tug him erect.

Breaking down at last, Baronne sagged to the foreign earth next to the man who had saved his life and sobbed, sobbed for Indians who had to defend their own heritage and Indians who pretended to be immune to human sentiment, sobbed for another sergeant named Scales, and countless other brave men.

Exhausted, his head collapsed against the big Indian's still ribs, hands warming the cheeks of a dead man.

PART TWO

6

Friends

As a gangly youngster who had as much need to fill out as to grow up, William Angelo Baronne had only one fistfight that he could remember. He hadn't grown up with a family so frustrated that its members needed to fight, nor had the Baronne residence in Southern California been located in a trouble-prone neighborhood.

In a climate rich in sunshine and baskets of produce, why fight? People had ample elbow room, and the extremes of weather were so moderate that even in the slums, the inclination was to yawn, stretch, and take a nap, or drift away to a convenient park to loft a football. Much later, it would occur to homesick, nostalgic Bill Baronne that people in his neighborhood, for miles around, seldom even remembered to lock their front doors.

It was a peaceful existence in which a maturing boy might take all the time in the world to decide what he wished to be—president even; this was America—before the war broke out.

The war in the South Pacific. Bill's daddy became Captain Angelo "Bear" Baronne and seemed to have not only left Southern California and his wife and son for good, but to have mysteriously exchanged his identity for something very different, yet special: an Officer Defending All the Folks at Home. The war was little Bill Baronne's first love/hate relationship, and he wasn't yet sure what to make of it.

Things hadn't been going too well in school for young William, either. The void he felt, created by his father's absence, had become apparent with his lower test scores. *Tests?* He didn't remember disliking the darned things so much before, but now? *God, please bring my daddy home.*

"What's that, William?" his teacher asked. "Did I hear you use the Lord's name?"

Her challenge was too much for little Bill. He began to shed a few tears, bowed his head with embarrassment. His emotions were uncontrollable.

The teacher seized the moment. Telling the rest of the class to read from page 12 to 20, she walked to Bill, grabbed him brusquely by the arm, and led him from the classroom. Once outside the door, she chastised him for interrupting the class with his outburst. Poor Bill—he had prayed to himself hadn't he?—was so confused that he finally broke out in real tears.

He spent the rest of the day in the principal's office, writing some goofy thing about why he shouldn't use God's name in the classroom and why he shouldn't interrupt when the teacher was talking.

He had figured the school bell would never ring when the principal, Mrs. What's-her-name, came to him and announced that his mother had just called to say, "Your father's home from the war." Well, nothing in the whole world mattered anymore except for his little feet peddling his darned bike as fast as they could.

"My prayer worked," he chortled, "I just knew it would."

The first report reaching them had announced that Captain Baronne had downed an even dozen Jap Zeroes before he too had been shot out of the sky. Straight out, and, according to the rest of the news that morning, shot straight to heaven or hell.

His mother had cried and sobbed and moaned her immense loss—until the Navy man had telephoned to say that Mother's husband—Daddy—was actually just fine. He neglected to tell them that soon Bear Baronne would be ordered back to the same war, as a forward air controller—a new experiment for the Corps, bringing pilots to the ground war to assist company and battalion commanders obtain direct air hits on the enemy. Big Bear would be working on the ground, under enemy fire. "He won't be doing any flying for the rest of this war," the Navy man reported. "But he's all right, only a little wet from having parachuted to safety."

It seemed that a small minesweeper had retrieved Daddy and, for reasons involved with the war, had been delayed in returning to base. "Radio silence prevented us from receiving the good news until now," the telephoner from the Navy added. It taught Bill immediately that the Navy Department, if it felt that it had to, could lie quite well.

The bees came at him voraciously. He ran from the small dormitory at Flintridge Prep, fleeing from all people around him and the headmaster particularly. Schaeffer had severely reprimanded little Bill over the matter of failing to make his bed that morning.

And it was the final straw. Bill Baronne's youthful spirit had finally been broken, all because of the way his family had had to move so often during that last year of the war. He was dropped back a year in school. He lost his lifetime chums, the boys he'd grown with through his first years of school. Now here, in another different school, he felt truly lost and alone—obliged to suffer alike the stings of the headmaster and countless hundreds of bees.

They seemed symbolic to the boy, although he wouldn't, then, have known the word. He had struck a beehive just outside the dorm—a hive that had been there all year, and one which he'd feared but had grown accustomed to. Out of anger, hurt, frustration, he'd hit the hive with his small fist—and ran, as fast as his legs would carry him. Straight to the school's swimming pool, where he'd arched his little body in a desperate dive. While Bill held his breath, the bees circled above him; he knew they were waiting for him to surface.

But that was one of his early feats, one he'd thought would be adequate to the task of protecting him. Even then he could remain underwater, holding his breath for more than ninety seconds, and the bees furnished him with another chance to break one of his personal records.

But when he found that the bees had given up and he emerged, gasping for air, Bill discovered that they had already stung him at least two dozen times. He'd been so full of adrenaline, and then soothed by the water of the swimming pool, that he had scarcely noticed. Now, the stings were painful, awful.

Carl Schaeffer, of all people, came to Bill's aid. As headmaster, he possessed the requisite qualities both to reprimand and praise, discipline and sympathize. Eventually Baronne would know that Schaeffer was a good man, but it would take years for *that* appreciation.

Schaeffer helped Bill back to the house and, with small tweezers and a soft, reassuring voice, he painfully pulled the stingers out one at a time.

It was later the same day, in his room, that Bill broke down in tears, near hysteria.

It had begun that school year, September 1944, at his regular school in Burbank. Sixth grade was going to be fun. He had enjoyed his schooling so far, had done well with his grades. He had many friends and often spent hour upon hour playing football, kickball, or basketball in the neighborhood park with the same boys.

Then his father had come home after his two tours in the South Pacific. They'd moved to San Diego to be with him until his discharge. Bill was placed in the local Catholic school, where he sat in classes trying to figure out what in the hell they were talking about. The religious accent was unfamiliar to him.

The teaching nun seemed to pray every half hour, and the noon lunch period drove Bill crazy. When the clock struck twelve, he was obliged to stand silently in the school yard for three minutes, saying a prayer. In the morning, they knelt in the classroom before school started, and prayed, during recess they prayed, giving thanks for food and time and God and studies and the men at war and the monsignor.

God, what do they want? My homework or my prayers? he screamed inside.

Three months later, at the end of his sixth year, the

family moved to Pasadena. The war had ended; things would return to normal. Almost.

Young Bill had to say good-bye to a girl he had met and liked. His first. *Girls!* They were different but nice. He really liked Christina, but he had to go and didn't understand it, said he'd write and so did she. It really didn't matter that they never would. It just helped the departure.

At Pasadena, his parents checked him into Flintridge Prep. On the day he arrived, the school tested him and promptly informed his parents that he would have to repeat the sixth grade.

"What?" he screamed when the news was given to him by Mom.

"Repeat the grade! The school says you haven't had enough of what they consider valuable for progressing through high school and then college."

Bill cried. He hid. He latched onto a bus which passed by the school daily and ran away.

But in the end, he attended classes. And performed poorly. He was, after all, rebelling. And he never did much better there, never accepted the prep school, couldn't accept repeating the sixth grade. Mostly, he hadn't wanted to lose his old friends.

Alone, he was crying softly in his room when another student stuck his head through the doorway and watched silently for a few moments while Bill wept. He'd buried his face in his hands and was simply sitting on the floor beneath his practice desk, sobbing uncontrollably.

"Hi."

Little Bill scarcely glanced up at the other boy. He went on sobbing, his shoulders shaking, because he'd tried to slow down and stop but couldn't. He'd devoured so much oxygen in his efforts that he was gasping for air as he cried.

The other student persisted. "Can I come in?"

A pause. Then Bill nodded affirmatively. Nobody would ever be like his old pals, he really believed just then, but he had nobody to talk to at all.

"They get all the stingers out?"

He nodded again because he still couldn't talk. He continued trying to curtail his anguished sobs, but it was just too much for him.

"My mom says it's good to bawl once in a while. But not all the time, she says." Only part of the boy's attentive watching was linked to curiosity. He'd cried that way himself a few years before. Suddenly he wanted to confide that to the boy named Bill Baronne. "I cried just like that when my daddy got killed."

Bill looked up. The other boy had a nice, soft voice. It didn't sound like it was making fun of him. He was the same age, and big like Bill. He was smiling.

"Mom said I should cry," said the stranger. "But she said that after crying once about anything, I shouldn't ever cry about that thing again."

"It's hard," Bill gasped—and then he wasn't crying anymore.

"The bees?"

Bill took a deep breath and then for two hours, talked about everything. He told his new friend about his family, about the other schools, about his friends, and about having to repeat the sixth grade. When he was through, the room was quiet for a while. He had stopped sobbing, but his eyes were red as stoplights and they felt sore. He could have hugged the new boy; he needed affection from somewhere. And part of him wanted to start crying again, but he didn't have to.

The boy put his arm around Bill's shoulders and spoke softly: "They made me repeat the sixth grade too."

Bill looked at him and wanted to smile. "True?"

The blond boy nodded and smiled. Suddenly he asked, "You want to go outside and play catch with my football?" En route, he called over his shoulder, "Most people call me Tommy or Tom but I wish you'd call me T.C."

7

The Core
of the Corps

"Marines are strange, unique!" Major John Pohl, an officer at the Marine basic school in Quantico, Virginia, strutted around his desk, his back straight as a board, his ass smaller than the pockets on his green utilities. "A good officer must be a deadly killer." He whirled on Captain Walter Forbes. "And oh, three, oh, two! Infantry."

"They can't all be infantry," Forbes argued.

"Bullshit! Look what's happened. We've got artillery officers and tank officers and supply officers and"—he nearly stuttered—"and we've got chaos." He walked to his chair and sat down hard. "Infantry, Walt. Every goddamned man must be infantry."

"No pilots?"

"Pilots are infantry on temporary duty."

Forbes looked up from his notes, shook his head, and smiled.

"You're laughing, you son of a bitch. You think maybe I'm weird like the publicity people."

"If you believe that."

"Of course I believe it."

Forbes curled his mouth and wrinkled his left chin, stretching his reddened Korean scar. "John, you give me the name of one goddamned pilot who's ever marched a foot after leaving basic school."

"That's just the attitude I'm talking about."

"It's the new Corps."

" 'From the halls of Montezuma—' "

"C'mon, Major. You're living with propaganda. Bullshit. Public relations." Walter Forbes walked to the window of the Quonset hut and grimaced at a platoon marching by. "Look, the infantry has the prestige during peacetime, pilots get it during war, and only generals make out with retirement." He faced Pohl. "And during war the infantry's shit. Now, that's reality."

Pohl stood, walked to Forbes. In a more gentle voice he said "It's the prestige that drives men into their MOS. Not shit!" He was rankled. "Maybe some think flying is glorious and others like tanks and still others the boom-booms. But I truly believe there are men out there who love the infantry and its life-style and what it stands for."

Forbes turned to face his commander. "Then, John, you're as nuts as the rest of us." He raised his clipboard. "And if we can get these people to believe as you do, then they'll be nuts, too."

Twenty-eight-year veteran Walter Forbes sighed heavily and lit a Chesterfield. Turning to the window of the metal quonset hut, he paused a moment, reflecting on his history in the Corps.

"Nineteen-twenty-seven, I was scheduled to be mustered out four years later, but with the Depression, I chose to remain."

Pohl stared at his friend.

"Twenty-one dollars a month was a helluva lot of money." He smiled amiably. "And what the hell did I know about finding work as a civilian?"

Pohl remained quiet, attentive.

"Now, after two goddamned wars and twenty-eight years, I'm just a captain." He turned to Pohl. "And you want me to turn raw college-graduate 'second johns' into—" He stopped short, spit a piece of tobacco out, and chuckled menacingly. "Into infantry officers!"

Pohl nodded. He was a fourteen-year veteran who outranked but did not have the experience of Forbes. By Corps standards, courage and bravery and strength aside, Pohl was said to be "about as insane as anyone in the military." Pohl was force-recon all the way. Jumped from aircraft and defused land mines and rode ashore from night-sneaking submarines. He was, a fanatical warrior in combat, earning every major hero ribbon available while he was in Korea.

"Not bad for one war," he had declared to his wife a week before she divorced him. He'd also earned a partial metal plate for the inside of his skull and an unhealthy, rarely acknowledged taste for killing.

Pohl looked hard at Forbes. "You're not just a captain, Walter. You're a captain in the goddamned Marine Corps!" He paused, unsmiling. "And one of the best I've ever known."

Forbes shook his head, returned to his chair. He picked up his list of new lieutenants, and concentrated on bringing the session back on track. "Three hundred and twenty, forty from the Academy, the balance from college R.O.T.C."

"Jesus!"

" 'Cept for a dozen . . . from P.L.C."

Pohl thumped his desk with his longer-than-regulation, leather-covered swagger stick. "Okay, Walt." He sat, sighed heavily, "I'll play the game. Who are these people? Any football? Basketball? Anyone for the base team?"

"Navy quarterback. Penn State halfback and an end."

"Barnett? Well, that's something. The team can use an All-American."

Forbes nodded. "There are a few linemen from West Coast schools." He thumbed the papers and mumbled admiringly, "Another halfback from Southern Cal." He looked up. "Not a damned basketball player in the bunch."

"No . . . coloreds?" Pohl nearly blurted "niggers," but he'd trained that word from his vocabulary.

"None." Forbes paused. "They like to be called negroes now. Some even prefer blacks."

Pohl disregarded the comment. "Political influence?"

"Two. One a senator's son. The other, just a rich kid."

"Make sure the senator's son gets into Wilkes's platoon." He rubbed his chin. "Any outstanding Middies?"

"Four." Forbes coughed. "Can you imagine? A free college education, then being called outstanding?"

Pohl laughed, "Walter, I know how you feel. And, well, maybe you're right."

Forbes sat back and looked out the window. The same platoon was marching back and forth, back and forth. "I wonder what these college boys will do when they're thrown into a real blood-splattering, guns-and-cannon battle?" His voice cracked. "From panty raids to platoon leader."

"They'll do the same thing we did—fight like hell."

Forbes exhaled smoke and coughed again, "Maybe . . ."

"Better quit smoking." Pohl didn't like cigarettes. "It's our job to give 'em the same training we had."

"Not mine. Yours maybe, but not mine."

Pohl raised one eyebrow.

"Unless they want to be privates first." He shook his head. "Dumb, *really* dumb."

"Dumb?" Pohl chuckled for the first time. "That's close to heresy, Walt. Depending upon who you're talking about."

"Lieutenants dying right and left and I accept a commission in the middle of that crap. That's dumb."

"You're alive."

"With lead in my ass. Still!" He hesitated, squashed his cigarette into Pohl's ashtray.

Pohl jumped to his feet. "Sure, these youngsters have been spoon-fed, but they've got something else going for them—and you can use that."

Forbes looked up, questioning Pohl's remark with a slight curl of his mouth.

"They've been motivated by schools and families and Jack Armstrong and Frank Capra movies. For God's sakes, Walter, we're getting men who believe." He leaned down to Forbes. "When you came in, Walter, what did you believe in? You tell me you had to stay because of the economy. That's not exactly patriotic. But these kids?" He spread his hands. "Hell, they've been prepared like no other generation in this country, save the founding fathers."

"That's not making it easier."

"It's not supposed to be easy, goddamn it."

"Well, sir, they've had it easy up to now."

"That's 'cause they've only known peacetime America, Walter. They've read about our wars, but by God all they can relate to is peace."

"Peace?" Forbes stood and prepared to leave. He looked out the window and watched Lieutenant McCarthy intentionally march his platoon into a Quonset hut. "Jesus, maybe it's just as well we have something to keep him humored during times of peace."

"We have to live with that, Walter." He braced his legs apart in a defensive stance, swaying back and forth a little. "And at the same time, we have to teach them to kill."

"The better to survive." Relaxing his military bearing a moment, Forbes let his head rock slightly. "Actually, as I understand it, I'm supposed to teach them to kill commies, specifically." He smiled tightly, placed his hat on his head, and picked up his clipboard. "I've been doing this for twenty-eight years, John. It's never stopped."

"The killing, or the surviving?"

Captain Walter Forbes finished buttoning his Ike jacket and left the office without answering.

8

Back to Basics

Quantico, Virginia, to the south of Washington, D.C., had been carved from an area of thick woods right on the Potomac. Civil War battlegrounds mixed with the relatively united Marine Corps to form its base and training areas. Summers there, they said, were hotter than hell, the winters colder than hell. The operative word was hell.

From the "frozen Chosin" to the malaria-ridden South Pacific, Marine Corps instructors had had experience in all conditions of battle. To them, they said, it wasn't hot enough. Neither, they said, was it cold enough. Few were brave or ignorant enough to debate either point.

The main gate to the training area was located at the end of a seventeen-mile road that wound crazily through a dense forest of trees and underbrush and quasi-swampland that some said had all been shoved up from hell.

But the entrance to the posh headquarters base was in the opposite direction, just off the main highway.

"Can you believe this?"

"Not yet. Love the way that guy saluted us."

"He has to salute us," T.C. laughed. "Jesus, this is one funky base."

"Mainside?"

"Yeah! I can't believe we leave one base just to come to another." T.C. jumped out as the Ford screeched to a stop. He motioned to Baronne. "Maybe Wilner will make us a special deal."

"Sorry, fellas," the official tailor answered. He placed his tape around Baronne's chest. "Hmmmm, a bit heavy? Let me see your papers."

Bill handed him the forms he had filled in with his

height, weight, and other measurements. Wilner read it quickly and handed it back, nodding. "Like everyone else, overweight."

"No way," Baronne said emphatically.

"You're at two hundred seventy pounds. If I make a uniform for you now, in two weeks it won't fit." Wilner was just as emphatic.

"I've weighed this all my life, Mr. Wilner."

Wilner laughed, "You haven't gone through Marine Corps training yet."

"What can they do?"

"It's what they don't do."

Baronne looked at the shorter, older man with curiosity. "I don't think I like that."

Wilner smiled, pulled the tape measure around Baronne's waist, and began the tedious measuring for another set of uniforms for yet another lieutenant. Dress blues and greens and khakis and whites.

"It's the food."

"The food?"

"It's terrible. Men come in here all the time, overweight when they get out of college." Wilner chuckled. "Then after a few weeks of running hard, sweating in this humidity, and trying to eat that cuisine they serve"— he pulled the tape around his own neck, and chuckled again—"they're down inches and pounds." He stepped back, sizing Bill up with an expert eye. "And you, my young friend, will most likely lose at least four inches." He nodded affirmation and smiled.

"Where?"

Wilner patted Baronne on the stomach, the chest, the thighs as he spoke. "Here and here and here. And that means I'll have to measure and remeasure and keep doing that until you're down where you belong—where you'll probably stay."

"I eat a lot."

"Not that Italian stuff, not here, you won't." He pressed a piece of paper into the young officer's palm. "Come back in two weeks, eh? We'll see who's right."

* * *

"Captain Wilkes is in charge of the first platoon." Captain Walter Forbes was strutting back and forth, exposing his lieutenants to their new surroundings, and laying down the ground rules for further learning.

Each basic-school class became a military company, and each company had four platoons, each platoon with its captain instructor.

Captain Benton Wilkes, first platoon, a graduate of the Naval Academy at Annapolis, was short, wiry, and tough. A known politician, it was assumed by most he would one day be commandant of the Corps. Few Marines usually expected that goal, since every four or five years only one officer achieved it. It was a dangerous career game. In a decade, only two winners, everyone else a loser.

Captain Barlow, the antithesis of Wilkes, was second platoon leader. A little overweight, he had singlehandedly killed over three hundred North Koreans in an effort to save an entrapped battalion of Marine supply clerks. His achievement had brought him a Purple Heart with cluster and the Navy Cross. His career would eventually lead him to Vietnam, where he would die as a lieutenant colonel in charge of an unusually aggressive battalion.

Captain Hammond was a new, recently appointed captain. His combat history was short but impressive. He had been captured by the North Koreans a few days after leading the last charge up Bunker Hill for Chesty Puller, and had been held prisoner for the balance of the war. Repatriated at Panmunjom after bitter debates between the U.S. generals and the North Koreans, who spent much of their time spitting at the American officers, Hammond eventually returned home a hero.

Captain Forbes would lead the third platoon.

The door to the company headquarters and Major Pohl's office, opened abruptly, slamming the side of the Quonset hut. It had been intentional. The lieutenants looked up.

The four captains stopped talking and ordered their platoons to attention. Training had begun; for a while they would be dogs in a kennel, a concept they had yet to realize fully. No one spoke. That rule they understood;

four years of college midshipman training had at least succeeded in that respect.

Suddenly from the blur of heat and Quonset huts, Major John Pohl appeared in front of the group, ramrod straight, in full green gab uniform, his golden jump wings jutting out above his many ribbons. There was the Silver Star with cluster, the Navy Cross, five Purple Hearts, two Bronze stars and three rows of campaign ribbons and—one more.

"Oh my God," at least a dozen lieutenants muttered. It was the Medal of Honor!

Without uttering a word, Major John Pohl had set the tone and the standard for his new class . . .

"Failure can come at any time!" Forbes was in the metal Quonset hut barracks, speaking to his new officers, who stood at rigid attention at their double bunks. Baronne and T.C. were in the second squad bay, near the south entrance to the long building. Their eyes were focused straight ahead, but their ears were tuned to Forbes. "You fail on the obstacle course and you're out! Give me poor grades in class and I'll dump you." He paced from one end of the barracks to the other, but he was loud enough.

"Tomorrow you'll take your G.C.T. test. Drop below one-twenty and you'll be packing your bags." Baronne's eyes widened and Forbes caught it. "What's your problem, Baronne?"

"Sir, what's a G.C.T?"

"Same as I.Q. General Classification Test. Think you can pass it?" He was gruff, his voice menacing. Bill remained rigid.

"Yes, sir!"

"That test, Lieutenant, will be the easiest you ever take in this man's outfit."

Captain Forbes was standing at the head of the river-cable crossing, dressed impeccably in starched green utilities. Forbes relished the obstacle course and the challenges it presented to the new officers. It was sadistic entertainment. The cable was the equalizer. Long, hard-ened steel worn over the years, always slippery, it offered the greatest physical challenge to his new charges. On the first day most would end up in the river. It was later that he would determine their progress, when he would choose those who would make it into the infantry.

T.C., first to the cable, hesitated a moment. "About a hundred, maybe hundred fifty feet."

"Gonna be hard to hang onto," Baronne muttered.

"No sweat."

Forbes watched Chapman swing out over the water, his backpack and rifle shifting awkwardly against his out-of-sync rhythm. Baronne and his other squad-bay bunkmate, Don Greene, another strong former collegiate football player who hailed from Stanford University, and who now stood alongside Baronne held their breath when T.C. neared the midpoint. He was moving slower with each hand-over-hand grasp he took.

"He's not going to make it," Greene said.

"Maybe."

"At that moment T.C. let go of the cable and made a sickening fall some twenty-five feet into the rushing water. Greene, Baronne, and the other lieutenants leaned over the embankment, their eyes bulging for a better look at T.C.'s fate.

T.C. was pummeling the water downriver, kicking, pulling his rifle and hanging onto his backpack, reaching out for a tree root while the water pushed him. His hand failed to grasp it. He bumped into another tree, rolled over, and grabbed a handful of brush. He stopped just long enough to rise to his knees and dive for the shoreline.

Greene turned to Bill. "Christ, if T.C. can't make it, how in hell can I?"

Baronne held his hand out to the cable, grinning. "Your turn to find out."

Greene jumped up and grabbed the cable. He didn't get far. His backpack and rifle became tangled with his left arm and the cable. He tried desperately to recover with his other arm, but the cable, slick and wet as a snake, would not cooperate. Drenched, he joined T.C. on the far shoreline, watching while others attempted the difficult challenge.

Bill, thinking hard, had an idea: "Sir! Must I hand over hand?"

Forbes, snapping his head around to glare expressionlessly at Baronne, simply waited for him to move out. He said nothing.

Taking silence for approval, Baronne turned to the cable, merely reached up—he was taller than Greene—and grabbed the wire. He began swinging his legs up and over, to hand-walk and leg-push across the river below.

Captain Wilkes joined Forbes. "How they doing, Walt?"

Forbes cracked a tight smile. "A long way to go, Benton." He looked at Wilkes with disenchantment. "God, it's such a long way."

Out on the cable, Baronne had stopped mid-river. The wire dipped lower now. His weight had caused the wire to sag deeply and swing more with each movement. His long legs were draped over the cable and his hands were scarcely on it. His heavy body, weighted with backpack, rifle, and utilities, was soaked with sweat. It dawned on Bill suddenly that he was slipping and there wasn't a damn thing he could do about it—he was going for a swim. Sighing deeply, he took a breath, gasped "Damn," and let go.

Captain Forbes looked at Wilkes one more time. "A long way to go." His voice was low and tired.

"You're what?"

"I'm taking this tray of shit to Major Pohl. If he can eat it, I'll eat it."

"Baron!" T.C. had switched to that moniker lately. Now he was nearly panicking. "He'll eat you alive!" He glanced quickly around the mess hall, then back to his friend. "He sure as hell won't eat that gee-dee garbage."

"T.C., they can't be serious about this shit. It's been four months now and it's always the same crap. Look at me, will you? I'm skin and bones."

T.C. laughed. "You been working too hard."

"No way. C'mon." Baronne rose, carrying the tray.

They left the mess hall and marched quickly to Major Pohl's office. As they neared the Quonset hut, T.C. slowed and stopped. He shook his head. "I don't believe this."

"C'mon. Chicken?"

T.C. narrowed his eyes, and shook his head. "You know better than that, man."

Bill walked adamantly toward the Quonset hut. For a moment T.C. held back a few reluctant steps, then followed.

"You're saying what?" Major Pohl straightened in outrage. "What's wrong with it?" He remained behind his desk, his Weimeraner next to him. He was letting the fact that two lieutenants had the nerve to complain about the food sink in slowly. Both he and the Weimeraner sniffed the air suspiciously.

"It's terrible, Major," Bill said honestly. "Not fit for human consumption, and it's all we ever get."

Pohl stood. "Jesus H. Christ. What kind of infantry officers am I creating? Pogey-baiters?" He stuck his fingers into the food and pulled his hand to his mouth. "Delicious," he said immediately. "You know what your problem is, Lieutenant? You're spoiled. You've been living off the fat of family and land for too many years. This is the Marine Corps, not your mother's kitchen."

"Sir, if you'd just—"

Pohl cut him off. "Just what? I'm not tasting it again."

T.C. jumped in. "Let the dog try it, sir. If it's fit for your dog, I guess it's fit for us."

Pohl answered quickly, glaring at T.C. "You really think you're at the same level as a dog, Lieutenant." It was no question, it was a statement.

T.C. did not answer. Neither did his tall, powerful friend. But they looked pointedly down to the dog, at the tray, back to the dog.

With a heavy sigh Pohl snatched up the tray and set it before his pet. Weimaraners were supposed to be the most intelligent dogs on earth. "Here, Sarge, here, old boy. Have a feast."

Sarge put his nose to the tray, and sniffed: first the mashed potatoes, then the discolored meat, finally what passed for vegetables. He barked, sat back on the his haunches, and discernibly shook his head.

Pohl was aghast. "Sarge, boy—eat it!"

Sarge only whined. Then he shook his head, dropped to his belly, and virtually buried his head under his lifted forepaws.

T.C. smiled, Bill chuckled. Pohl picked up his phone with his face a terrible mask and ordered the officer in charge of the mess hall to his office. He would change the meals for now, he decided, fully understanding they would probably drift back to their current tasteless conditions in less than a week's time.

He would also chat with Walter Forbes later about keeping an eye on this young lieutenant who had just given him his first notice that he would be a leader, *of sorts*, he thought, *and not a follower*. That much was good for a Marine Corps officer. *But oh, God,* he added to himself, *there's still much, much more.*

9

Ethnic Wars

Standing obediently, in the R.D. White School cafeteria line, Bill stared dreamily ahead of him. He sometimes needed to be nudged by a red-haired little girl behind him to shuffle forward with the others. The third grade: he'd dreamed of that for what felt like all his young life. On the day his mother had held his small hand tightly and taken him to R.D. White to enroll, Bill couldn't imagine ever being older, or bigger, or more fortunate.

Until today. While Bill was inspecting the lunch dime he'd cupped in his palm, realizing for the fist time that the design was always the same from dime to dime, John Watson snatched his dime away.

John, three years Bill's senior, had bent his hand back to steal the dime and it had hurt. Despite the fact that John happened to be older, larger, and known as a fighter, little Bill chased him throughout the government-green cafeteria, through the lines of long tables, and out onto the blacktopped playground. "Gimme my dime!" he shouted, charging after the chortling Watson—and with a flying tackle that astounded both boys, Bill knocked the older youth down. He began to pummel him, all the time working assiduously to get his lunch money back.

They were tumbling on the ground, slugging one another with wildly flung punches that stung more than hurt when Miss Davis finally caught up with and stopped them.

Instantly, without batting an eye, John Watson told a lie with such sterling conviction that only an experienced teacher could have doubted his sincerity: "The little wop pushed me."

Bill Baronne gaped at the bigger boy, stunned more by the mysterious name—he'd never heard it before—than he was by the outrageous lie. His innocent, wounded eyes met Miss Davis's questioning glance, and for a fleeting moment he believed that he'd met something his parents had often discussed warmly, something called "justice."

"I can't believe a little third grader would start something with a massive old sixth-grader like you, John," she murmured, doubtful. *Although,* she reflected, *William is going to be a very big boy.* She stared at them for another contemplative moment.

Then she marched the two of them back to the cafeteria, where she tugged a couple of napkins from a container, wetted them, and handed one to each of the young combatants. *They're both responsible,* she thought, unwilling to make more of it than it deserved to be. "William," she began her admonishment, "shame on you for getting John Watson all dirty. Not every boy at school doesn't mind if he looks shabby."

That night at the dinner table, Bill asked his father, without warning of any kind, "What's a wop?"

For a long moment there was a valley of silence that pressed against each Baronne like close, clammy woods. Mother glanced at Daddy, looked away.

Then his father gave him the answer, and Bill had never forgotten the sense of outrage immediately born inside him.

"A word that no longer has meaning and which has no meaning, at all, for you." Captain Baronne was choosing his words with extreme care. "You're a born and bred American citizen." He cleared his throat. "And so am I. We're Americans. Not Italian, not wops."

"But our name is Italian, I know—"

Daddy smiled. "Our heritage is excellent, Bill. Our family blood is wonderful. But, my son," the father hesitated before continuing, clearing his throat considerably, "what you met today is called prejudice. It means, well, hating with no reason. Prejudice is evil and stupid. It's mankind's curse."

The word "curse," sounded neat to Bill. He'd seen voodoo movies and had tried putting curses on a cat, a dog, and a passing squirrel. "Who put a curse on us?" he asked eagerly.

"A powerless curse, most of the time," his father had replied. "made by ignorant people who need someone else to blame for their failures. But, William," Daddy had sat up straight, waggled his index finger—he still wore part of his captain's uniform and looked splendid—"living in America, you should be an American. If you wish to be Italian, go to Italy. You see?" Daddy winked. "Prejudice is dumb."

"You sound," Bill said slowly, picking his words carefully, "like it isn't that way anymore."

"People, well, they're getting out of the ghettos." He lowered his voice, glanced at Mother and then into the distance. "You know, in the Pacific, it didn't matter. bullets killed us all equally. Irish, Italians, Germans, British, it just didn't matter. I think to some extent the war has brought us Americans a lot closer."

"Then what happened to my son today?" Mother asked, speaking for the first time.

Father closed his eyes, searching for an answer as he shook his head slowly. He answered mostly to himself, "I had hoped we left all that behind us when we moved out here to California. No, now my own son—in Los Angeles yet!—somehow reawakens it all." The father stood, a giant above the dining table. "It cannot be ignored."

And so the Baronne family moved again. To a small suburban city on the outskirts of Los Angeles County, where there were fewer problems, or prejudices.

Until Quantico and Lieutenant Wilson.

Grown-up Bill Baronne had learned to rein in his anger, to keep from chasing Johnny Watsons whenever they came at him—teasing or testing, prying or simply causing trouble. Wilson, however, could not be ignored.

"Hey, wop, shine those shoes till they're shiny as your face." As Wilson chuckled, T.C. reached out from his groundfloor bunk to touch Bill's left leg cautioningly. "You spica d'English, wop?"

T.C. frowned as he saw Bill trying to shrug it off. "Cool it, Wilson, okay?"

For an answer, Wilson yawned, stretched and moved toward them a few paces. Bill didn't glance up; he knew what Wilson looked like: tough, wiry, with a body that seemed to drift, the way a boxer's could. Wilson had bragged about being a schoolyard bully who never lost. His father had urged him to fight for the big bucks, he was so good. "Yo, Eye-tye, can you talk?"

Watching them, Don Greene lowered the phonograph needle to Webb Pierce's "You're in the Jail House Now." Other new lieutenants raised their heads and ambled toward the developing confrontation.

Bill's gaze moved to the mirror of his seven-foot green locker. Finally he looked up. Despite his experience, Wilson was fifty pounds lighter, almost seven inches shorter. Despite his experience, Bill let the flash of anger pass.

"Hear about the wop war-surplus rifles? They're in perfect shape—never fired, dropped only once."

T.C., flinching, pushed down on Baronne's leg. "Back off, Wilson, we don't appreciate your crap, okay?"

Wilson's contempt was obvious. "Can't your pet wop talk?" he snarled.

Bill's eyes narrowed. "Right, that's enough."

Wilson threw up his hands in mock surprise. "It talks!"

"Dammit, back off, Lieutenant," T.C. admonished the man.

"Will you listen to that?" Wilson said wonderingly. "Baronne's personal bodyguard. And bunk mate. And God knows what else."

The exchange had consumed only a few minutes. But for Bill, "wop" stuck in his craw like a broken bone. Where was it written that he had to take this from such an asshole? Smiling, shifting slightly on his bunk, over T.C.'s, he leaned out to the brawler and motioned with his index finger for Wilson to come nearer.

Immediately Wilson did. When he was within reach, Baronne swiftly thrust his right leg up. His heavy boot slammed into the other man's chest. In almost the same motion, he'd dove from the bunk and crushed Wilson to the floor.

He meant that to be it. Instead, Greene, knowing better, increased the record player's volume.

John Watson had been play by comparison. The teacher near the playground had kept them from hurting each other. Yet Baronne's attitude had changed since then. He'd had Marine Corps training, the years of football, and knew what pain was. He also knew how far to push someone else, or himself.

Now he yearned to use his knowledge and beat Wilson to a pulp. Now this bully was all the bullies in the world.

But Wilson, who'd learned his boxing lessons well, moved nimbly before Baronne, sticking his left jab into Bill's chin and circling him, the right hand cocked. Bill had only donned boxing gloves once and had not learned how to fistfight with or without the gloves. He didn't care for anything they represented. When Wilson's right cross slipped in hard, Bill's left eye quickly began swelling.

And when, off balance, he left the other lieutenant a clean shot that sent Bill reeling against the bunks behind him, he responded with what he knew how to do best: He put his shoulder down and tackled Wilson just the way he'd done during his years as a high school linebacker.

Flailing, the two crashed against a row of wall lockers and fell hard to the deck below them.

Rolling, punching, and kicking, they slumped back solidly against the bulkhead, still throwing punches. Now they were breathing heavily, sweating profusely in the humid air.

Around Baronne and Wilson, the other lieutenants cheered them on. When they clambered to their feet, using each other for balance, the onlookers gave them whatever room they required.

Then somehow, no one quite saw it happen, their heavy bodies were careening into a set of bunk beds. Their combined force brought the beds crashing to the deck, along with an open can of cordovan shoe polish. It landed upside down on Bill Baronne's white dress cap—the one he'd been preparing for the upcoming inspection.

"My God!" The realization of what he'd seen from the corner of his eye kept Baronne from even feeling the next punch. "The inspection!"

In ten minutes they would have to be standing at attention in front of the Quonset hut, dressed perfectly in dress blues.

"He's in the jail house now," ol' Webb crooned.

Baronne, drawing in a hasty gulp of air, saw Wilson stand again, asking for more. Immediately he dropped both shoulders, and with a football scream he charged into the other young man so hard that he squeezed Wilson between two sets of upright wall lockers. Wilson emitted a yell of agony—"My ribs, you broke my ribs!"—and both the lockers and Wilson crashed to the deck . . .

Walter Forbes had survived two major wars, more because of his size than his luck. For a Marine, he was short. Stocky, bullish, but shorter than anyone else in Baronne's basic school class.

It was a damned good thing, too. Four or five of the dress white caps worn by the tall lieutenants were black or cordovan on top, depending which shoe polish had been knocked over during the fight.

The inspection dampened their anger. It was the time for the platoon to join together. Their common adversary stood in front of them, judging each individual as he reflected on the group. It was a way of making allies out of the temperamental, often highly strung lieutenants.

"Baronne," Forbes shouted, standing before Bill. "Can you see? Can you see yourself?"

"Yes, sir!" Baronne barked back.

"Well, what the hell happened?"

Bill paused. "I fell, sir."

Forbes knew better than to laugh, which was his first inclination. In 1929 he had offered up the same line. Every year since then he had heard the same line. He knew too that if Baronne ever made it to the field in charge of other Marines, he would hear the same excuse and probably subdue his own urge to laugh, remembering this moment.

"You fell? You fell?" He turned to Wilson. "And you, Lieutenant?"

"Me too, sir!"

"I ought to court-martial both of you," Forbes growled. Feigning anger, he paced up the first row of lieutenants and then back to Baronne and Wilson. "This platoon will remain at attention."

Fifty lieutenants knew they had passed some kind of test. They weren't sure what, but watching Forbes walk back to his office, they were all convinced it had affected him positively. So they would stand at attention quietly, definitely. Tomorrow would be Saturday and they could do whatever they pleased.

" 'Been two hours, Walt." Pohl looked up from his record books.

"We don't want to snap their character in two—just strengthen it."

"It's good training."

Pohl eyed Forbes carefully. "You're not punishing them, are you?"

Forbes chuckled. "Nope. Communicating."

Pohl nodded and returned to his paperwork.

"Another hour ought to do it," Forbes grinned. "That'll give 'em enough time to get caught in Friday's D.C. traffic."

10

Rabbits and Other Game

"Got 'em!" T.C. yelled.

"Yeah! 'Attaway!"

T.C. ran to the dead rabbit and picked it up by the ears while Bill snapped a picture.

"Hey, Bear, put the camera on that rock and take a picture of us, why don't ya?"

Bill screwed the small timing mechanism to the camera and set it on the rock. He ran to T.C. and stood with him facing the camera, each mighty hunter holding an ear high in the air, the rabbit hanging between them. The camera snapped the picture and the photo ended up in T.C.'s wallet, a picture he flashed often to show people his good friend, William Baronne.

"Nope, the rabbit. That's me on the left."

"No shit?"

"No shit."

It had helped them laugh at the tough hours of football training and brought guffaws from other lieutenants during basic school. Time passed quicker, the humor harmless, but effective.

"I wouldn't have."

"Same here."

"You wouldn't have what?" It was another lieutenant marching alongside Baronne and T.C., listening to their idle chatter.

"I wouldn't have played football if Pohl had been the coach."

"Yeah. He sure is a son of a bitch."

"Right. And look at our boots."

"Why do we spend hours on end rubbing a goddamned

bottle top into the polish when the fucking shine is wiped out with this—''

"Friggin' assed powerline mud?'' T.C. finished with a chuckle.

"Besides, mine don't fit.''

"How many socks you wearing?''

"Three pair.''

"Leather's stiff!'' T.C. looked down at his feet, then back to Bill. "Hey. You ever hear of Endicott Johnson shoes?''

"No.'' Bill was on to him, understood the reference to their boots and the company that manufactured them. "You?''

"Not me—never heard of them.'' T.C. howled at his own absurdity.

"Damn, who in hell would live in this godforsaken state on purpose?''

They continued to walk without speaking for a while.

"Column is slowing.''

Baronne looked up from watching the moving feet in front of him. He'd been concentrating: one step, then another, then another, on and on. "Crap, T.C.,'' he said suddenly. "You know, I've lost twenty-five pounds on these powerline jaunts?''

"No, I don't think I ever heard it,'' T.C. said, trying to keep a straight face. "I hope the music's better than the lyric.''

Captain Forbes, from at least fifteen rows of lieutenants ahead, commanded, "Take ten.'' The men collapsed on the spots where they stood, breathing heavily at first, slowly recapturing their energy. Baronne looked up to see Major Pohl approaching with his weimaraner, Sarge.

"Baronne! Empty your canteen into a cup for Sarge. He's thirsty.''

Pohl walked away, leaving the dog. It stared at them as if wondering when they would obey the order. Bill saw that T.C. had a mad light in his eyes and wore an ear-to-ear grin. Both men recalled the same fact: Weimaraners were reputed to be the world's smartest dogs. Yet what they saw before them was merely an impatient, over-bearing mutt. T.C. grinned.

Suddenly Bill realized what amused his friend, and remembered what he had in his canteen. "This pooch may not care a lot for scotch, T.C."

"But orders are orders." Chapman, sprawled on his back, tried not to laugh too loudly. "If Sarge is so human, he may like good scotch."

He watched as Baronne poured half his canteen into a metal cup and set it before the animal. Sarge sniffed deeply; then he lapped it up.

"That's going to be one drunk dog," T.C. cried with hilarity.

"Aw, Jesus, if Pohl ever finds out, my ass'll be mud without bubbles."

T.C. watched Sarge finish and weave away from his cup, decidedly weaving. T.C. laughed too hard to talk. "Aww, fuck," Bill told him, "we've all had it. But maybe Pohl won't figure it out. Maybe he'll assume Sarge is just dizzy from challenging people to spell the name of his breed."

Dog, scotch, laughter, and four-letter words dispelled any inhibitions Don Greene may earlier have had. Bill and T.C. had a new crony as Greene sat down between them, amused as only a friend would be. "Now, why didn't I think of that?" he wondered. "What was that stuff?"

"Keep your asses down," Horrible Harry Maxwell urged them. "You won't get hurt so badly if you're hit in the head." Then he roared, "No woman wants a man with a holy ass." God, Maxwell loved to laugh loudly at the expense of these new officers.

"The Indians were never like this," Greene barked, referring to his alma mater's football team. He looked to his right, saw Bill, T.C., and the other lieutenants moving steadily, smoothly, hugging the ground. To his astonishment, both T.C. and Baronne were wearing large grins, almost laughing. "What the hell's so goddamned funny?"

T.C. looked back at Baronne, then to Greene and answered, "You don't think they're shooting real bullets over us, do you?" He laughed loudly. "God, Greene, those gotta be blanks."

"Then what in Christ's name is that whizzing sound I hear overhead?"

T.C. bent his neck back and looked up. "Shit, babe," he gasped, blanching, "they *are* real!" Again, blanks. T.C.'s imagination was too vivid.

Baronne had inched forward, laughing hoarsely. Until he saw the real thing, in terms of combat, he sometimes motivated himself by pretending he was half-mad. "Hell, T.C., serve 'em right if they did pick off a few of us. Think of the repercussions in the press, all that G.I. insurance being paid." Smirking, he crawled away from the barbed wire and toward the river cable crossing.

It took six weeks for them to learn the art of preparing for Monday morning without consuming their full weekends. True, there had been those few hours driving to Fredericksburg, Virginia, checking out the girls' college in that Civil War town. Nice southern girls. Too nice. Sweet. Syrupy.

And those hours spent learning how to get back out of Washington, D.C., after getting into it.

"Damned streets must have been designed by some drunken Frenchman," Greene said with a scowl.

This weekend would be the payoff, because they were ready, really ready, for Monday morning. Rifles were shined, boots polished, utilities pressed, bunks superbly made—they were ready for the next week. The trick, they had learned, was to visit the "small stores," that name given to the military-goods shop where the lieutenants purchased their socks, skivvies, shirts, virtually everything they must have for their "clothing on the bunk" display and inspection. And then buy a second set of everything.

Monday they'd merely turn one set—the items used that week—into the laundry and on Thursday morning pick them up. The system insured a fresh set of starched clothing on hand for every Monday morning's mandatory "junk on the bunk" inspection.

Six weeks to learn what everybody else in the entire Corps knew.

"I wonder," T.C. reflected after that, "if we ever learn to kill anyone. Since we may need to."

"Probably not," Baronne replied.

"No, I mean learn how," he pushed the car faster. "Not do it."

"Neither."

"There you go again." He glanced at Greene. "Drives me nuts with that."

"What?" Green smiled at T.C.

"Saying things that don't mean anything."

"I understood Baron," Greene smiled again. "Double entendres without the sex."

"Bullshit."

The fire-engine-red Ford customline convertible rushed across the bridge, and after T.C. negotiated the circle, they headed off toward the Willard Hotel.

"What's there?" Greene asked.

"Stewardesses." His expression was smug. "Simply awaiting their men in uniform."

"They're waiting for airline captains?" Greene chuckled. Baronne smiled.

So did T.C., privately. He'd show 'em. After all, hadn't he been Baronne's personal bird dog at U.S.C.? Big Bill Baronne, the Bear, a good-looking guy but shy as hell. Every date Baronne ever had at U.S.C., T.C. arranged for him. Here he was, doing it again.

"Bear, when you gonna ask the ladies out yourself?"

Greene turned to Baronne. This was new to him. "You timid or what, Bill?"

Baronne curled his mouth in a little smile. "Aww-w, when the right one comes along it won't take much."

"God!" T.C. reacted. "I got him some of the best-looking girls in college." He slapped the steering wheel and laughed. "Remember the blind date Kazinski and I lined up for you?"

"Yeah, I remember."

T.C. turned to Greene. "Kazz didn't know her, but took her name from a girl he had dated to our spring formal." He grinned. "Now, remember, Greene, that's a weekend affair. Away from school. Overnight." He couldn't contain himself. Baronne shifted uncomfortably. "Anyway, her name was Joyce. A blind date." He glanced at Baronne. "But I was told she was gorgeous. A doll. Perfect for Bear." T.C. laughed so hard he began half choking.

Greene looked curiously at Bill. "She was a dog, huh?"

"No. Not a dog, exactly." He wanted it dropped right there, but he managed the tight little shy smile everybody was growing accustomed to. "Well, Greene, dammit—she was exactly four feet, five inches tall."

Greene wrinkled his brow in an effort to keep from howling. "Are you serious?"

Baronne nodded, reddening. "If she was that tall."

"Lord, it was funny, Don," exclaimed T.C. "When they were out on the dance floor together, faced just right, it looked as if Baronne was out there dancing by himself!" He cackled infectiously.

Green grew serious. "Was she a nice kid?" he asked Bill.

"Yeah." Baronne leaned back into the small car seat. "Rich too." He smiled, glanced at T.C. He had never mentioned that before. "Her father offered to set me up in business when I get out of the Corps."

T.C. flashed a stern glare Baronne's way. "You son of a bitch. You never told me that."

"It didn't matter." For a long moment Bill watched the scenery as T.C. drove, then added with quiet dignity, "Because I'm never getting out of the Corps."

They fell silent in T.C.'s vehicle as they glided into the Willard Hotel parking area. As the trio of new lieutenants passed through the lobby, headed doggedly for the bar, they paused before a full-length mirror. It was the first one they'd seen in months, and they were horrified by their appearances.

"Oh, Jesus, T.C., look at me," Baronne moaned.

"You lost so much weight you couldn't make the back-field, Bear."

"What a bitch," groaned Greene. "Look at our tiny little shaven heads. We look like we're ready for the frig-ging electric chair. Look, how our skinned skulls, sort of attached to our—"

Bill and T.C. shook with fresh laughter. "Yeah, we look just like—"

"Bowling pins!" Greene finished it for them. "That's what."

Chuckling, they shrugged it off and entered the bar, a little more self-conscious than when they'd driven up to the hotel.

The bar was almost empty. T.C. glanced around, moved to the stools. "Gonna be hard to bird dog for you tonight, Baron." He smiled at the bartender, who joined them quickly. His civilian eyes bored into them.

"What'll it be, Gyrenes?"

Damn! They'd been spotted. No uniforms and this guy knew right away they were Marines.

"We're wearing civvies, so how in hell—?" T.C. be-gan.

"You gotta be kidding." The barkeep was round and tough-looking. He had a blue tattoo of arrows and a heart dripping blood on his left bicep. "I been at this bar since '47 and you guys are just cookie cut-outs." He wiped a glass with a cloth, set it down, and picked up another. "The enlisted have tattoos that look like neon lights, and all they want to do is get drunk. The officers"—he looked up at them and paused—"well now, you officers look real shiny. Squeaky clean. And all you want to do is get laid." He placed the three beers in front of them with glasses and smiled. "On the house. 'Bout all you'll get free to-night, gents."

T.C. glanced at Baronne, who was similarly expres-sionless. But they knew each other well enough by now that the irritation each other felt was clearer than spoken language.

"Now, take those dames—if you got the balls for it."

The bartender indicated some women at the other end of the bar. "And you can take them if you got the bread."

T.C., wondering if they were the ones he'd arranged dates with, reddened and scrubbed at his blond skin-cut. "They're hookers?"

"Hookers?" The barkeep invented a shudder of revulsion. "In my nice little bar? No-o-o-o." He winked and left them, drifting away to the bottles lined up at the back of the bar.

The three Marines drank their beers quietly.

Then, without approaching the play-for-pay ladies, they left him, his bar, and the kind of action they knew ruined more Gyrene lieutenants than almost any other.

11

Thinking Marine

"Someday, Bear, we're going to wake up and discover what this is all about."

"What's that?" He peered thoughtfully at T.C.

"This running and hiking. Crossing that goddamned river and sitting in classrooms listening to all the bullshit about old wars and heroes and battles and saving Mother America from disaster."

"I guess."

"Guess? Jesus, Bill, all we've seen so far is the politics of war. Politics by itself doesn't kill. Bullets and bombs kill."

"Not without politics first."

"Bullshit," Don Greene added.

"We'll find out soon enough . . ." Baronne tried again to listen.

And Major Maxwell droned on as T.C. bitched, "God, what a boring voice."

"These are real mines, gentlemen." Major Maxwell had a gift for stating the obvious. "Fail in handling them and someone gets hurt, usually the person attempting to disarm the unit." He paused for effect, and glanced at the now attentive class. After he had moved his classes into this area, none of them dozed off. "The procedure is simple. You've all studied it. You've all passed your written exams." He turned to Benton Wilkes. "Captain Wilkes will lead you to your mine, beyond that barrier." He indicated a pathway leading behind the cement barrier.

"What does he mean, 'our' mine? I didn't order the fucker," Bill grumbled.

"Never mind that," T.C. said, going along with the others. "What about 'failed'?"

"You weren't paying attention." Bill made an exploding gesture, fanning out his big hands. "Phff-f-ft! *Boom.* Dead and no need to be buried."

Maxwell picked it up, "Captain Wilkes will return to the, um, safe side. I have no intention of losing a good man just because one of you clowns did not properly study the mock-up this morning." Maxwell hesitated and glanced around. "Any questions, gentlemen?" No one replied. Without the slightest warning he jabbed a finger at Don Greene. "Lieutenant, you are first."

"Oh, Christ."

"I don't think you'll find Him here," Maxwell said with raised brow.

For over two days they had been studying the mines, but Greene remained nervous. Captain Wilkes thoughtfully stressed that they had "never lost a lieutenant before and we don't want to start now."

The other lieutenants stepped back several discreet paces as a solemn Greene followed Wilkes behind the barrier, out of everyone's sight. On the other side, he found himself in an open field sporadically laced with small yellow stakes jutting up from the damp ground.

"Pick a mine," Wilkes encouraged. "Just don't step into any of the other areas."

Greene nodded. "Pick a mine." Like it was a fucking candy shop. He turned back to the minefield, brightened. Why step over a live goddamn mine to reach another one? Obviously, he thought, taking the first in line was safest. *Shit, they really set us up for this dangerous crap . . .*

He strode to within a few feet of the golden stake, lowered himself to his shaky knees, then noticed Wilkes disappearing behind the barrier. *Not precisely a confidence builder,* he grumbled, and moved down closer to the explosive encasement. He attempted to inch his way to it, stopping for a second to sweat. Very, very deliberately Greene pulled his bayonet from its sheath.

The handle of the long blade was quickly soaked with

Greene's sweat, making the long knife slippery, especially dangerous. He wiped the bayonet on his utility
jacket; it remained wet. He was perspiring from his
palms—his goddamned palms were sweating! He looked
back to see if either Wilkes or Maxwell was watching.
They weren't. *Oh, damn.* He bent down over the mine
and carefully inserted the bayonet into the ground to find
the "hidden death."

He felt the blade touch metal. Don stopped, placed his
hands in the loose, moist, and sandy soil, and felt the
mine—exactly the same model as the mock-up they had
studied. He stopped. He was sure the mine was activated
by a pin/spring combination, but he still had his doubts.

"The pin, shithead! Do I insert it or pull it out? Ohhh,
my God! A spring. What's a fucking spring doing—? Shit!
What'll I do with a spring?"

He froze for several moments, mind racing, unaware
he'd spoken aloud. It was that erector set. "I remember—
all those holes and screws, and nuts. Crap, I hated that
damned bastard. 'Build me a crane, Donald,' Father ordered. 'It's easy, kid.' Jesus, I hated that crane, I hated
those little tiny screws, those nuts—those damned
springs." Sweat poured from him. "I could only get the
sonuvabitching erector thing to raise. But 'Lower the
crane, too, Donnie.' Where the fuck are you, Father?
You lower the fucker!"

He suddenly realized he'd been talking to himself
aloud, and looked furtively around. Still nobody there.
Don lowered his head to his chest. "It won't lower,
Daddy," he whimpered. "It won't, it won't."

He'd never seen water flow from his palms, his fingers,
like that. He hadn't known they could. Greene shook his
head; there was no time for daydreaming. *God, I could
die here,* he confided to an audience of One. An instant
later he turned his head sideways to shake away some of
the hot sweat dripping into his eyes, scorching them; then
he looked down at the ground. "Wait a minute. You
pushed the pin, that was it. When there was a spring,
you pushed the pin, inserted it, right? Right?" It was just
like that damned erector set, it was that frustration all

over again—but maybe no worse than that. Don squeezed his eyes together and gritted his teeth. He wriggled his hands, just slightly.

And heard the click.

But no explosion. Still, that wasn't all of it. It wasn't over.

"You take your hand away now, buddy," he told himself aloud. *What if the bastard explodes?* He grinned and answered himself aloud, "Then you take your hand away quickly." He was down to joking with himself; it was all he had left.

Greene didn't even inhale or hold his breath. He snapped his hand out from under the ground, away from the mine. And when it didn't go off, he knelt there for a second, waiting for something but uncertain whether it was God or Satan. Then he collapsed over the mine in the grip of an icy, clammy chill.

After Captain Wilkes led shaky-legged Greene away from the mine field, he brought in T.C.

T.C. watched Wilkes leave, just as Greene had. He stood over his stake, knelt down, and pulled out his bayonet, showing more confidence than Greene. A little cocky, he curled a tight smile when his bayonet struck the mine with sickening force and he shoved his hands to it.

"Spring loaded," T.C. saw. "Pin in or out?" He paused and looked around. "Pull the pin when there's a spring, right?"

Wrong!

There was the loudest goddamned explosion T.C. had ever heard in his life. Immediately he crumpled to the ground, his face ghostly white. His hands collapsed in on themselves, had no strength. His confidence was shattered.

The primer cap, the only explosive the Corps allowed during anti-demolition training, had exploded, barely causing the sand to move, but it effectively exaggerated in the mind of a student the horror of his certain death if he failed.

T.C. lay there a few seconds, recapturing his senses. He looked up, realizing he'd been had by the instructors.

"Those bastards!" he shouted. On rising, one knee gave way.

Thursday was obstacle-course day. When training began, it had been Obstacle Course Day, Black Thursday, but eventually the course had become easier for the swiftly maturing men. Black Thursday had become something of a lark.

At the cable crossing T.C. moved ahead of Baronne and raced rapidly across the wire, easily dropping to the other side.

As Bill reached up to the wire, Forbes asked coldly, "Still using gloves, Baron?"

The air was far more biting than it had been in summer. Bill's hands didn't sweat as much of late because of additional weight loss. He was seventy pounds lighter than when he'd reported for training, mistakenly believing that he was in great shape. Now he stripped off the gloves, crammed them into his pack, and smiled coolly at Forbes. Reaching up for the cable, he hand-walked across almost in a leisurely manner, never missing a beat as he raced to the other side.

Wilkes stood alongside Forbes. "Quite an improvement, eh, Walt?"

"Yeah. Now if we can just get them all to think Marine a hundred percent of the time."

"Shit, Walt. You don't do that. They have to pick it up themselves."

"But they don't know I can't make 'em." He turned back, watching the improving officers nimbly cross the cable. In the distance, he saw the lithe Baronne and shorter, blonder T.C. running gracefully toward the barracks. "They'll need every ounce of that gung-ho, semper fi shit they can get."

Friday evening signaled the beginning of weekend liberty. They were always called to formation and admonished. Warned. Cautioned.

"Drive carefully."

"Stay away from D.C. broads."

"Be in formation Monday morning at 0500."

They were closing in at last on the final period of their training. More fieldwork—shooting and learning about tanks and weapons and artillery, mines, and armament. They were working harder, moving quicker, responding more easily to orders. Responding without questioning.

Marine Corps training was having its affect. Pohl addressed them before liberty: "Monday, at 0600, you will be involved in the largest field exercise we have had at Quantico to date!" He paced before them, back and forth, barking his emphasized words. "L.V.T. landings, tanks, artillery and air support." He stopped and looked them over with misgivings. "A few of you may be injured." He lowered his voice, shook his head dramatically. "Always happens." He raised his voice again. "It's your final exam."

12

Sword Rattling Works

Arlington Cemetery and Fort Myer represented the same venue to William Baronne. He passed through the same gate to reach them. Two names, same place: home of the Tomb of the Unknown Soldier and those who were known for dutifully guarding it. Fort Myer, an Army base, did not seem to have a purpose other than housing the shrine. The tomb was guarded day and night by sharply dressed Army personnel who marched back and forth as rigidly as possible across the rather small concrete-slab monument.

"A little crazy," Bill thought. "We guard a dead soldier—a public-relations gimmick leftover from the World War I—and don't always care enough about the living ones." He'd spoken his thoughts aloud but to himself. It made him recall Professor Johns, who had spoken so cynically about the tomb: "The politicians know how to sell wars."

Baronne had never agreed with Johns. He felt that his history courses had taught him differently. After all, wasn't his degree in history? "The real reason we guard that tomb," he'd told his fraternity brother Lyman Kazinski one day, "is to show the world that we care."

"Public relations?" Kazinski asked.

"Public relations," Bill answered.

Kazinski's barracks were a few hundred feet behind the Unknown Soldier. As Baronne walked beyond the tomb, out across an open area, and through some of the thousands of hallowed Arlington grave markers, he looked more the military man than the soldiers marching above the dead soldier. His Marine Corps uniform was tailor-cut for his lithe one hundred-and-ninety-five-pound body. He walked erect and proud.

It was his first public appearance wearing his new uniform of a second lieutenant. For this his instructors hadn't prepared him for what to expect.

As he entered the barracks, responding to directions given him over the phone by Kazinski, an Army soldier toward the end of the bunk area shouted: " *'Tenshun!*"

Since 1951, as a midshipman, then a Marine officer, William Baronne had been trained to ram himself upright at the sound of that command. At basic school he had better do it quickly! It was only natural, then, that he rammed himself against the bulkhead where he stood.

"We're calling attention for you, Lieutenant," the same voice spoke loudly.

Bill wanted to melt into the wall; everything he had ever learned disappeared in a flash. *What the hell can I say?* He had missed that lesson somehow. After dragging, embarrassing seconds, he managed to speak. "At ease," he gulped.

"It's okay Lieutenant. We get a few first-timers in here," the soldier nearest him said, containing a smirk.

"Private Kazinski here?"

"Yes sir. Second level," the soldier answered. He turned back to his locker, then again to Baronne. "They'll call for attention up there too, Lieutenant."

Bill took a breath, smiled at the soldier again, and headed up the flight of wooden stairs. The caution proved true; attention was called again. This time he handled it like a twenty-year veteran.

Kazinski, leader of numerous college panty raids, quickly approached Baronne. "Bear! My, don't we look all gung-ho?"

Bill looked his friend up and down while they shook hands. "Not too bad yourself, Kazz."

"Girls are waiting in the lot. Yours is a ringer for Yvonne DeCarlo."

"Taller than four feet?"

"Aw, that wasn't on purpose, Baronne."

They exited the barracks, marching into the parking

area with perfect military precision. Yvonne DeCarlo lost the beauty contest to the girl in the car. Elizabeth was, by all standards, an eleven. Bill slowed his pace, his shyness intensified by her beauty. "Jesus, Kazz. What do I do with her?"

Kazinski chuckled and clapped his arm. "She'll give you a hand figuring that out," he promised. He led the way toward the girls.

"I'd like to get a hand for not being awkward around women for once," Bill whispered.

They strolled through downtown Washington, D.C., Baronne again captured by its magic. To him it was forever an exciting place. It wasn't the bars located at almost every other doorway, or the hookers walking the streets, or the countless restaurants, or even the disproportionate ratio of women to men that fascinated and intrigued him.

For the first time Baronne found himself trying to say why. "We are walking on spots George Washington probably trod," he said to Kazinski and the girls. "Plus Thomas Jefferson and—"

"John Wilkes Booth?" Kazinski worked at sounding irreverent.

Baronne colored when the other date giggled. "C'mon, Kazz, look at this city—it's historical. There!" He indicated everything around him. The foursome had stopped between the Washington Monument and the Lincoln Memorial. Bill turned from the tall spire to the smaller structure with the great, seated figure. "It's here, all of it, to tell, to show, our children. That we remember. That Marines care." He swallowed hard.

"Good God," Kazinski growled, "you really eat this crap up, don't you?"

Elizabeth, his date, smiled, but she did not laugh. She did remind Bill of actress DeCarlo, star of *Salome, Where She Danced.* Her swirl of dark hair also had a faint reddish cast to it, her slightly slanted eyes were green, her figure was sensational. She gripped his hand tightly, impressed by her fervor despite herself. "It's not so bad that he loves serving his nation."

"You bet." Baronne exclaimed. "Cook's tour for you people."

Bill had made friends with the security people in the Congressional buildings and possessed after-hour passes to the inner sanctum. He relished sitting in Senate meeting rooms and fantasizing about the country's past and future and his own small role with all that. He wanted to be a part, to have something to say.

"And someday I will have something to say—or contribute."

"I'll bet." Kazinski stared at the statues in the long hallway while they walked toward Senator McGinnis's office.

"Here." Bill stopped, pointing into the office "Your senator's office." He chuckled. "Bet you never thought of writing him, Kazz."

"For chrissakes, I don't even know who he is."

"You ever consider he might vote to send you off to war?" Bill smiled, Elizabeth frowned.

"That's when he'll get a letter from me," she exclaimed.

They walked on, following Baronne, who enthusiastically pointed out every statue, picture, and office on their way to the Senate chambers.

"Fills my soul with energy, Kazz," he said exultantly.

"I think, Baronne, that you're just a little weird," Kazz muttered.

"I think it's nice," Elizabeth gushed slightly.

"You ever think these characters might send you off to war?" Kazinski was serious as he turned his head to Baronne.

Bill stopped walking, smiled, nodded his head a little. "Yes." He turned and looked down the hallway, then opened the Senate chamber doors, exposing the colorful interior. "It's okay with me. I'm career, Kazz. Thirty years. You can count on a war during that lengthy a period." He stepped into the chambers, followed by Elizabeth, Kazz, and Sue, Kazz's date.

"You can count on it happening," the G.I. said. "But it won't happen to me."

"Why does war have to happen at all?" Pretty Elizabeth clearly did not like the conversation.

"Public relations." Kazinski smiled.

Baronne smiled, shook his head. "Not all that funny," he murmured.

A short distance up Pennsylvania Avenue, three humorless men sat in the Oval Office. They awaited the commandant of the Marine Corps.

It seemed fitting during the Fifties, after two recent and terrible wars, that a general should be the nation's caretaker. After all, the public reasoned, the first president of the new American republic, which had also needed to fight some bloodily expensive battles in order to carve out a niche for itself in the world, had been a general: Washington himself.

Dwight D. Eisenhower had helped to deliver the world from a war in Europe that would have annihilated liberty as we know it. He had been put into the White House because he'd told his country—indeed, the world—that he'd deliver the United States as well as the United Nations out of Korea.

If you thought about it, it made sense. Apparently day-to-day politicians did not have the answers. Maybe they did not know the questions. Wasn't it the team of Dean Acheson and Harry Truman who'd announced to the whole world that America would *not* defend Korea? Hadn't that induced the stubborn and single-minded North Koreans to attack the South? No general would have ever talked that way. So a general became president.

While Bill Baronne and his party visited the buildings on Capitol Hill, Ike was engaged in a meeting with brothers John Foster and Allen Dulles. Allen, even more solemn than John, was the director of the CIA while bespectacled John was the secretary of state. These powerful men ruled, in effect, everything the U.S. did on foreign soil.

At first the conversation was relaxed and pleasant enough. They reviewed the current election campaign—Ike's second—proposing that the president hold back from too many unneeded public appearances. And besides,

John Dulles encouraged him, the country remained positive about Ike and "your contributions to the free world."

"They perceive Adlai," the secretary contended, "as too isolationist and independent for these difficult times. Too unknown a commodity in foreign affairs. Hell, just last week Adenauer himself said he would find it difficult to keep West Germany free without you leading America."

"They're afraid Acheson might return as State," Allen put in. It was, in point of fact, what the chief executive and the two brothers feared.

Ike reflected for a moment. "Boys," he said softly, "we should have knocked the piss out of those Russkie bastards after we crushed Hitler." He drummed his fingertips and sighed. "But as good soldiers know, once you've peaked, victories are hard won, and, I might add"—he looked up at both Dulles brothers—"costly."

"That brings us to tonight's agenda, Ike." John Dulles always called Eisenhower "Ike" in private, Mr. President in public. The press addressed the president as Ike, except at the new televised news conferences. Eisenhower never discouraged either practice. Ike was a victory symbol to his country. He'd come close to being deified. The country was at peace and prospering. "I Like Ike" campaign stickers, buttons, and posters seemed to be everywhere. "I'm expecting General Hook any moment," he said abruptly. They would wait.

"I'd like to continue our 'sword diplomacy,' Ike." John looked owlishly enthusiastic.

"So long as the press backs the concept." Ike revealed his flashing, youthful grin. He genuinely liked this Dulles, thought he'd have made a good soldier.

"It works." In an almost Trumanesque motion, John shot up both flat hands. "It keeps us from war."

"But you can't simply go on aiming the gun, Foster," the president reminded his old friend. "Someday, God forbid, you might have to pull the trigger."

"Then," the secretary said firmly, owl eyes hardening, "we'll pull it."

Allen Dulles, shoulders hunched on his side of the table, had in mind certain reports that had reached him from different channels. "Ike, there could be more guns aimed at us than we have at our immediate disposal."

With a glance toward the ex-general, Foster Dulles exclaimed, "No one has more guns than we do."

"On the surface, then," Ike murmured, that alert gleam in his eyes again, "no one wants peace more than we do. Correct? Correct, gentlemen?"

"Sir." Allen sat straight in his chair. He bore a family resemblance to his famed brother, but knew that both John and Ike considered him over-educated, over-informed, disposed toward rashness; in particular, Ike thought him too impatient. "There are rumblings concerning our ability to fight again. From . . . the field. A question of our, um, desire to fight again." He yearned to describe certain other rumblings reaching him. "It's the paper-tiger dialogue that's bothering me the most."

Ike looked sharply at the younger man. "You still angry with my decision in '54, Allen?" He was more circumspect than the CIA director.

"Honestly?" he demanded. His hand closed into a fist. "Yes. Yes, sir."

Ike was sighing heavily when General Hook entered the Oval Office, sitting quietly, listening. Hook found the president's silent gaze upon him disturbing, a message of sorts.

"The Viet Minh looked too strong for the French," Foster began.

"No. Not so, Foster. We know that wasn't the reason," Allen interrupted his brother.

Ike leaned forward, "I didn't give the French the planes at Dien Bien Phu—"

John Foster hammered, once, on the table. "At the time, Ike, that decision was sound."

Allen declared, "Operation Vulture would have ended the war."

"For the lord's sake, Allen," John sputtered, "we've gone over that before—" He stopped short, glanced at Ike, and breathed slowly, "It would have been nuclear holocaust."

"Our allies think we no longer have the desire to fight," Allen retorted. "To wage a necessary war."

President Eisenhower's mouth was working. "We've never had the desire to fight, Allen," he amended. "But we have always had the ability. God help us, we'd better keep that ability."

"We still have it, Mr. President." Hook peered soberly from face to face.

Ike turned to him, shrugging. "I am diametrically opposed to any deep or lasting involvement in Southeast Asia, General. However, it does start to appear that we may—"

"Have to do something," Foster Dulles finished. He'd been doing that for years.

We may have the ability technically, but do we have men willing to fight? wondered the CIA director. He hadn't liked much of what his organization heard whispered around the nation lately.

"We may need to use reserves, General." Ike said, eye-to-eye. "Experience most likely will be required, eh?"

General Hook's lip curled faintly. "The Marine Corps, Mr. President, has had little trouble in filling its ranks with volunteers." He raised his chin proudly. "We are still at ninety percent strength."

"A hundred percent might not be enough if we permit this to get out of hand. General, you see"—the president reached into a box containing dominoes and spread them about on his desk—"you have a row of dominoes to set up, follow me? You knock over the first one and what will inevitably happen to the last one, sooner or later, is that it too will go down. If Indochina falls to the damnable communists, then Burma and Thailand"—his round, everyone's-grandfather eyes suddenly blazed—"the whole Malay Peninsula must follow!"

There were several beats of silence. Everyone stared at the black-and-white tiles until John Foster Dulles narrowed his eyes as he turned to stare at Hook. "General, are you aware of our financial involvement in Southeast Asia?"

13

Final Exam

"They'd hide in trees and holes and snipe our guys." McNeil was relating stories again about the Japanese in World War II. "They were chameleons in a jungle we didn't understand and could seldom see clearly."

"But you beat them, Colonel. You won."

"We lost a lot of fine men learning how." He rolled his head back and forth, and made funny sounds with his throat. "And then came the kamikazes. A desperate ending to a desperate war."

"Thought they hit the ships?"

"They did. I was on the *Wasp* when we took one of those,"—he caught himself, kept himself from saying "slant eye"—"planes on the starboard side. The damned thing blew into a million pieces—killed a lot of men."

McNeil continued his stories, explaining to his Marine class that death too often became so commonplace, it was numbing, that simple survival became paramount.

"Survival in itself often became the victory."

Baronne watched a World War II Corsair F4U scream across the beaches, dropping napalm, firing 20-mm. cannons into the sand below. He was beginning to understand some of what McNeil meant.

"A person could die in that fire." Bill turned back and looked at the small, weathered LVT he was about to enter, sitting among other LVTs in the hold of the larger, parent LSD.

"Shit burns." T.C. was impressed.

"Pilots have it made. You know that, don't you?"

"Then, let's be pilots."

"Too tall," Bill muttered, winking at his old friend.

He seldom mentioned that he was many inches taller than the not-quite six-foot T.C.

The lieutenants had just boarded the sizable, rectangular landing-ship dock at 0700 hours. This would be a series of firsts and one ending. Their first amphibious landing, their first simulated combat conditions, their final exam. They neared the end of their unforgettable training.

Baronne and T.C. glanced up at Major Maxwell, who was beginning to blast his orders through a bullhorn.

"The LVT will rise after it sinks. It will then move toward the beach." Maxwell paused to look at them. His charges were paying attention. When things got serious, they paid attention. "The aft bulkhead opens at the beach. You will then exit. Hit the beach and form up."

"Maybe it's the tank troops who have it made." T.C. looked down at the LVTs with concern. "LSTs are a helluva lot larger."

"Small fuckers."

"Tankers?" T.C. suggested.

"The LVTs." Baronne shook his head.

Thirty combat-outfitted lieutenants, loaded with backpacks, rifles, ammunition belts and canteens, helmets, heavy boots, and considerable trepidation, boarded Baronne's LVT. The small boat became smaller. Tight. He looked at T.C. "Take your backpack off." He turned to Greene, command coming so naturally to him he didn't notice he was doing it. "You too." He paused. "Pass the word on."

Forbes was observing. "William Baronne," he told Major Pohl, "will be a helluva leader."

"Like his father?" asked Pohl.

The main hatch closed snugly, throwing the interior into absolute darkness. Then a small light clicked on. The LVT driver, a Navy enlisted man, spoke up:

"This light is the location for the escape hatch." He flashed it on and off. "If we don't come up after diving off the LSD, you will single file, push through that hatch." He paused, waiting for his message to sink in, then continued. "We'll be underwater if that happens.

When the hatch opens, water will pour in faster than beer piss in a toilet. About five of you might get out.''

"Let me out of here. Oh, God. I don't want to go. I don't care! I want out!" Lieutenant Wexler, situated at the front of the LVT, screamed hysterically. He had panicked.

The driver moved grimly through the officers, forced his way to the front, and hit a lever causing the doors to open. A painful burst of light shot into the LVT. Bill, T.C., Greene and the others watched while Wexler, swinging his arms and shrieking, was escorted firmly out of the vehicle. Abruptly the doors closed again—to total silence.

"Pass the word," Baronne ordered Greene, "hands on the shoulders in front of you. If we sink, follow the man ahead through that damned hatch."

The LVT's only exposure to possible enemy fire from the beaches was about ten inches of steel. The balance of the small boat was designed to ride underwater to protect the men from enemy small-arms fire. *Before* they hit the beach.

Baronne's vehicle followed others off the end of the LSD, entered the water, sank, and held—for ten long seconds.

"Jesus," T.C. muttered.

"Reminds me of when a baby sitter locked me in a dark closet with my brothers."

"You're kidding. What'd your folks do?"

"I don't think"—he hesitated, then continued, smiling—"they ever found out."

"Scary."

"This is what you call scary."

The LVT popped up and began its journey to the beach.

"You really didn't think it would sink, did you?" the coxswain asked, chuckling.

"Bastards," T.C. mumbled.

Lieutenant Colonel Baxter T. Pyne watched the landing from the shore. He'd been a Marine Corps hero on Saipan and at Iwo Jima. He was also the commandant's favorite "rank rising officer," as it was termed. He had been a lieutenant at Saipan when Colonel Hook was in charge of the assault. Since then Pyne had drawn tours of duty in Korea, the Philippines, and Washington, D.C. He was about five ten, smoked fat, stinking cigars, and never, in contradiction to the code of the Corps, appeared neat. He was a fighter first, a Marine second. His brilliance was never challenged, however; he would be a good field general someday.

Pyne was on the small hillside with General Hook and one Captain Powers, a Marine pilot assigned to ground air-control duties, watching the field exercise developing in an open, burned-out field below them. The LVTs had made their landings, and the F4Us were still making diving passes, firing blank bullets for effect.

"Pilots are low today, Frank," Pyne spoke to the pilot.

"Bachelors!" Powers growled. He didn't use many words because he didn't believe they were necessary. It was a habit developed from flying fighter planes and having to speak into throat microphones quickly, to the point. His problems with alcohol were also well-known, but Powers was liked and the brass did their best to protect him by keeping him on the ground.

Below and in front of them, tanks began to appear when the F4Us departed. The young officers had advanced quickly from the beach to the wooded area and were themselves watching the tanks approach.

"You wouldn't," T.C. teased.

"Why not? Look at 'em. Two tanks all alone with their goddamned crews huddling over a fire. Whimps."

"So now you're Major Pohl?"

Baronne didn't answer at once. Then he said in a low voice, "No rules against stealing tanks."

"Christ Almighty, Bear! You'll get us all killed."

Bill laughed and pushed off from the tree he was leaning against. Cocking an eye, he nodded his head toward the tank. "C'mon, old pal."

From the adjoining hillside, Pyne watched with a curiosity developed from years of working with young officers. His fascination with youthful ingenuity never ceased. "Do my wondering old eyes deceive me, or is that lieutenant about to cumshaw a tank?" His tone displayed his anticipation and delight.

"Just like the old days, Colonel," Powers rejoined with a grin.

Almost sashaying, Bill Baronne moved lightly to the old, mound-like Sherman, and a moment later climbed stealthily down the hatch. T.C., shaking with silent hilarity, was behind him. Bill paused only a moment. Then, with an ease and deftness that surprised him, he edged the tank forward and drove it away, its crew running behind it and shouting curses at them.

Pyne turned to Hook, smiling from ear to ear. "It's really great to see that we still get an occasional arrogant, naturally bred Ma-rine."

"Greene," Bill was yelling, "get your ass on this mother!" At once Greene, waving to other officers, clambered aboard the tank, laughing loudly. But not for long. Another tank came at them head on and stopped Bill's forward progress. The hatch of their adversary pushed open, and Captain Forbes stuck his head through. His helmet boasted a white stripe around the rim. That signaled he was an official umpire for the combat exercise.

Baronne had already reached down into his tank and discovered a small brown sack of white flour. It represented a mock shell.

Without hesitation he threw the sack directly at Forbes.

The flour splattered against the tank, raising a lovely white cloud. It sprayed a coat all over the green steel and Forbes's green helmet.

Forbes was not happy. T.C. ducked out of sight into the tank, moaning.

Bill cried, "War game rules, Captain. You're dead."

"You can't kill the umpire, Baronne. Now get your ass out of that tin can and back to being a foot Marine!"

He was pissed at the act, but not the action. The young officers had shown panache.

On the hillside, General Hook asked Pyne: "Who's that captain, Baxter?"

"Forbes. Good man. Up from enlisted ranks. Battle-field promotion in Korea."

"Good instructor?"

"The best. He'd be an asset."

"He's yours, then. Anyone else?"

Pyne turned and smiled at Frank Powers. "Our aire-dale here." He turned to the field below him. "And a few of those lieutenants."

Hook smiled. "Take the arrogant ones. You're going to need them." He looked up to the sky, down to the lieutenants then, back to Pyne. "It's going to be different this time . . ."

14

No Heroes, Just Marines

On a raining, pitch-black night, Baronne found himself encouraging three other lieutenants on the edge of an artillery range.

"The mission is easy enough. Get across the open field while artillery shells fly overhead, and reach the road leading back to camp."

The four of them sat under their ponchos, huddled together in wait for their appointed departure time.

Bill glanced at them, reflecting to himself that Lieutenant Wilson had calmed down in the past three months. He wasn't so quick to fight everyone anymore. Lieutenant Feister, joining them from another platoon, would team with Wilson in their search for the distant road. Bill and T.C. would venture out together.

"Five minutes." He broke the silence.

"I don't like this shit," T.C. responded.

"Is it real artillery?" Feister asked suddenly. In the dark, his broad shoulders and his pale, freckled face posed an incongruous sight.

Wilson stared at each of them. He said nothing but seemed uncharacteristically nervous.

"It'll be fine," Bill chuckled. "They fire over us. To let us know what it sounds like."

"Except they shatter sometimes," T.C. said, discouraged.

"How do you know that?" Wilson demanded.

T.C. looked back at him disapprovingly. He'd developed zero respect for Wilson over the past hard months. "The sergeants told me—"

"It's like the damned LVTs. They won't sink and these shells won't shatter." Baronne made a disgusted face.

"LVTs do sink sometimes," Feister mumbled.

"Jesus!" T.C. breathed.

"What about all those artillery holes out there? I mean, I've seen 'em in daylight. Those fuckers are deep." Feister was clearly apprehensive.

T.C. responded. "Full of water by now. What a bitch, Baron. I can't see a frigging thing."

"Don't worry. There's no time limit. We just have to get across the field and wait on the other side." Baronne stood, indicating they should do the same. "It'll be a snap for you, T.C. Just a little broken-field running." He pulled his rifle up. "Let's go! Two groups."

"God, It's fucking scary," T.C. mumbled. "Bill, I have a confession to make." His old sense of humor caught up with him and he finished his comment with a phony blubbering noise. "I'm skeered of the dark."

Bill touched his arm, sensing the real apprehension. "Stick with me, T.C."

Baronne had hated the dark ever since they'd gone camping, near China Lake in the Mojave Desert. It had really been dark then. No moon, a sprinkling of stars that had probably died ten thousand years ago, and their insignificant little camp fire. Crickets, bobcats, slithering snakes, and yowling coyotes made constant sounds.

"Here," Bill's father had told him. "You sleep here, all right? Tuck down into your bag and you'll be okay."

Little Bill had watched as his father returned to the fire and his two friends. They had come to search for gold in the dry, sandy riverbed half a mile away. Suddenly Bill couldn't handle it and left the sleeping bag, scooting over to his father. He was clearly scared. His father reached out and touched him gently on the shoulder. "Okay, little bear, come here. Stick with me."

The affection had kept the boy from crying aloud.

"Gosh, these holes are deep—really deep."

"Probably slimy too, alive with things," Bill chuckled.

T.C.'s voice came to him again through the darkness. "How many shells hit this area?"

"A lot."

"Bill?"

"Yeah?"

"Maybe we should hold hands in this dark." T.C. snickered. Then, "for chrissakes, I can't see a thing."

Baronne half laughed. He was eager to make it across.

"Damn!" The bark of anger from his old friend again shifted to a tone of rising terror. "Hey, Bill, I'm slipping! Going *down!*" T.C. gulped. "Aw-w-w, shiiiiiiiit!"

Baronne froze, trying to see what had gone wrong. "T.C. ?"

"Help . . ." T.C.'s voice had also dropped from somewhere around his big pal's shoulder, Bill realized, below ground level. "Bear, dammit, I can't move!"

Baronne half-knelt, squinted against the swarthy gloom. "What the hell . . . ?"

"Get me out of here—please!"

"Where are you?" Bill demanded, irritated. And frightened.

"In the fucking hole, man. And"—he groaned, sounds of exertion now—"I can't even swim in here with all this goddamn shit stuck to me!"

"Keep swearing, T.C., all I can do is hear you. I can't see shit." Baronne shielded his exposed face from the driving rain with cupped hands.

"Dammit," T.C. exploded, "I'm under all the shit." He stopped. The heavy, noisy rain continued.

Baronne caught the desperate note in T.C.'s annoyed banter and sank to his knees, crawled as quickly as he dared through sloshing mud toward T.C.'s voice.

"Over here. Quick. I'm slipping again. Aw, damn."

T.C. sounded close. Baronne shouted into the wet, black night. "Remove your BAR, T.C. Raise it up for me to grab." An artillery shell hid his added remark, "—if I can see it." The flash from the distant shell illumined the hole in front of him, but that was all Bill could perceive: one hole, no T.C. He edged toward it. "You in there?" No answer. "T.C., dammit . . ."

No reply. Nothing. Simply the drenching rain, occasional wind. Blackness.

For a second Baronne remained motionless, thinking, trying urgently to hear anything. He was wet, disoriented; by now he was a trifle confused and afraid for his friend. All sense of direction was gone, and in the darkness there would be no chance—once he located T.C., if he could—to find their way through the morass of bombed-out holes and glue-like mud.

"My God, T.C.," he shouted, getting exasperated with his fear. "Have you drowned or what?" A chill coursed through his body.

"Bear? Baron?"

Bill glanced up. "T.C. ? Where are you, man?"

"Bear, I think I've broken my goddamned leg."

Baronne moved to the frantic, frustrated voice. "Ah, Christ, what the hell's happened in there?"

"I dunno, Bear, but I'm up to my frigging neck in muddy water." He held up his automatic rifle. "Here!" He pushed the barrel toward Bill and held onto the stock. He grabbed it, tried to pull T.C. out of the hole. It was too slippery. "It isn't working, Bear. My leg won't support me," T.C. cursed colorfully. "Bullshit mud," he finished.

Baronne dropped his backpack and, putting his bayonet onto the front of his rifle, began to enter the hole; he stabbed the blade deeply into the muddy slope of the pit. He moved down with great care, holding the rifle for support and reaching out for him. "Hand me your pack." T.C. struggled to get the pack to him, succeeded. Baronne threw it up and out of the hole. "Now your belt." He threw the belt out of the hole.

Then he took T.C.'s hand, grasping his wrist as T.C. did the same, forming a lock against the slippery mud. With all his remaining energy Bill began pulling hard, trying not to pay any attention to his friend's moans of pain. "One step at a time, T.C.," he urged.

It seemed impossible by then, but they began moving upward. Slowly, torturously.

And after a nearly timeless period in the neighborhood of ten minutes, they made it to the top.

Baronne yanked T.C. over the edge and together they collapsed, back to back, leaning against each other, onto the muddy ground. Above them artillery shells began to whistle past, bursting flashes of light down-range again. Their breathing gradually returned to normal.

"Bill? Got any scotch?"

Baronne reached for his canteen without replying. He pulled it from its pouch and handed it to T.C., who took a long, hard swallow. "Major Pohl isn't going to like this. I mean, my leg is killing me."

Bill began to chuckle, low and throaty. "You musta been tackled a thousand times, T.C., but *you*, you gotta break your leg falling into a frigging hole!" He laughed. It fell quiet again for a few moments. Finally Bill said soberly, "He'll probably court-martial your ass."

T.C. took another swig of scotch. "I wanta thank you, Baron. I'm dying and you're making jokes."

"Can you walk?"

T.C. tried to move his body a little; he reached for his twisted leg and emitted a short, almost-canine yelp. "Shit! Aw God, it hurts!" He shook his head, then lowered his voice into a desperate wail. "No. No! Not now, not this close!"

Baronne sighed. "I carry you back."

T.C. drank deeply from the canteen again and then tried to hand it back to Baronne, who waved it off. "Just keep it. I brought two." He reached for the second canteen, pulled it out of his backpack, and started to down the contents. T.C.'s voice was small. Neither man had made any attempt to leave.

"Bear?"

"Yeah?"

"I ever tell you Lieutenant Wilson was a Golden Gloves champ?"

Only the rain and artillery shells answered.

* * *

At daybreak, the morning light fighting its way through the clouds, T.C. began to stir. The scotch had done its job, killing his pain somewhat and putting him to sleep. Baronne was still sitting against T.C., his knees drawn up to his chest. He hadn't slept a wink all night.

"T.C.? You awake?"

"Yeah."

"I gotta get you out of here—now." Bill leaned forward slightly, forcing T.C. to fall backward without warning. T.C. caught himself but not before renewed pain reminded him of his condition.

"Awww, hell."

"Still hurt?"

"Yeah." He rattled the empty canteen. "Christ, what'd I do, Bear? Drink every drop?"

"I wasn't offering the rest of my scotch." Baronne stood and slipped into his pack. "C'mon." He carried forty-five pounds on his back with his own rifle and back-pack, belt and canteens and helmet, rain gear and sleeping bag and poncho. He resembled an old drummer who passed from village to village with a world of pans strapped to his bent back. Now he'd add T.C. and his gear to the burden.

"You know, don't you, that the Corps doesn't expect this and therefore will not appreciate it?"

"Yeah." Baronne'd only half heard what his friend said. Collecting his energy and his bearings, he felt as if he were on the verge of understanding something profound about himself. "It's just that I . . . ." Abruptly Baronne chuckled. "Can you believe it? I've come to expect to do things like this." He grinned. He'd become a man, he saw. A responsible Marine. His father would be proud.

He reached down and carefully eased his friend over his shoulders and began to walk through the gripping mud, around the holes, toward the road in the distance. He didn't feel tired, or even pressed or weighted down.

He felt nothing physically, because, he perceived, strangely thrilled, I want to do it . . .

Although early in the morning, it wasn't bright. The sun was not yet full and the clouds were confusing the exact time for Baronne. Why was the jeep coming toward them have its headlights on?

"Who's that, for chrissakes?" T.C. asked from his more or less horizontal position over Baronne's shoulders.

"Dunno." Bill stopped as the jeep pulled up. It was Major Pohl and Captain Forbes. Pohl appeared upset.

"Who's that, Lieutenant Baronne?"

"Lieutenant Chapman, sir!" He shifted T.C. a bit. "Broken leg, sir!"

"Put that man down," Pohl commanded.

The young lieutenant shot an incredulous look back at him.

"Now!" Pohl shouted.

Baronne carefully lowered T.C. to the ground, feet first. Without crying out during the process, T.C. grimaced in pain. Suddenly on his one good foot, he grabbed Baronne for balance.

Major Pohl stepped up close to them. "This is not a game. This is for real." He paused, clearly trying to contain himself, but his words remained clipped and emphatic: "Every officer is on his own." He caught a breath, relaxed somewhat. "When you're in the FMF, gentlemen, the enlisted are going to look to you. You will walk with a broken leg, if you must!"

I wonder if he's going to shoot him, Baronne thought.

But Pohl spun, strode aggressively back to his jeep, and climbed into it as Forbes fired up the engine. He pointed at them. "But you will never let anyone else carry you. You're officers in the United States Marine Corps, goddamn it."

They sped off, coughing up dust.

Baronne and Chapman stood for a few moments, unmoving. "Think he's pissed?" Bill inquired.

"It's hard to say." T.C. looked at his oldest friend,

grinning. "You know, I was just beginning to enjoy myself."

But Baronne had turned to peer into the distance at the dwindling jeep. Something in his posture and the look of wonderment on his broad face made T.C. rethink what he'd heard.

They said it together, in a breath: "Major Pohl just called us officers in the United States Marine Corps."

15

Graduation

"That's it, Bill. Hold your wing level with the horizon."

Bill looked out the right side of the cloth-covered Aeronca's cabin area and matched the bottom of the wing to the flat horizon in the distance. The small plane didn't move fast, but it certainly moved quickly enough for a thirteen-year-old boy.

He held it there a few minutes and then took his eyes off the wing and the horizon and looked straight ahead. He was heading into the mountain over Griffith Park, just a few miles from the little airport he had left.

"You see, you have to look everywhere at the same time. Otherwise, you'll hit something."

Bill moved the stick back slightly and attempted a turn to the left. His father added power, something Bill hadn't yet mastered. The plane rose somewhat and slipped to the left, missing the mountain by hundreds of feet.

"Want to land it today?"

"Do you think I can?" he said eagerly.

"Do you think you can?"

It was a helluva question. He thought about it for a long time, continuing his flying in a circle to the left. He looked below him and saw the empty land, the long flood-control ditch they called the wash, designed to take rain water through Los Angeles to the ocean instead of into the city. He watched men working on a new house on Riverside Drive and a bus moving slowly down San Fernando Boulevard.

"Yeah . . ."

"Okay, take it back." His father jiggled the stick to

tell Bill when. The plane leveled off and then he was looking for Glendale Grand Central airport.

It wasn't hard to locate. The runway was next to the wash, just south of San Fernando Boulevard. In 1946 there were few buildings or houses or people to clutter the picture. The airport was near the stables where he'd learned to ride horses.

He aligned the plane with the runway centerline and aimed it for the ground.

"I'll get the power for you today."

Bill only nodded, he was too busy to speak. He watched while the runway came up at him. It was moving fast, he thought. Suddenly it was coming at him too fast. His eyes opened wide and he yelled wildly, simply, to his father: "I can't!"

Angelo Baronne seized the controls and, powering the little plane, pulled it back up into the air. He returned it to the flight pattern, then told his son to take the stick again. "You said you could do it. Now, let's see you try again."

Little Bear took the stick, placed his small feet firmly on the rudder controls, and took a deep breath. His father spoke as softly to him as the noise from the engine would allow.

"It's easy. Look at the other end of the runway, William. Don't look down where you're going to touch."

Bill followed instructions and saw the runway wasn't rising toward them as quickly.

"Now, hold the airspeed at forty, right where we learned. That's it. You can do it, Bill, because you said you could do it."

And when William had and his proud gaze met his, Angelo Baronne knew that his oldest dreams might be slowly moving toward fruition after all. Like so many other ex-military pilots, he'd purchased a small airplane upon his return from the South Pacific. "To teach everyone how to fly," he'd explained, so zealous about the miracle of flight that he'd become a missionary. And he understood the nature of challenge, of danger.

And like so many other Marines, he'd enjoyed watching that inner strength grow in others, watching them become real men. Angelo wanted badly for his thirteen-year-old son to be one of those men.

As the grown Bill Baronne stood at ramrod attention on the parade ground, the Marine Corps Hymn playing only for him and for the other graduates, he was bemused by his father's old dreams filtering through his own youthful mind. It was so much better when one's parents said what they hoped for, even if you found that you could not deliver. For Bill, he had been trying to become a man for a long, long while. Soon General Hook would be congratulating them. For a moment the images of Angelo Baronne and the general merged, and Bill realized exactly what Hook had just said: "We challenged you, and you accepted. You have succeeded because you thought you could."

Baronne, misty-eyed but smiling, muttered aloud, "Sounds like my father."

"Sh-h!" Greene whispered hoarsely from nearby. "You'll get us booted."

Then somebody yelled squads right, and Baronne's big body moved where it was supposed to go. He found himself raising his sword as he approached the reviewing stand and marched by. His heart was in his parched throat.

And then, just as suddenly as it had begun, it was over.

General Hook was snapping to attention on the dais. Incredibly, Bill thought, he was saluting them. "You may, now, proudly call yourselves United States Marines! Congratulations, and *semper fidelis.*"

Baronne left his old friend, T.C., and Don Greene behind on graduation day. T.C. had his broken leg and could not go; Don had been assigned officer of the day. So Bill borrowed T.C.'s car and drove to Fort Myer, where he picked up Kazinski, and together they met their dates.

Elizabeth was as beautiful as ever, even more like Yvonne DeCarlo than Bill had remembered. He was glad to see her and yet felt badly, knowing he'd be transferred out of Washington within the following week. She was someone he'd like to know much better, and in three months he had only seen the sloe-eyed Elizabeth six times.

They drove aimlessly. Kazinski was in the back seat, passionately kissing Susan. To Baronne's embarrassment, Kazz was already petting, as usual. His casualness bothered Bill.

"He was that way in college," he told Elizabeth, glancing briefly into the backseat, "and he's still that way. Sorry."

"Seems to enjoy it, doesn't he?" Elizabeth smiled. Then she moved close to Bill and began kissing his ear and neck. While he drove across the bridge and into McLean, Virginia, headed for a favorite place to park, talk, neck, and be alone, he began to try very hard to think through his real feelings toward Elizabeth.

Soon they were parked. Elizabeth, infected by Bill's mood of celebration, responded more passionately than she had before. To his astonishment, after she had moved her cool hand beneath his shirt, she was moving it down toward his belt and locked one finger around it, pulling. "No," he whispered, wondering if he might be mad. "No . . ."

"Christ, it was so close," Baronne confided later to T.C.

"So that why you've been going to mass so regularly?"

"Well, yeah." He glanced at his friend. "Confession every Saturday for a month, too." He couldn't get the picture from his memory. The girl was something else. Not only passionate and aggressive but beauteous. Lips of fire and breasts that he imagined begged him, pleaded to him: "See the wonders of my body."

He'd never attended another spring formal. He couldn't have handled another weekend away with his fraternity brothers and their dates. Not his date, anyway.

"God, Chapman," he reminisced, "she came into my hotel room and after we'd poured down a few scotches and some screwdrivers, well, I'm not sure how it happened, but we wound up in the shower together.''

"You poor guy," T.C. said sarcastically. "Life's so frigging rough when you're six five and an All-American, Jack Armstrong boy."

"So we were sitting on the edge of the bathtub," Bill proceeded, "my left leg dangling in the tub and my right one on the floor—and she sits astride me." He paused, marveling at it again. He saw that T.C.'s eyes were wide open in total attention. "Well, she began kissing me, feeling me all over." He shrugged suddenly. "Maybe you're right. I guess it was all only natural for her."

T.C. hurled a pillow at Baronne. "You should be so lucky," he hooted.

"Father said I was, well, fortunate."

"Your dad said that?"

"No, idiot. The priest, in confession." Bill lifted his gaze toward the window and looked off into the distance. "Said I showed I was strong enough to back off, to pull out—and save both of us from sin."

"That's all he said about it?" T.C. prodded suspiciously.

"That, and ordering me to say a few hundred Hail Marys or so."

"You're your own man," T.C. said slowly, possibly admiringly.

. . . "You can't be that Victorian." Elizabeth shook her head in astonishment, moved only an inch or two back. "You're a Marine."

"I'm me," he insisted. "And, well, it's the way I was brought up."

"But *I* want to bring you down," Elizabeth teased him. Her blouse had come undone at the top, her eyes were beautiful with desire. Her hand was raised above his lap as if awaiting the slightest signal. "Bill, you're human."

He made a face, then looked into the rearview mirror. Kazinski's girlfriend was barely visible except for one naked shoulder and one raised, shiny knee. Kazinski had gotten her spread out as comfortably as possible in a Ford

Customline convert rear seat, and was hovering over her, stripped down to his G.I. skivvies.

"Let's get out of this car for a few minutes."

Elizabeth looked hard at him. "I don't believe this."

He was around to her side, smiling, opening her door and reaching for her hand. "That's the problem. I do believe it. C'mon."

"But we—I thought—"

"Walk. Just walk, okay?"

She nodded, slipped out beside him. They were off a deserted road, and the night was warm and humid. She resisted taking his hand and he saw that she was embarrassed, possibly humiliated. Elizabeth was not easy, he decided, but she was sexually aware, at the very least. They strode quietly toward a wooden fence several yards from the car.

"What is it, Bill?" Her face was close to his, but the passion mirrored in it was no longer sexual. "How come you don't want me? Am I—"

"Nothing like that," he cut her off. "It's because it isn't right." He peered into her intent features. "You know that."

For an instant she held his gaze, then broke it with a reluctant nod. "I guess I didn't realize there were any men left who gave a damn about right."

"Do you know how hard it's been to be a Marine officer in training?" Bill studied her face and took a deep breath. He hated telling her this. "Do you know how difficult that can be when you feel like everybody knows you're a virgin?"

"You're kidding me!" Elizabeth gasped. "You mean, you've never . . . ?"

"Nope. But what's wrong with it?" He fought to keep his voice calm. "Do you give yourself away to anybody who asks?"

Anger flared in her green eyes. "No, I don't," she whispered. "But do you think I'm a virgin, too?"

Baronne pulled her to him and held her in his arms. "Look, kid, I'm sorry. It's none of my—look, I only meant—"

She hugged him and shivered. "It's all right." She had trouble getting the words out. "I forgot, I suppose, that we've only known each other for a short while, but I really do like you, see?" She looked up at him, tilting her pretty head. "No, William, what I mean is"—she paused—"I love you."

At that instant Kazinski had an orgasm in the backseat of T.C.'s car. *Probably,* Bill thought, *it was heard in New York too!*

But a moment later, Elizabeth Mallory and William Baronne were too busy kissing on the short wooden fence to give a damn.

T.C. was packing his duffle bag when Baronne returned to the Quonset hut. He stopped, grinned at Bill, and turned his head back and forth to feign scanning the barracks. "It's no longer home, Bear. Ever see it so messy?"

"How about the day of the fight!" Bill thought of Wilson, then opened his locker and, drawing a deep breath, pulled the small envelope from the crack in the hinge.

The future lay inside.

"I've got temporary orders to Camp Pendleton. They're staging me somewhere, but they don't say where." T.C. grinned and averted his gaze. "Infantry, though."

"Yeah?" Bill ripped his orders open as Jon Morris stuck his head around the lockers.

"Flight school, the whole squad bay!" He pulled back, smiling, and Baronne and T.C. and Don Greene heard a loud whoop.

Greene sat up. "My orders are confusing. Hang around here a few days and find out." He smiled. "That's what the damned things say."

Baronne smiled, read his orders. His fingers shook.

"Well?" T.C. queried.

"Oh-three-oh-two. Infantry. F.M.F. Pacific. Ninth Marines." He lowered the papers, dazed. "T.C., I'm going to Japan."

T.C. eyed Bill tightly, squinted back sudden tears. This

could be the last he saw his friend for a long time. He cleared his throat. "Think she'll wait?"

"Would you?" But he hated that joke and nodded grudgingly. "Yeah, she'll wait." He looked up, knowing it was time to say good-bye to a person who was the other half of his life. "T.C. . . ."

Wilson's head came around the edge of Bill's locker. "Hey, Baronne," he rasped, "you got a minute?"

Bill glanced at Wilson, his old foe, and didn't reply. T.C. quite noticeably raised a middle finger to Wilson to fuck off, but the aggressive lieutenant pretended not to notice. "Okay," Bill agreed.

Outside the barracks, Wilson put out a hand. "No hard feelings, okay? Huh?" He tried to smile. "Just cabin-fever crap, right?"

"Sure, right. Where you headed?"

"Artillery." Wilson's handshake was brief, tentative despite the grip. "Buy you a drink someday."

Captain Forbes had been busy making phone calls when the depressing telegram arrived. He'd seen death, lived with its specter. He had killed other men, but this was different. There was more to it than just a death.

In those last months a young man had come from immaturity to manhood. Had, in Walter Forbes's opinion, become one helluva leader. Now, only a few days before he would see his son, discover the growth and the thrill of him having become a man, Angelo Baronne had died.

Where was it, Guadalcanal, Saipan? No, Bougainville. It was on Bougainville that Angelo Baronne had finished the course. Forbes shook his head sadly. After being shot down, Captain Baronne had joined Forbes's outfit as a forward air controller, the first in the Corps. Wounded badly enough to keep him from flying, the rugged son of a bitch had been put on the ground by the Corps to call the shots for fighter planes and dive bombers.

Yet Angelo Baronne had been all pilot. He'd exhibited small regard for rank. He'd lacked elitism totally, respecting enlisted men as he had respected officers. For that reason alone, at least in the beginning, Sergeant

Forbes had become a battlefield comrade of Captain Angelo "Big Bear" Baronne.

Forbes remembered visiting him once after the war in Los Angeles as he'd passed through from Hawaii to Camp Pendleton. They had talked about the past with some nostalgia, drank considerable fine wine, and parted—never to see one another again.

It wasn't easy for Forbes, but it was exciting, watching Captain Baronne's carbon-copy son mature as a student officer in one of the longest basic-school classes ever held: thirty-two difficult weeks.

He wondered if William Baronne, partly his product now, would win as many medals in his whole career as his father Angelo had won in four years of combat.

Twenty-nine-year veteran Captain Walter Forbes rose, placed his hat on his head, and walked stonily out of the office door.

Bill had two weeks of free time before reporting to corps headquarters at 100 Harrison Street, San Francisco, for transfer to Japan. So Forbes had explained his past relationship with Bill's dad and provided assistance, through the Air Force, in getting young Baronne to his home quickly.

The funeral, even as funerals went, was saddening. Bill's mother had been deeply in love with Angelo, as were all the children. William wore his dress blues; his father would have liked that. Yet the tears that came so easily—impossible to hold back—seemed to conflict with the bravado of the crimson-stripped uniform.

He was the oldest of the children by many years, but his two brothers and three sisters had grown somewhat, reaching out for their own adulthood. Still, only Bill was leaving the nest.

He spent a week comforting and helping his mother, explaining to her that everything would be okay, he would be okay, Dominic, her youngest son, always the baby, would be okay. Finally he had to leave. She cried as much at that departure as she had at the funeral a week before.

"Be careful, Bill, be so careful," she wept. "So young, my little boy . . ."

"I'm not so little, Mama," he answered quietly. But she knew better. She had lived with the war and watched William's father age so rapidly. And now her boy was going off to God knows where.

"Mama, I'm just going to Japan."

PART THREE

16

Understanding

The sound of wheels against rails clicking rhythmically, unceasingly, finally put Bill to sleep. He was sitting in the seventh silver car of the California Zephyr, north-bound. A few stops—Santa Barbara, San Luis Obispo, Monterey—then San Francisco.

His book rested against his chest, his hand half covering the title, *The Last Parallel*. Martin Russ had fought in Korea and knew a great deal about the war, more than Baronne did. More than Bill wanted to know, actually. And so the monotonous rhythm took its toll and put him to sleep.

He dreamt of odd things as his mind finally relaxed after his depressing trip home, after eight months of intense training, after four years of college. Sometimes it seemed to Bill that he hadn't had a free breath in all that time.

He dreamed of Elizabeth and hand grenades and his mother and his father and parachutes and bullets and planes and homework he hadn't completed. He dreamed of not being able to locate his school locker, and forgetting the location of his classrooms, even his schedule. "My God," gasped Bill dreaming, "where's the English class?"

The train moved quickly along the coast. Waves washed the shoreline, seagulls sailed overhead, and a catamaran could be seen now and then, the ocean clean and pure and vast. Yet Bill missed most of it in sleep.

Someone was tackling him, hitting him. Was it Wilson again? No, maybe that brat, Watson. Foggily lolling his head, his hand ran almost independently over his short-cropped hair. Consciousness returned and he was rubbing the sticky, clammy feeling from his eyes and cheeks, yawning and finally gazing out of the window. Again someone tapped him, and he turned.

He found himself looking into Tom Chapman's familiar, laughing eyes!

Baronne scrambled to sit up, all but pinched himself to be sure he was awake. He'd left his oldest friend behind. But T.C. held up his orders, waving them and chuckling. "San Francisco, Ninth Marines," he exclaimed, sitting next to Bill. His smile broadened. "I'm going to Japan, too."

Baronne fought to gain full consciousness, still monosyllabic but with joy quickly starting to fill him. "Not Pendleton?" T.C. shook his head. "Japan?" T.C. nodded.

They laughed so hard someone across the aisle cleared her throat conspicuously until they settled down. Suddenly their orders were only requests.

"Jesus, Baron, I'm glad we didn't have to hike through this city every day." Walking from Marine headquarters at 100 Harrison Street to the hotel, Baronne and T.C. were amazed by the San Francisco hills and the wharf, the diversity and number of people, and the cable cars.

At the hotel they changed from their uniforms to their civvies and asked the concierge where a good place to eat might be. "Amelio's," he answered without hesitation. "North Beach area."

The food was excellent and the service even better. Neither man had previously devoured a five-course meal, and neither had had the chance to relish the impeccable service that accompanied it. Four years of making do with meals in the fraternity house plus the past eight months of Marine mess-hall dining had, according to T.C., turned Amelio's into "a real sexual experience."

"No way," said Bill, vaguely disturbed by the suggestion.

"How would you know?"

Afterward they walked the wharf, chatted with some

girls and some walkaway crab hustlers, and visited Aliotos' fish grotto. They had a drink there, then took a cab to the Top of the Mark.

"This place was in *Bridges at Toko Ri,*" Baronne remarked.

"Great flick!"

"My father—" Bill paused. It was the first time he'd mentioned his father so casually since the funeral. He looked down, abashed. "He told me everyone met here before going overseas during the war."

T.C. looked around, saw the harsh interior, the exciting view outside, the small and somehow exclusive crowd. "I guess it must have been romantic."

Bill smiled, nodded, drank his scotch.

"Ever wonder what it was like?" T.C. asked idly.

"What?"

"The war. World War II."

Bill looked at his friend and shook his head. "No."

"I have."

"Why?"

"Dunno. Guess I didn't want to be there."

"I used to cut out the campaign maps."

"In the Sunday papers?"

"Yeah." Bill chuckled. "I thought maybe I could follow my old man around the Pacific."

It was quiet a few moments. Then Bill added softly, "But most of the maps were of Europe."

They didn't use their beds that night. Instead, impressed by the wakefulness of the big city, they rode the cable cars until the system shut down, dropped into bars until they were afraid they couldn't drop out, and finally purchased their own bottle of scotch. Alone in their hotel room, they sat quietly drinking it until it was time to leave. They were slightly hungover but not miserably. Their youthful sense of anticipation and hot-flowing adrenaline were enough to keep them functionally sober.

Since midnight, the green Marine Corps bus had been at work, picking up scores of the enlisted men who were bound for the Far East. It was nearly filled with the dozing men when, at 4 A.M., it found Baronne and Chapman waiting in front of the Marine Memorial Hotel.

T.C. stepped aboard first. His duffle bag sagging to the floor, he hesitated and then whispered to Baronne, "Jesus, Bear, I haven't ever been around enlisted before. Just officers."

"Stick with me. They don't bite."

They moved down the aisle and, finding two seats adjacent to each other, crammed their bags into the overhead storage area and sank into their seats.

"We're on our way." Baronne leaned back, smiling.

Across from them, Technical Sergeant George Bender, a Marine hero at Tulagi, Gavutu, and Tanambogo on Guadalcanal, and later at Iwo and in Korea, watched the two lieutenants as they settled in. He always loved teasing newly commissioned officers. The campaign ribbons on his chest inevitably intimidated them. He leaned toward Bill. "Lieutenant, sir?"

Baronne opened his eyes. He was tired and had quickly sat back to let his body recapture some energy. "Yes, Sergeant?"

"You need a kerchief, sir?"

Baronne remembered: "It's the enlisted," his father had stressed, "who really run the services. Officers are in command—don't ever forget that. But it's the enlisted who make it work." Dad had stopped and smiled. "Remember two other things too: You must keep them in line, and"—he had paused to underscore it—"keep them on your side."

"How?" he'd asked his officer father.

"You will find out quickly enough. Hell, there's no special formula. At that instant Dad stopped smiling, had become serious and lowered his voice. "Except you cannot permit the enlisted to insult or challenge the rank."

He stared at the man wearing the stripes. "What for, Sergeant?"

"Oh, nothing much. Just that it looks a bit damp behind your ears, sir."

T.C. cocked one eye open and rolled his head to see what would happen next.

Baronne was angry. Only with difficulty did he stay cool. "The only rag you might have to loan me, Sergeant, probably has blood on it."

It was crude, tough talk from a shiny-new lieutenant. Bill absolutely would not accept this sergeant's ridicule. For a hard moment he sustained locked eyes with Bender, and tightened his lips until they became a white line.

Bender got it finally. He faced forward and remained quiet for the balance of the trip.

The sun was cracking the clouds, lighting the Vacaville landscape of onion fields, star thistle, and scrub brush when the bus pulled off the highway at the Travis main gate. It took less than three minutes for the Marines to off-load. They moved quickly and efficiently into the bare-walled air terminal.

Sergeant Bender allowed the two officers to exit ahead of him and gain a little distance before he stepped from the bus and found himself face-to-face with his friend, Sergeant John Scales. Like himself, Scales was a decorated combat veteran.

"You what?" Bender said, amazed.

"Sprung a bunch of poges from an ambush. Burned the shit out of my hand holding the gun barrel, too."

"Alone?"

"Yeah. But I didn't know that. Shit, I thought my squad was backing me up."

"Alone?" Benders was disbelieving.

"Yeah," Scales laughed. "All by myself. They gave me the medals 'cause I was all alone."

He had also taken two bullets in his right leg, Baronne later learned. His Navy Cross led the banner of ribbons on his chest, the colors standing out gloriously against his khaki uniform and black skin.

"Black don't help."

"Why should it?" Bender asked.

"I mean, the medals don't cancel anything out. I'm a man of color." Frustrated, he caught Bender's arm and they paused enroute to the terminal. "Still get called nigger. I hear it, George! Not to my face, but I hear it."

"Not from me, man."

Scales flashed a smile. "That's why I like you, George. Why, you didn't even know I'm a black man."

They shook hands in front of the terminal. "You trying to make friends with that honky lieutenant, George?"

"Uhhhhh, uh." Bender shook his head. "I don't think he's the kind of officer to fuck with, Scales. He's quick with his mouth, got a temper, I think."

Scales nodded. "This new breed. Shee-it!"

"Trouble is, he knows we're enlisted. Doesn't forget it for a minute."

"A smart ass, huh? Aw, Jesus, the ninety-day wonders. Training ground heroes, you dig?" He stopped his rather standard lines for a moment, looking around humorously as if someone might have hidden them: "You see any negro officers around here? Fuck no!"

Bender allowed himself a look around. "Would they be any better?"

"For me they would, brother."

Bender chuckled. They accepted coffee from the Air Force woman at the small counter in the center of the waiting area and strolled to a section of chairs.

"Where you headed this tour?" Bender asked.

"Ninth Marines. You?"

"Same."

Across the terminal, T.C. and Baronne were gazing out a large window to the aircraft ramps. C-97s were lined along the tarmac, some of the planes ingesting cargo, others boarding military personnel and a few dependents.

"How come those civvies are going?" T.C. wondered.

"Army and Air Force get to take their families everywhere."

"Bullshit."

"It's true," Baronne stressed.

T.C. turned to him, changing the subject. "When we supposed to leave?"

"Six."

"It's six now."

"We have to be on time. They don't."

T.C. glanced at a sergeant walking toward them. To his rear, two first lieutenants accompanied the sergeant. The tallest was holding a briefcase with a small dangling chain and handcuffs attached to it. Astonishingly, they walked directly to T.C.

"Lieutenant Chapman?"

"Yes?"

One of the lieutenants promptly handcuffed the briefcase to T.C.'s wrist without speaking.

"Hey!"

"You're a courier, Lieutenant," the sergeant informed him. The barest flicker of a smile followed.

"Deliver this to General Sharp in Tokyo," announced the lieutenant who had been carrying the briefcase.

"The general has the key. Please follow us, your flight is leaving now."

T.C. snatched up his duffle bag, looked back at his friend, and was nearly dragged away, leaving Bill a bit dazed but nonetheless amused.

"See you in Jap land, T.C. !" he called.

He was led to a military air transport service C-97 as Baronne watched the dramatic exit through the window.

Inside the plane, T.C. met Air Force Sergeant Bill Blake. "Make a bed out of 'em, Lieutenant." He motioned to the hundreds of mail sacks which consumed the interior of the aircraft. "We have coffee, rolls, and a sandwich for your meals. Flight will take about twenty-four hours." He smiled, noticing T.C.'s look of sudden surprise. "Yes, sir, twenty-four hours. Two stops and a slow plane." He paused. "By the way, we usually lose one or two engines enroute. Nothing to worry about; it'll fly itself." He turned and walked unhurriedly back to the cockpit.

T.C. hesitated for a count of three, looking for comment. "Jesus!" he said at last, finding his old reliable recourse for speechlessness.

Abruptly the plane bucked. He was tossing his duffle bag against the bulkhead and caught himself on a piece of rough metal protruding from the exposed fuselage. The plane's brakes released and the large ship taxied forward. T.C. had to move quickly and stumbled over several mailbags toward the interior of the cabin.

"Hey, look out!" The voice seemed to come from inside of a large mail bag.

Feeling half haunted, thinking about old stowaway movies, Chapman inched forward—and discovered Don Greene emerging from a bag. He'd found himself a comfortable niche among the bags, covering himself against the cold at the high altitudes.

"What in hell?" T.C. gasped.

Greene, out of his hole, nearly howled his greeting upon seeing an old friend. "T.C. ? Lord God Almighty, what are you doing here?"

"Well, what in the hell are you doing here?"

"This is what I had to wait around Quantico for, for chrissakes. I'm a goddamned courier. Been on this piece of shit airplane since last year, it feels like. Man, it's o-l-d and s-l-o-w." Relaxing, he leaned back against his mailbags. "Seen Baron?"

"Oh, yeah." Chapman grinned. "He's back in the terminal. Waiting for his flight."

"You look like hell," Don offered.

"Feel like it. Haven't been to sleep for two days."

He crashed back onto the bags and loosened his tie and rolled up a free mailbag. Yawning, he waved farewell to Greene for the time being. They could talk later.

17

Wake Island

It's lonely at the top, remember. Baronne stood silently, simultaneously tall and feeling painfully insignificant and alone, watching through the window as T.C.'s C-97 took off from the runway headed west without him. *Generals must send men into battle knowing many will be maimed for life, or die. They don't like to do it. They don't even want to do it. They just have to.*

He glanced around, looking for other officers. Hundreds of men crowded the air terminal, but all of them appeared to be enlisted men. "It's lonely at the bottom of the chain of command, too," Baronne muttered.

He heard feet quickly striding toward him and turned. The captain approaching seemed to have materialized from nowhere. "Lieutenant Baronne?"

"Yes, sir!"

"Your orders, Lieutenant." He handed Bill a small packet of papers and smiled. "You've got your hands full."

"Sir?" Startled, he wondered why he had his hands full.

"You're in charge of those enlisted men, all the way." He pointed. "Eleven of them."

"In charge, sir? All the way where?"

"All the way to the Ninth Marines." The captain continued speaking and Baronne stared at the bunch, gradually getting the idea. "They are, well, a salty bunch, Lieutenant. Don't let them get to you, but get 'em there."

"I'll watch it," he replied with more confidence than he felt. "Thank you, sir."

The captain eyed Bill intently for another moment,

smiled tightly, and walked off. Baronne gazed again at the eleven men and saw, standing in the midst of the group, the NCO from their bus ride in, Sergeant Bender.

Great, he thought sourly, sighing and moving toward the men. *Just great.*

Moments later Bill's C-97 rolled down the runway. Lifting its overloaded cargo bay and passenger compartment into the air, it strained hard against the weak, aged engines, the small props working. The pilot, Air Force Captain Sam "Spade" Digger, switched the no smoking light off, motioned to the copilot to take over, leaned back in his seat, and promptly fell asleep.

Flight Engineer Daniel "Pappy" Shugart shook his head. He handed Jerry Howard, the copilot, his coffee and returned to his gauges to keep an eye on the number three engine.

The one that always quit.

"We're four thousand pounds overweight," Howard commented.

"Be okay, Lieutenant, if you can burn off the fuel before she quits again." Shugart glanced at their snoring pilot.

Howard nodded and increased the fuel mixture. "That'll help."

"Digger burn himself out again?" Pappy asked.

"Too much booze and too much ass. Gonna catch him someday. Level and ground him." He shook his head gently, then asked, "Those Marines in the back give you any trouble?"

"No, sir. They're fine. Dependents in the back could be a pain in the ass, though. Fat lady with a bunch of kids."

"Maybe I should burn off a few more gallons," Howard laughed.

"Bucket seats are shit," Baronne swore under his breath as he tried to conform his body to his seat on the plane.

Once settled, he dozed off, aware only of the hum of the engines. From his own flying experience he could tell that one, maybe two of the engines were rough. He awakened but kept his eyelids half shut.

In front of Bill, the enlisted men had turned their bucket seats to face each other in order to play poker. A loud, obnoxious, drunk, and heady game of poker.

It was the time for a new second lieutenant to look the other way. A time to watch, learn, listen. To step in as a raw silver-bar recruit and attempt to end the antics of these veterans would be leadership suicide.

Only one, a Sergeant Berry, impressed Bill just then. Eventually he learned that his estimation had been right: A World War II Navy submarine hero, Berry later joined the Corps and served with similar heroism in Korea. Seaman Berry it was—a man born at sea by world-class sailing parents, where he spent his youth learning the oceans of every nation—who guided his commander's Silent Service sub through the narrow Straits of Tsushima separating Japan from Korea, helping to win for the men of his boat a presidential unit citation. On board the *Wahoo* he found himself embroiled in the longest submarine battle ever—fourteen hours with a heavily armed Japanese convoy—in which they were able to sink the four primary and valuable ships—over thirty-one thousand tons of Japanese war supplies and warriors.

But it was his guidance, his ability to plot through underwater mine fields into Tokyo harbor, enabling his boat to sink major "sons of Nippon" combat ships in front of the Japanese people, that brought him attention.

After that war he transferred to the more exciting Corps for the bonus money. Quickly enough, he found himself at Inchon, where he was wounded seriously enough to sit out the balance of Korea at Parris Island, South Carolina, as a drill instructor.

Later Baronne learned about Scales, Barnes, Dellon, Bender, and the others, finding there wasn't a shirker in the lot. *For some reason,* he thought, *the Marine Corps sure seems to be sending a bunch of heroes to Japan.*

The airplane was not sound-proofed, and the engine buzz penetrated the cabin with a loud and steady hum, mixing the combination of the Marines and kids across from them into a chaotic cacophony. The children were climbing over the seats, scrapping with each other, and the fat mother was making no effort to discipline them.

Finally Sergeant Berry slowly put his cards down. Turning toward the overweight woman, he called, "Lady!"

There was no response. Perhaps, Baronne thought, watching quietly, she didn't trust men in uniform. Or perhaps she could no longer hear an adult voice. "Hey," Berry tried again, louder, "lady!" At last she looked icily toward him. "You see this lever?" His hand rested on a large, bright-red lever jutting up from the deck below him. Quite clearly it was marked: WARNING. EMERGENCY USE ONLY!

"Yes, of course, I see it," she snapped.

"If you don't shut those brats up, I may just pull this red lever." Berry gave it a slight, experimental tug. "Those clamshell doors will swing open, and both you and your little darlings can get a close-up look at the sky." He spoke in an oddly affectionate, soft tone of voice and ended by smiling at the fat woman, who clearly freaked. The enlisted roared their laughing approval, but all the woman had done was wave to her brood and frown at Sergeant Berry.

"You're a crazy man," she told him, frantic but unwilling to be reasonable without a second opinion. Immediately she leaned across the aisle to Bill Baronne and slapped his knee hard two or three times. "Lieutenant, Lieutenant!"

Baronne cranked his eyes open, the soul of politeness. "Ma'am?"

"Aren't you going to control these men?"

Baronne leaned forward to Berry. "Sergeant, if you do pull that lever, what will happen?"

"They'll be sucked clean out, sir."

Bill sat back and looked at the lady. "Better do what he says, ma'am," he advised her, and folded his arms.

The fat lady was exasperated but whipped. She waved her titanic arms wildly for her children to sit and to connect their belts. They argued, but when they looked at

Baronne silently glaring back at them—as his own father had done with him at such times—slowly, one at a time, they settled down.

In the seats ahead of the card game, Sergeant Bender turned to Sergeant Scales. "That ain't no ninety-day wonder, John."

Scales just grunted. Bender added, "I've seen worse."

The C-97 continued on its way, its engines monotonously droning on and on. After the number three quit, they made a landing at Hawaii and, in two hours, continued on with a planned stop at Wake Island. But Flight Engineer Pappy Shugart knew the number three would break down again.

"Wonder if there's a C-97 in existence with four good running engines?" Howard asked Pappy.

"Most only have two good engines."

"Then, what we need to do is scrap a bunch of fuselages and marry all the good engines to the best airframes."

"Wouldn't work."

"Why not?"

"Well, sir," Pappy began, "everyone knows when you mess with a good engine it quits. You'd find yourself up here with all four engines stopping at once."

Howard grinned and nodded. "Makes sense." The plane hummed on.

Near Wake Island the pilot, Spade Digger, came to life.

"I've got it," Digger barked. He jiggled the control wheel first. Blinking out the cockpit window into the intensely bright heat, he aimed the plane for the short, water-bound runway. Tide was out so the runway was at its longest, the length he would need for takeoff, but a length unnecessary for the landing. "Fuck," he growled. During takeoff they would be overloaded from the refueling. The weather at Wake was hot and humid, killing the lift on the inefficient, underpowered, life-threatening C-97 by about thirty percent. "It's a back-assward world."

After deplaning, Baronne headed toward the small

shack which served as a terminal and was joined by Sergeant Berry. "Ever see anything like it before, Lieutenant?" He gestured around the small atoll. It was a blaze of color. "Four hundred Marines held off the whole fucking Jap navy for fifteen days with goddamned M-1s and guts." He laughed and took a deep breath. "And after that, they sent a radio signal saying 'Send us more Japs!' " He looked up at Bill. "Begging your pardon."

"Nice legend, Sergeant. But hasn't Jimmy Devereaux—the CO at the time—denied that?"

Berry only grunted. No greenhorn, second John was going to rob him of his visions from the past.

"Thanks for the tour, Sergeant," Bill smiled.

They entered the visitors' shack and found most of the others downing chilled beer. "Beer, Lieutenant?" Berry asked.

Baronne nodded.

Bender and Scales watched from the wooden bar as Berry walked up to them, Bill a step behind.

Bender asked quietly, "Beer?"

"Two," Berry answered.

"How about some to go?" Bill asked.

Bender brightened. "You serious, Lieutenant?"

Baronne nodded. "Not always." He reached for his beer and smiled.

"Like scotch?" Bender asked hopefully.

"Get it," Bill said.

As Bender walked off to get the scotch, Pappy Shugart approached. "Two more hours at least, fellas. Number three's down pretty bad."

Terrible news. The heat was stifling, their khaki uniforms hot. On Wake, military bearing as a way of life had had to go. It was too hot to survive any other way.

"Now, I know this little place right down the road," Berry began, eyes bright.

Scales cut him off. "Road? Man, the runway is a little road."

"No kidding, John. Out where that Jap supply ship beached itself. The one with its nose still up in the air. Well, there's a touch of shade, and nice, shark-infested water pools for you to dip into.'' He smiled. ''I tell ya, it's a tropical fucking paradise!'' Berry glanced around at the others. ''And it isn't bad for shaking some snake eyes, either.''

Wake Island could be traversed in under a half hour. Twenty minutes, when the tide was in. With Bill's non-committal acquiescence the men walked to the rusted-out destroyer and huddled under the only spot of shade on the island. They rolled dice and bet their meager pay-checks, drank beer, and shouted.

''It'll be about three more hours, men,'' Shugart said, arriving later, glancing at his watch. ''We'll have to wait for low tide. For what little runway is left, the plane's simply too heavy.'' He shook his head and turned to depart.

''Hey, it's the fat lady that did it.'' Berry called, chuckling. ''C'mon, Pappy, get into the game, all right?''

Shugart hesitated and shook his head. Then he grinned and knelt with the others, taking the dice dropped into his cupped palm.

For two hours they consumed their beer, energy, and money, looking much as though they were the remains of the four hundred Marines who had fought on the is-land. When they returned to the small, hot, uncomfort-able, weather-beaten terminal, they had lost their erectness. They were loose, disheveled, a little drunk. On this atoll, far away from anyone except a brand-new second lieutenant, they had let it all hang out.

It's a fine line, Angelo Baronne reiterating in his son's memory.

Bill had simply watched approvingly. *It seems to me,* he thought, pleased, *that there are times when the best or grandest of us can just let our Irish pennants hang out.*

When it was time to chance it, the old wreck of a plane lifted off the runway with some ten feet to spare. As before, Captain Spade Digger gave the controls to Lieu-tenant Howard and promptly passed out.

To the rear of the C-97, the fat matron and her bois-terous brats again came to life. Immediately Berry clutched the lever, shouting pointedly, "Hey, lady, remember?"

Her lips formed the words, damn you. Baronne, on the kibbitzing outskirts of another poker game, thought with amusement, *She's really ticked now!*

He wasn't prepared for what the fat lady did next.

Muttering, "I'll show you hooligans," she yanked the cord above her head; it rang an alarm next to the flight engineer. *She thinks it's a goddamned bus, by God,* Baronne smirked to himself.

Pappy Shugart shoved aside the cabin curtain and, clearly showing the effects of an afternoon pleasantly spent with beer and dice, ambled up the aisle to them. Pretending not to know who'd summoned him, Pappy stopped, hovered over the card players, and squinted down into Sergeant Berry's hand. "He'll take one," he announced, pulling a single card from the hand and, tossing it down, promptly headed back to the pilot's cabin.

Amid the laughter, the fat lady could no longer handle it. Surrounded by her staring children, she lowered her face into her pudgy hands. "Aww-w fuck it, just fuck it. The pilot's probably sozzled, too."

18

Sake, Rice,
and Pyne

Tokyo International Airport impressed Baronne. The runways and ramps and passageways were crammed with planes and people. Once inside, the brightly lighted terminal was chaotic beyond description. His letters home would sure have to reflect that!

But if the terminal was chaos, the street traffic was sheer hell. "They don't have any traffic signals or cops, or street lines or direction or laws!" The Maine private who'd picked Bill up, spoke in defense of his own driving, his jeep weaving in and out of traffic which traveled in both directions on both sides of the main road. Bill flinched imperceptibly at each near collision.

When he arrived at Fort MacArthur, just outside Tokyo, he was quartered in a spacious but stark room with a comfortable bed and other amenities. His first experience of the way officers were treated here was a pleasant surprise.

Later he wandered into Tokyo with Army Lieutenant DeWitt. DeWitt was a recent West Point graduate assigned to the Army base to assist personnel passing through the area.

Which, unfortunately, Baronne would be doing.

"I leave tomorrow morning," he told the Army lieutenant, "at 0500."

DeWitt was already aware of it, he said. "But you aren't going to find any of this at Camp Fuji, Baronne."

"I don't follow you."

"This is all show—backdrop. Like a fake filmed Western tavern. Besides, it's the Army.

"You're Army."

"Sure, right. But my old man was in the Marines during the war." DeWitt shrugged. "He thinks I'm some kind of . . ." He shrugged again.

"That you're not up to his standards?"

"Yeah, that's got it." He chuckled ruefully. He grinned at his newfound chum. "You want to see this city?"

"Show away, DeWitt-*san!*"

They dined at the Imperial Hotel, which was world-famous as architect Frank Lloyd Wright's contribution to Japan. They dropped in at curio shops, walked the Ginza, and drank both Asahi beer and Akadama wine and sake until both of them became a trifle drunk and Baronne went back to his fancy quarters.

At 0500 he was awakened by the orderly. He had been in bed all of two hours. "Oh my God," he muttered to himself, dragging his body to the shower. Reaching up, he turned on the hot water and promptly flooded his head. Then he turned on the cold water and allowed it to run over the throbbing blood vessels that coursed roughly, painfully through his cranium. "Jesus," he swore, "never again."

"Goddam potholes!" At the wheel today was a Corporal Sanchez, who hailed from East Los Angeles and drove the jeep wildly, amazingly ducking some of the fissures in the street. "The people here pay their taxes each year by filling the holes in front of their houses."

"They seem to have more than their share of tax evaders," Baronne quipped, his night before ripping his head apart whenever Sanchez failed to miss a gaping hole.

"The rain washes their work away the next day," Colonel Silvers told him. "Mad" Jack Silvers was the inspector general for the Corps on the island and was enroute to the three Fuji camps, North, Middle, and South Camp, to inspect the units stationed there. He sat imperiously beside the jeep driver, behind him Captain Frank Powers. Next to Powers, a young second lieutenant.

"Their runways aren't much better," Powers added.

Silvers glanced toward Powers. "It's not the runways, Frank."

Sanchez interrupted the conversation cautiously: "VMO-2 is at North Camp, Captain." He spoke directly to Powers. Then he glanced at Baronne. "Ninth Marines are at South Camp, Lieutenant." The jeep hit another hole and jolted everyone. They straightened as Sanchez continued, unnoticing. "Headquarters are at Middle Camp, Colonel." He paused, looking at Silvers and continuing in a confidential voice. "I guess you return to Tokyo in a few days, sir?"

"I do. After the C.G. inspections."

"C.G. ?" The acronym was new to Baronne.

"Commanding general inspection," Powers was quick to explain.

"You'll get used to them," Silvers added.

"Never!" Powers rebutted, seemingly unafraid of the colonel's rank or position. "Gruesome stuff, sir."

"Not so bad, Captain. We just want to know things are in order."

"He means clean," Powers translated.

"And working properly," Silvers concluded.

The jeep pressed on, stopping finally at the halfway point for a lunch break. The officers sat on the tatami floor at a small table in a Japanese facility built for the military traffic who provided its sole customers. They talked of where they had been and avoided speaking of their destination; the past was safer. Powers spoke of the days he fought in Korea, flying FJ-3 Furies, and Silvers discussed his adventures with General Holland "Howling Mad" Smith.

"Sir, is that where you picked up your nickname, Mad?" The question had been blurted out, conversationally, by Baronne. For a second he thought he'd gone too far.

But Silvers only smiled. Powers lifted his chin and spoke bluntly. "What it is, he gets mad at inspections. Furious."

"Don't pay any attention to Frank, Lieutenant."

Somewhat to Baronne's surprise, Colonel Silvers and

he became quite friendly during the long trip. Silvers seemed to like him for his honesty and straightforwardness. *Perhaps,* the young lieutenant pondered, *he also finds me terribly young and innocent. I've met one fine gentleman who is an inspector general,* he realized. *And one who's an alcoholic pilot.* It was one interesting Marine Corps!

When they finished their sake and fried rice, containing bits of white meat, Powers opined, ''Probably cat meat. But I don't want to know for sure.''

Afterward, they continued on to the camps high on the slopes of Mount Fuji. They arrived during the late-evening hours. Bill was dropped off from the jeep first, reaching South camp ahead of the others. Grabbing his duffle bag, saluting Colonel Silvers and Captain Powers, he strode with renewed confidence into the headquarters office of the Third Battalion, Ninth Marines, FMFPAC.

There he met Lieutenant Colonel Baxter T. Pyne, USMC.

Later, he often wondered if his entire life hadn't changed that day.

19

Welcome to the FMF

The three camps, South, Middle, and North, were remnants of America's victory over Japan during World War II. They were carved into the side of Mount Fuji, a mountain with traditional religious significance to the Japanese. Provided at first, for the conquering heroes to keep an eye on the Japanese, later maintained to use as staging areas for any possible war actions which might take place in the still volatile Far East. But the camps were under threat of closure as President Eisenhower received more and more pressure to return them to the Japanese Ground Self-Defense Force.

The president soon would acquiesce. Politics and economics would soon move the Marines out of Japan. But to ensure the transfer, the Japanese agreed that the JGSDF could remain for defense only. With this agreed, time began to run down.

Colonel Pyne intended to be ready.

Baronne stood at strict military attention before the Third Battalion commander. The colonel's plywood-sided, rice-paper-walled office was not like anything Bill had seen before. He waited for Pyne to read his military record and acknowledge his orders, but the older superior took his sweet time.

Pyne finally looked up. "Regular commission. Career, Lieutenant?"

"Yes, sir."

"Thirty years?"

"Yes, sir!"

Pyne rolled his moist, stubby cigar from one side to the other of his rather meaty mouth as he eyed his new lieutenant, probably thinking of his own early days. "Gonna be commandant someday?"

Baronne remained at attention, but he didn't *want* to answer the question. His mouth worked. "Well—"

Pyne relieved the pressure finally. "Your first week of that long career will be a busy one." He reached thoughtfully to the ashtray with his stogie. As a tank clattered past his small office, the solitary bulletin board on the olive-colored walls trembled. He looked steadily back at Baronne. "Lieutenant, you have command of the weapons platoon, I Company."

Baronne wasn't quite sure what a weapons platoon was. He remained silent, though, knowing he would find out soon enough. Pyne continued, appreciating the way the lieutenant paid attention: "See Captain Stroh. One other thing, Lieutenant." He eyed Bill intently. His eyelids were somewhat narrowed, indicating that an important message was about to be imparted. "It's easy to get along out here, Baronne," he drawled. The narrow gaze became a warning squint. "Just as long as you do things my way."

Pyne even took his time about excusing Bill to let the point set in.

He found that his new billet was a fairly small room located in the bachelor officers' quarters. He touched the rice-paper walls with his fingertips and shook his head in wonderment. He'd already come a long way. But the other officers seemed blasé about the arrival of one more lieutenant.

"You can get those things pressed at the camp laundry," a voice interrupted Baronne's musings as he unpacked. The other man had piercing black eyes and a glossy black handlebar mustache. "I'm Jack McCarthy, hi. I remember seeing you check into basic school when I was graduating."

"Hi. Thanks for the tip."

"It's all right. Getting settled okay?"

"Yeah, thanks."

"What's your assignment?"

"Weapons platoon, I Company."

"Stroh? Aw, God! Welcome to the FMF, anyway. But the man's a son of a bitch."

Baronne paused in slipping a hangar into his green gab coat and looked McCarthy in the eye. "He the only one?"

McCarthy laughed. "Guess you've met Major Dorn?"

"No."

"Well, he's a lot like Stroh. Except Dorn comes by it naturally. Stroh is just fucking nuts." He pushed away from the wall and glanced at his watch. "Gotta go. Troops waiting for me to check out their gear." He walked through the door, then stuck his head back in. "You ever stand a C.G. ?"

Bill shook his head. The saturnine McCarthy made a clicking sound with his mouth, winked cautioningly. "Killers," he said, and walked off, leaving a new FMF second lieutenant with a new command wondering what in the hell would be next.

Baronne was expected in Captain Stroh's office at 1400. Rather concerned, he started for there, but outside the BOQ, he stopped to appraise his new surroundings for the first time. A huge water tower hovered above the camp like a bloated bird of prey. The green barracks and macadum streets were so immaculate that they seemed somehow ominous. The jeeps and trucks that passed by were also impeccably clean. "Must be the product of inspections," he murmured. He saw a crack platoon of Marines marching by, rifles just so on their shoulders, then moved toward the office of the man McCarthy'd called an s.o.b.

Outside Stroh's office Baronne again hesitated, remembering what Sergeant Bender had said to him when he'd stopped by to visit his new platoon after his interview with Pyne. When his new gunny sergeant turned out to be Bender, Baronne's heart sank.

The sergeant, however, was both respectful and snappy now, making it clear that Bender had accepted Bill as the new boss.

"Platoon's got problems, Lieutenant."

"Such as, Sargeant?"

"Weapons, sir. They're old, rusted out, don't work. Think you should mention it to Captain Stroh before the inspection, sir!"

"Of course," Baronne had lightly assured him, glad that they wouldn't be at war.

He stood at brisk attention at the appointed time, staring down at Stroh while trying not to make his height conspicuous. With almost thirty years in the Corps behind him, the captain had a lean body like a coiled spring, and his leathered face behind his handlebar mustache gave him something of the appearance of an old Western marshall. He looked mean as hell, promptly said he was, added that he didn't give a shit for anything much. "I sure as hell don't even give a piss about reading the military jacket of a rookie second john." He only wished to pick up his pension "and fuck everything else, Lieutenant, do you read me?"

"Sir!" Bill stayed military. "If I may, I'd like to point out that the weapons don't work. I think we must replace—"

"Goddamn it, son, it's your fucking platoon now and I do not give a rat's ass what you think." Captain Stroh's face burned red; his voice quavered with fury. "Don't you think I know the fucking weapons don't work? But you see, since you need me to repeat it, I don't give a shit! You just make goddamn sure they're clean for that inspection. And when that chickenshit colonel asks you if they work, you better sure as shit snap to and say yes!" Stroh banged his gnarled fist heavily on the desk. He paused only to breathe. With the blood vessels in his neck standing out like strawberry candy, he added, "Or your second john fucking ass is mud."

Baronne wondered for a second if Bender had set him up for this. He doubted it. Horseplay was one thing; Bender's career was another. Besides, other superiors had appreciated his determination. "Captain, sir, not one single weapon in the platoon will fire. Respectfully, I—"

"Can't you hear, you greenhorn fucking college brat? Come here." He was up on his feet, rushing around his desk. For an instant Baronne believed he might smack him. "Come on, come on."

Bill, bewildered, obediently trailed after the older man into the company street. He gesticulated wildly. "This is my last command, Lieutenant, and my last fingerfucking inspection. In two measly months I'm out of this chickenshit outfit, and no motherhumping slipshit colonel is gonna screw up my record—and no lieutenant!" He got control of himself with difficulty and lowered his voice to a near imitation of reasonableness. "They are old weapons, boy. We used 'em on Iwo, and at Inchon. And we'll by God use them again. Tomorrow, however, allllll that matters is that they are clean." His voice rose on the last word, then got louder. "And you had sure as shit-shooting better inform that inspector general that they *work*."

"And what if he tries to, um, operate one, Captain?"

"That dumbass son of a bitch?" Stroh snorted. "He don't know where the fucking muzzle is. He's a goddamned desk jockey, a poge."

When a truck, rumbling along with a thundercloud of noise and dust in its trail, furnished the captain with the chance, Stroh departed and left Baronne alone in the street.

"Lieutenant?"

Bill spun, surprised by Sergeant Bender's abrupt appearance. Stroh had jarred his nerves and he needed time to think.

"Sergeant Scales has joined our platoon, sir." He coughed, then added, "Are you aware, sir, this battalion is short of, um, officers? Lieutenants?"

Baronne scarcely heard him. He edged back to the curb, shaking off his help. He knew that the question he was about to ask would amount to a plea for help: "Is it always this way, Sergeant?"

"Certainly not. We are supposed to be ready to leave for combat at a moment's notice. Something—" Bender stopped. He had come close to insubordination.

"Go on, Sergeant," Bill encouraged him.

"It's Captain Stroh. He leaves here in two months and

we get stuck with the weapons.'' He looked Baronne right in the eye. ''You get stuck with the blame, Lieutenant. Assuming you even get past this inspection.'' His eyes followed the truck as it turned the corner and disappeared. ''They're so goddamned rusty inside, nothing'll ever make 'em work,'' Bender continued, reminded again of the weapons.

''We have to stand that inspection tomorrow,'' Baronne sighed, remembering his day spent in a jeep with the inspector general.

''And next week, Lieutenant? Did you know Colonel Pyne had appointed you aggressor commander for the exercises?''

''No. But I'm not surprised.'' Bill drooped in resignation and shook his head. ''Our colonel does move quickly.'' He chuckled hollowly, trying to relieve some of his new pressures. ''With broken weapons, I wonder what we ought to do? Shout bang bang bang? Point our index fingers like kids?''

Bender didn't smile. He was in his realm and had been there before. Clearly, Bill thought, the sergeant was genuinely worried about what they'd do if orders to a combat zone came down.

Slowly they trudged toward the platoon office. Bender spoke suddenly, softly: ''Begging the lieutenant's pardon, but can we talk?''

I thought that was what we were doing, Sergeant Bender.''

Wearing a slight smile, he followed the young lieutenant into the platoon office, discreetly choosing his words. He'd been responsible for introducing more than one new officer to the FMF. In Korea he'd received a new one every other week and taken them by the hand, guided them through the morass of bullshit received in training, and eventually showed them the truth. He invested a lot of valuable time, introducing the new officers to reality, trying to give them time to adjust, to observe, to absorb, so that they might operate efficiently as good officers, as good Marines. And then, sadly, pathetically, he'd watched most of them die in combat. He closed the door behind them.

They moved around the footlockers and past the clerk's desk to Bill's makeshift affair of two sawhorses and piece of plywood. Bender stood opposite him. "Lieutenant," he said, hesitating.

"Feel free, Sergeant," he smiled. "Forget the wet ears."

"I wonder if you would like me to run the platoon a few weeks?" he said abruptly. He searched Baronne's eyes for a reaction. Not all second lieutenants were receptive to his approach. "I mean, so you can get a feel of what's going on here."

"That's a good idea." He remembered his father's injunction that the enlisted were the main cogs in the wheel. "And, tomorrow, Sergeant, what would you do if you were me and you were asked—certain questions?"

Bender half closed his eyes and rolled his head from side to side, as if stretching his neck to alleviate a fresh tension headache. Immediately he had put himself squarely on the spot with his brand-new second lieutenant, and he wanted to be neither ingratiating nor a liar. He wanted to add that military people never volunteer anything or for anything. He wanted to reach out to this kid, to yell, "Tell the son of a bitch—if he asks any questions at all—that we'll probably fucking die because of some goddamned retiring captain couldn't or wouldn't do his job properly."

Instead he chose to stand on his simple answer.

"Yes," Bill replied quite softly. "Of course."

20

Silvers' Lining

Mount Fuji was majestic in her ownership of the sky over Japan. On a clear day she could be seen from virtually everywhere. From South Camp she was overpowering—her snow-capped top, her distinctive slope reaching down to the Marines who were standing at attention on the parade ground, waiting to be inspected by Colonel Silvers.

For a month the Marines had prepared for this inspection of inspections. New equipment was impossible to obtain, so hours of work went into refurbishing antiquated rifles, jeeps, tanks, even canteens.

The weapons platoon of I Company spent most of its time scraping the rust from the exterior of the .30-caliber machine guns, Browning automatic rifles, and .45-caliber pistols worn by the squad leaders and the platoon's only officer, Lieutenant Baronne.

Colonel Silvers had completed his inspection of the battalion when he approached Baronne's platoon, flashing a glance of recognition, a gesture not missed by Bill as he expressionlessly held his position.

Captain Stroh walked to the right and slightly back of Silvers. Colonel Silvers was a vastly experienced veteran of combat, inspections, and the politics of the Corps. He was an expert at his job, and did his homework. That was why General Sharp had assigned him to the job. That and their long-time relationship. "If it wasn't for Silvers," Sharp had explained to his staff, "Tarawa would have been a different story."

"Morning, Lieutenant," Silvers began. "We meet again."

Stroh's expression changed, Bill noticed.

"Morning, sir. Weapons platoon ready for inspection!"

Silvers nodded, holding his gaze on Bill's. "Walk with me, Lieutenant." Baronne turned, and together they marched to the first Marine in the first row. He stood at attention over a .30-caliber, tripod-mounted machine gun. Silvers spoke quietly to Baronne. "Any . . . problems, Lieutenant?"

At perfect military attention, listening intently to every word, Blender formed a thought in his mind which he sought to project telepathically: Tell the man, Lieutenant—you got to.

Baronne had not replied as Stroh pushed to the front, trying to edge Bill neatly aside as Colonel Silvers received a .45-caliber pistol from the Marine over the machine gun. Perhaps Stroh could intimidate Baronne, back him away, and prevent any need for the lieutenant to answer.

Baronne answered, "Yes, sir!" He nearly choked. He felt Stroh's murderous gaze.

"Then, Lieutenant," Silvers said quietly, commandingly, "tell me." He returned the cleaned pistol to the young Marine.

"Weapons, sir, don't work." Bill's throat was dry as dust. He paused, feeling the heat from Captain Stroh, and looked Silvers in the eye. "None of 'em work, sir!"

Silvers returned Bill's polite but steady stare. *None of them?* Questions of the young Baronne's sanity raced briefly through his mind. Either the boy was suicidal, or announcing the leave of his senses if the weapons did work. His gaze filtered thoughtfully to Captain Stroh and back. Then he turned to the corporal standing over the machine gun. "You know how to operate that weapon you're hovering over, Corporal?"

"Yes, sir," the lad gulped.

"Well, then, let me see you pull the bolt back and load the weapon, son."

The Marine leaned down and pulled on the bolt. Unsuccessfully.

Baronne said again to Silvers, "The weapon doesn't work, Colonel. It's rusted shut." He looked around the platoon, into the eyes of his men who at that moment took their new lieutenant into their lives and wanted desperately to return their own loyalty. Against all odds, he was speaking out for them. "None of the weapons work, Colonel, and they were issued to these men that way, sir."

Silvers watched the corporal again attempt to pull the bolt back without success. He nodded and turned quite calmly, to Stroh. Mad Jack quickly illustrated the source of his nickname, both in his abrupt judgment and in the almost gentle hiss of his words: "You, Captain, are relieved of this command. Now!" Silvers had reached beyond his normal authority, making the impact of what he had done even more impressive to the younger, inexperienced men among them.

Stroh's struggle with his fury was unforgettable. Hands clenching into fists, he clearly wanted to reach out and strangle Bill. But he behaved militarily, saluting Silvers before whirling to march off toward his barracks. Unjustifiably proud, still tall, crimson-faced.

Silvers turned to Major Dorn, the battalion adjutant who had filled in for the absent Pyne. "I want Stroh out of here—today."

"Yes, sir," Dorn's voice cracked.

"And I want to meet the new company commander for I Company before I leave," he said, indicating Bill.

"That would be the lowest-numbered, um, available lieutenant in the battalion!"

Because they were short of officers, after their losses from Korea, Second Lieutenant William Baronne—for now—became the youngest infantry company commander in the Marine Corps' Far East division. It happened within weeks of his graduation from basic school, and he heard the orders himself, staggered by what Colonel Silvers had done—and enormously grateful.

"Our plane lost two of its engines just short of Hawaii," Greene chuckled. "So we had to lay over for three days. In Paradise! Man, Baron, the women, the beauty of the place—it's fantastic!''

"He went out of his mind," T.C. put in, grinning. "Never saw a guy get turned on so much so quickly." He sighed ruefully. "And me, Bear, with a goddamned briefcase handcuffed to my wrist the whole time."

"Drunk every night. A new broad every hour." Greene was pulling his gear from his duffel bag as Bill stood at the doorway to his new quarters.

"When'd you get here?" T.C. asked.

"Few days ago."

"What's it like, Baronne?" Greene pushed him.

Bill shrugged. "It's okay. Had a big inspection yesterday already."

"We heard," Don muttered with a glance at his big friend. "Driver told us we got lucky that the plane was laid over."

"Maybe." Bill looked to T.C. "Checked into battalion headquarters yet?"

"Sure." T.C. reached into his pocket and pulled out his crumpled orders. "Clerk told us to come back this afternoon. To see Colonel Pyne. But he was gone."

My friend, Baronne mused, *as long as I do it his way.* He smiled. "Colonel's all right. He doesn't bite.

"What they got you doing?"

"I Company."

"Which platoon?"

Bill waited a few beats, relishing his answer, but no matter how hard he tried, he couldn't hold back the smile. "No platoon. The company. Ah, I'm in charge—the CO."

Greene stopped tugging gear from his bag, astonishment washing his features. T.C., open-mouthed, eased away from the wall. "You?" they said in a breath. Bill merely nodded. "How do ya like that," Greene growled. "He gets here a few hours ahead of us and fucking makes company commander."

"Well, it's just numbers," Baronne said easily. "Mine's lower than yours."

T.C. sat down on Greene's bunk. "It's okay with me.

Congratulations. Now we don't have to work with that s.o.b. Forbes or Pohl, anyway.''

Bill moved over and sat next to T.C. "T.C., these are rice-paper bulkheads. You can hear the officers talking eight quarters down." He smiled broadly. "And you'll hear their snoring, breathing, whispering."

T.C. looked at him and squinted his eyes. His friend was telling him that for a reason. "You're not telling me—?"

"Forbes. Your favorite Marine. Checked in yesterday, T.C. Seems he and the colonel are old buddies."

"Jesus!" T.C. moaned.

21

Spiders

There were Ghengis Khan and Harry of Monmouth and General Korechika Anami and Baxter Pyne and knights and tanks and spider holes and planes and soldiers and now Marines.

There were George Washington and Ethan Allen and Stonewall Jackson and Sergeant York and John McAuliffe and Billy Mitchell and Chesty Puller and Merrill's Marauders and Colonel McNeil and Bill's own father. Books, movies, and stories were all playing a part in Baronne's work, too, because Bill was also creative, adaptable, spontaneous. He appreciated testing and experimenting with ideas—then reformatting and rearranging until his concepts worked, until he was sure things were going to work. He was capable of drawing on the past experiences of others, comingling their successes with his own ideas and applying them to his future.

He had read about Che Guevara and felt he understood the challenges facing the people who couldn't defeat Guevara and the new insurgent strong man in Cuba, Fidel Castro. Guerilla warfare was clearly the future, including urban warfare. It would take, Baronne was convinced, more maneuvering, more planning, instead of the straight-ahead assault used in all wars before his time.

"The world has changed, and adversaries within that world. Weapons will change, along with their use." Baronne was waxing philosophical for the benefit of his only available audience. "Nations seeking greater power will find themselves fighting other struggling countries—often supported and supplied by a superpower."

"Men stay the same, basically. And bullets are bullets, Lieutenant," Bender offered.

"They go on killing just the same," T.C. pointed out.

"But the battles," Bill argued, "will necessarily become smaller. War is always the same political, hellish mess, but combat will become more confined, to fairly limited terrain, and probably with less decisive outcomes. We can't plan on fighting the Iwos and Verduns much longer."

At first his ideas encountered resistance. His men eyed him with doubt. But because Baronne had become the officer in charge, he'd win. That fact did not always diminish his feelings of triumph.

"Total surprise is the most powerful wedge a commander can employ, as you all know. But when surprise just isn't possible, strategically planned and placed smaller surprises, within the perimeters of battle, can suffice." His facial expression firmed. "Maneuver warfare is what they'll call it."

"Baron, it boils down to being a goddamned field problem," T.C. pleaded. "You can't know what will happen until it's starting to happen."

"Ghengis Khan," Bill said, as if he had produced a magic trick or word. "He invented every tactic in the book, and centuries later, Napoleon fell victim to Khan's greatest trick of all—and in Russia!"

"I can't wait to hear it," T.C. sighed, giving up. "What was his trick?"

"A draw play." He smiled. He had studied this and felt cocky. "Let the enemy advance too quickly for their own men to support them. Draw them into a ring of fire. Isolate them, then, run over them." He smiled. "Preferably from the rear."

T.C. shook his head. "I'll tell you who's gonna get run over from the rear. You. This is," he hesitated, glancing at the others, "it's too creative for the Corps, Bear. You know that."

They were standing on the ridge line, looking through their binoculars, scanning a valley below. "Everything's in place, sir," Scales interrupted, joining them.

Baronne nodded. He continued to search the area through his binoculars.

Bender lowered his glasses. "Lieutenant Chapman's right, skipper. This ain't exactly kosher."

"Were you always kosher in Korea, Sergeant?" He dropped his binoculars and gazed steadily at Bender. "Seems you made a few heads swivel, too."

"I got my stripes back." He colored, realized he was overstepping. "Sorry." Then he blurted, "But the lieutenant doesn't play fair when he argues, sir!"

"You actually read Bender's military records?" T.C. asked.

"I did." Bill looked around the group, nodding. "Everyone's. Sergeant Bender did live to tell his story." Presently he raised the binoculars again to his watchful eyes. "Heroism, I think, never seems to be by the book." For a few seconds he gazed at the field below, thinking. At last he glanced at his old friend. "You ready?"

T.C. nodded as Sergeant Scales inquired, "What about the decoys, Lieutenant?"

"At the first sight of aggressors, they will pull back over that ridge and appear to fall into the valley behind." He pointed to the area indicated. "But instead they will run over here and catch them on the flank." He nodded to indicate the new area. "When they're halfway up the hill, spiders will catch the rest." He moved around Bender. "Let's see if the colonel's battalion knows about guerilla warfare."

Bender and Scales looked at each other and mouthed simultaneously: "Guerilla warfare?"

An HRS helicopter passed overhead at that moment, swooping low, banking, slowing, and then circling once before departing.

"They're looking for us, skipper," Bender shouted above the racket. As the spotter helicopter disappeared over the ridge at a crazy angle, a new noise was added to the tumult: the sound of fifteen Boeing twin-engined combat-troop carriers—helicopters flying low and ascending from the valley below. Baronne saw them land

and debark their cargo of four hundred crack combat troops. *Hard to remember this is an exercise,* he thought.

"That means there are five hundred more somewhere else," he said. Bill's expression altered little as he slowly lowered his field glasses, his mind racing. "Of course, our left flank! Scales, your machine guns in place?"

Scales nodded.

A tinny voice sounding: "Red One, Red Three, Bear? Over." It was Don Greene calling from his foxhole, where he had been waiting at the left flank all morning.

Bill smiled. Don's use of his name in the transmission was taboo. He picked up the prick-six radio. "Go ahead, Don." To hell with taboos.

"We got a bunch of 'em down here. Came in on trucks. 'Bout two hundred."

Baronne whipped out his topographical chart and spread it in front of him. With his finger he followed the lines he had drawn earlier. "What in hell are they doing there?"

"Pyne's reserves, Lieutenant," Bender said, moving closer to his commander. "In Korea he always did that. Then, when the enemy least expected it, he threw fresh men into the fight." He smiled. "Attrition, Lieutenant. Firepower and attrition."

The radio crackled as Bender finished. It was Sergeant Berry. "Lieutenant Chapman there, sir?"

T.C. grabbed his radio. "Chapman." He stayed prone.

"About three hundred coming into the gully."

"I'll be down." T.C. rose to a crouch and waved to Bill. "We've got mortars and BARs in there. Dug in."

Scales added, "And two of my machine guns."

Baronne waved Chapman away. "Take off!" As T.C. ran, Bill shouted after him, "T.C. ! Shoot 'em in the back." Then he grabbed his radio and commanded Greene, "Don, do your thing when you hear the first shot."

"Troops coming!" Bender's voice crackled.

Baronne whipped around and scanned the valley below them. He recalled his late father's warning about keeping his eyes searching constantly, "or risk getting hit by something, anything." He grabbed the PRC-6. "Okay, Scales, let your squad show itself now. And Don Greene—stand by!"

Bender was getting excited. "They are walking right into your hands, Lieutenant," he shouted.

"It's textbook perfect, Gunny."

"They are the textbook, Lieutenant. You," he added with hesitant respect, "are different."

"That's why we're going to win."

"That's why, Lieutenant, you're going to piss off the colonel."

"Maybe." He heard a muffled chuckle.

"Marines don't take kindly to innovation. You could be the quickest short-timer company commander in Corps history."

Baronne thought back to the day before, how he had pointed out the ridge line and the gully, the valley and the flank areas to Sergeants Bender, Scales, and Berry.

"I want everything to be ready. Spider holes where we've marked 'em here." He jabbed an index finger to the chart. "And here. And along here." Then he'd focused on Scales and T.C. "I want the gully traps and the weapons dug in and hidden exactly where we staked them."

Then he had turned to Greene. "Don, I have no idea if anything will happen here. There's no way to predict it." He pointed to an obscure position on the chart. "But I want you there as a flank guard just in case."

"This gonna work?" T.C. had asked him in a whisper.

Bill had merely smiled. Bender and Scales, eyeing each other, experimented with conciliatory smiles. "Lieutenant, sir," Bender put in, "these are experienced combat people. The colonel, the sergeants, and the men—"

"It's okay, Sergeant." Bill's smile had spread infectiously. "It'll work."

Greene shook his head. "But where am I gonna get the tank you want?"

"Requisition it," Baronne retorted.

"They don't just—"

T.C. tapped Don's arm. "He means, like in basic school." He chuckled.

"Oh, Jesus . . ."

Baronne straightened to his full height, sighed, and then looked steadily into their dubious eyes. "They won't know where we are until we trap them, I tell you. Explain to your men what we're doing, all right? Fill them in. Make each man an active part of it."

And so they came early, dug holes and laid mines and trip wires, and arduously prepared the area for Lieutenant William Baronne's first combat-training exercise. The troops did as they were told, but never stopped shaking their heads. Bender and Scales spent a good part of the day over a small fire brewing coffee and drinking it and smoking and chuckling covertly at the new officer and his tactics. They doubted him, but found it all humorous. Lives were not at stake and they went along with Bill without a sustained debate. The day of the battle would expose him.

In any case, having worked with new lieutenants in the past, each sergeant was determined to teach young Baronne those things they wanted him to know. They would do it their way. Time would be on their side.

"Coffee, Lieutenant?" Bender had asked as Baronne approached the fire.

"Sure, thanks!" His grin was boyish.

"It's gonna be a long day tomorrow, Lieutenant."

Bill only smiled. "You don't believe this will work, do you?"

Bender looked at Scales and coughed. Both shrugged. Bill caught it, but didn't feel shaken in the slightest. It was clear in his voice when he spoke, and the sergeants looked at him curiously. "The marriage of our knowledge and our energy," he said softly, "will work out well."

"I hope you are right," Bender replied at last, still disbelieving but, to his credit, willing to learn something new.

* * *

The vastly experienced Sergeant Bender remembered the young officer's quiet ways, his poise and self-assurance, as the oncoming aggressor troops—many of them similarly experienced combat veterans, some of whom Bender knew—walked into his lieutenant's trap. With growing surprise he saw the aggressors follow the decoys straight up the slope of the small hill, inevitably walking right into their predesigned ring of fire.

Bender, marveling, shook his head.

Colonel Pyne was watching, too. He stood on another hill with Captain Powers and Captain Forbes, intensely searching through his field glasses.

"What's that s.o.b. doing, Walt?"

"Not sure, but I doubt he's running away, Colonel. He's a bit arrogant but capable. Lots of balls during our field exercises at basic."

Pyne scoffed softly.

"You picked him, Colonel," Forbes chuckled. "But, of course," he added, "he's still untested."

Powers spoke up. "O-E coming, Colonel."

As the small Cessna recon plane passed overhead, Powers spoke into his radio. "See anything, Charlie?"

The plane flew over the ridge line and, dipping its wing, turned slowly into a three-hundred-degree arc. "Doesn't seem to be anyone down there." Then, with surprise, "Hey! They're running to their right flank!"

Pyne reacted. "Jesus Christ, will you look at that? The son of a bitch is smarter than we thought."

"Where's the rest of his men?" Powers yelled into the radio.

"Don't see anyone." The plane dipped low and searched new areas. "Shit, Frank, That's all there is."

"Bullshit." Pyne mustered a smile. "He's up to something. Let's get 'em."

Pyne's forces moved forward rapidly. They arrived at the hillside and began their climb.

"Christ!" Charlie yelled from the plane. "Spider holes!"

Pyne and Forbes saw what was happening and couldn't believe their eyes.

Behind the aggressors the ground itself seemed to come alive. Baronne's men came from nowhere. Hiding in holes, covered with makeshift lids of plywood, dirt, and grass, they popped up on command and instantly began shooting the entirely bewildered, far more experienced aggressors in the back. Other Baronne men on the hillside also materialized from underground homes.

The aggressor force was hopelessly surrounded. At once, umpires wearing their familiar military helmets with white stripes declared the entire aggressor corps K.I.A: killed in action.

And in the long, shallow gully, T.C.'s men rolled from holes dug in the side of the sloping hill. With machine guns and mortars and BARs, they shot their aggressors in the back with precisely the same victorious results.

Don Greene, without firing a single shot, captured six truckloads of troops. He had commanded the tank that he and Baronne "requisitioned" the night before from the tank company at Middle Camp Fuji.

Standing beside Bill Baronne on the ridge line, Sergeant Bender stared in astonishment as men he knew were sharp veterans walked first into the trap and were then adjudged "dead" by knowledgeable military umpires.

Grinning broadly, aching to slap the young officer on his back, Bender turned to Baronne with delight. Things were becoming a little more interesting.

"The colonel ain't going to like you, Lieutenant."

22

My Life,
My Career, My God!

Colonel Baxter Pyne was a true Marine Corps combat hero *and* a friend of the division commander and the commandant, *and* he was known by everyone else in the Corps. He had killed the enemy for his country and saved his own men and sent men to their death, and had been wounded and fought with bayonets and mortars and rifles and tanks.

Mostly tanks. Although an heroic infantry officer, Baxter had turned tanks into significant offensive weapons. He had developed tank warfare with infantry alongside as a weapon only Army General Patton before him had understood.

But Pyne's greatest asset to the Corps was his ability to train new officers and prepare them for things to come.

"And things are coming," General Hook had explained to Pyne. "You'll have to prepare a battalion of new officers and fighting men, and develop some young combat leaders in the enlisted ranks as well as the officer." That was the reason why Colonel Pyne had hand picked Bender, Berry, Scales, and the others, and the reason Walter Forbes had joined his battalion.

And why Lieutenant Bill Baronne stood across from Pyne in his office the morning after the mock battle.

"Scotch?" Pyne asked.

Bill nodded. "Thank you."

"Major Pohl told me you got his dog drunk on scotch." Baronne, sipping the drink, smiled carefully as Pyne continued. "He knew, Baronne. Fact is, as much as he loved that goddamned mutt, he had to admit that he thought—a bit cruelly, in my view—that it was pretty funny." Colonel Pyne paused. "Suited his own personality."

Bill looked at the older man wide-eyed. "He ordered me to do it, sir."

Pyne chuckled. "I imagine I had better keep my eye on you, Baronne. He ordered you to give his goddamned pooch water. But he didn't know you had scotch in your canteen." Pyne sipped his drink. "You could've been kicked out of the Corps for that."

Baronne nodded. Pyne leaned back in his chair and eyed his lieutenant for a moment while Bill somewhat nervously sipped his drink.

"This is just a big game to you, Baronne?"

"No, sir."

"Ever see anyone killed?" He paused as Bill shook his head. "Shot at?"

"No, sir."

"Where'd you learn those tactics you used yesterday?"

"Books, Military-history books."

"You some kind of nut? A fanatic?"

Baronne smiled, relaxing. "No, sir! I enjoyed reading them. I also read about you. And your tanks."

"You kissing my ass?" Pyne chuckled. "Never mind." He leaned forward. "Think all that—your ideas— would work under fire?" He picked up his drink, swallowed it dry. He poured another. "Ghenghis Khan didn't have today's goddamned weapons, you know."

"Yes, sir, I know. However"—he hesitated to consider what he was about to say—"my ideas aren't based on weaponry, ahh, that is, excessive firepower as much as they are on, well, values. And—"

"Values, by God!" Pyne blinked, gathering himself. "Sorry, Lieutenant. But I haven't heard that word from anyone in a considerable time."

"What I meant, sir, is that guerilla-type warfare is destructive as hell. To the other side. It can be efficient. And such tactics tend to keep as many of the guerillas— hopefully, mine—alive as long as possible." He hesitated to see how the colonel was taking it, looking Pyne directly in the eye.

But Pyne would not interrupt so quickly again. It had

always been his practice to let his military students talk it all out.

"It seems, from what I understand about today's politics, that battles in the future will either be small and contained or so overpowering they'll render infantry useless."

"Such as?"

"Nuclear weapons."

Pyne sat back and sighed. "They overruled that in Indochina back when the French were in trouble."

"Yes sir." Baronne set his cup back on Pyne's desk. "So, basing our training on conventional weapons, I would prefer to devise tactics, a sort of flexible-creative-warfare tactic, that will keep me and my troops alive."

Baronne's reference to his guerilla-style tactic had sent a pulsating beat through Pyne. "First, Lieutenant Baronne, creative warfare can be deadly warfare to you and your troops. Second, this guerilla stuff you keep referring to is for revolutionists. We aren't revolutionists. We are defenders—" He stopped, shook his head lightly. Then he looked at Baronne and said more quietly, "It's more likely you're talking about limited war. Small unit stuff. Skirmishes. That's what they're called and that's pretty much what it is.

"But all those battle commanders you mentioned won for the most part because they had a larger army. They won through attrition, the way most battles arc won. In fact, rather than battles being a victory for those commanders, the other side simply lost." He stopped for a moment and let his words settle in before continuing. "That's probably my point. Battles are usually lost, not won." He sipped more scotch and then continued. "But for the moment, using your choice of terms, what happens if it's rcal gucrillas you're fighting? Guerillas, Baron. Revolutionists. Remember, you will have a conventionally trained rifle company, which in turn will have conventional weapons. What do you do if you're up against unconventional guerillas? Primitives, actually." Pyne didn't allow Bill time to answer or react. Instead he again leaned forward, in confidence. "Baronne," Pyne's voice tensed, "there has always been something missing in our conventional training. Probably in most of those books you read, too. And you had better recognize it. Recognize it before you go charging off hell-bent.''

"Sir?"

"The other guy wants to live, too. Really. Don't pay any attention to the press guys reporting about fanatics. Even the enemy's PR. When we captured Japanese—and we captured a helluva lot of 'em—we discovered that they really wanted to survive. Same with the Koreans." He relit his cigar. "So, how does your thinking fit with all that?"

Baronne reflected a moment. "I never believed the soldiers of all those armies in the past wanted to die, sir." Then he sighed heavily, preparing to argue with the colonel. "Neither do I accept victory through attrition alone. I want to live through it all, and I'm going to assume my troops want that, too." He looked out the window and then back to Pyne. "I would hope to exploit my enemies weaknesses and mistakes. And"—he smiled shyly—"like yesterday, create some confusion on their part." He dumped the smile and pulled his folded yellow tactics card from his breast pocket. "I'd probably forget all this. Fire and maneuver tactics would disappear. I'd be forced into adjustments."

"Maybe," Pyne muttered, remembering his own adjustments on Saipan. He sighed, ready to wrap up the discussion. "I've learned, Baronne, that mistakes can go either way. And you're right when you believe they're deadly." Pyne seemed wistful.

"Well, sir, if I'm correct," Baronne said, understanding that his position was tenuous at best, "—and recent history has demonstrated I might be—how can there be a better defense against guerillas than one that starts with a current understanding of their tactics?"

"Well, you'd certainly better understand the enemy's thinking." He lowered his voice and looked Baronne directly in the eyes. "But what about you? What do you understand about you, Lieutenant Baronne? When those first shots are fired, meant to kill, how will you react? You?"

"Hopefully, sir—"

"It can't be 'hopefully' in combat, Baronne. Listen,

all those clever theories of yours are just crap.'' He winced. ''Yes. Just that. Pure shit if you're afraid to die. If you can't handle watching others die. What you must begin to perceive is who and what you are.'' His voice dropped to nearly a murmur, and Bill had to listen hard to follow him. ''Lieutenant, you have to be ready, in yourself, to command men to their death, no matter what your theories so confidently say. And sometimes—most of the time, you have to figure that you're already dead. Useful, but without the chance for—''

''I see,'' Bill murmured, thoughtfully.

''No, not yet, you don't.'' Pyne twitched with slight irritation. He narrowed his eyes and stared hard at Baronne. ''You can't enter the heat of battle if you don't enter the fray figuring, that should you survive, it's as if you have undergone a reincarnation.'' Pyne paused, watching Bill carefully. ''And if you allow any fears you harbor to dominate, Lieutenant''—he was leaning back in his canvas chair, now, summing it up—''all your complex theories have become useless. And most of your good men are dead.'' He spread his hands, dipped his head to signal he was backing off just a bit. ''Now, a touch of fear is necessary, or so some say. But intelligent courage under fire—that's mandatory.''

Bill's eyebrows curved, his forehead wrinkled. He realized how much he'd been absorbing in the presence of this Marine Corps battle commander. Somehow he had lost sight of the fact that the Colonel Pynes had been out risking their lives, learning by leading men, when he was still in diapers.

Pyne poured a little more scotch for both of them. ''Ever hear of Indonesia?''

''Yes.''

''Quemoy? Matsu? Formosa? Laos? Ever hear of the Huks?''

''Formosa and the Huks, sir.''

Pyne had a motive. ''Baron,'' he began, ''I've only got two other career officers here. One's an airedale who's drunk half the time, and the other was your instructor at Quantico.'' He sighed. ''They're the best. Both of them.

Frank Powers can guide an air strike with napalm next to your fingernail and not hurt you. Captain Forbes should be cloned. But they've both put in two wars and almost thirty years each.''

"Bill remained still, watchful.

Pyne looked out the small window and watched a jeep drive by, stirring up dust in the hot air. "That leaves you as my only career officer in this whole battalion." He looked back to Bill. "The only one young enough . . ."

"To hang around for a fight?"

Pyne nodded. "You had better get damned serious about training your men and yourself. Basic school introduced you to what you need. Here in the FMF you'll have to draw on those sergeants I brought over. And Captain Forbes." He exhaled. "You'll also have to train the new officers in your company. Can you handle that? All of it?"

"Yes, sir!"

"I'm not sure what we're getting into, Baronne. But if we don't take it to them, we'll most probably end up with a bucket full of unadulterated—!" He allowed the invective to hang unsaid. He stood briskly, slapping on his cap. "Lieutenant, we are probably going to enter a few little operations while we still have a president who understands the military, appreciates it." He raised an index finger, almost winked. "And, Lieutenant, victory!"

"Yes, sir!" Bill leaped up simultaneously, and saw Colonel Baxter Pyne retrieve his swagger stick. Motioning that their meeting was at an end, Pyne walked without further comment from his office and out into a waiting jeep.

It wasn't any of young Lieutenant Baronne's affair to know that he was heading out the main gate toward his favorite Japanese whorehouse, called the Bar America. Even military careerists didn't live by the dead alone, Pyne told himself, and smiled at his private joke.

23

Look the Other Way, Colonel

Gunny Bender was the oldest man in the battalion. He had seen it all. He was tall, straight as an arrow, and all business.

"Possess their minds, skipper," he urged Bill, "and they'll be serious about this. If you own their minds, they'll respond. Without question."

"While the bullets are flying?"

"Especially while the bullets are flying. It isn't fair any other time."

"How," Bill asked in all sincerity, anxious to learn, "does one man come to own another man's mind?"

"You never can own another's mind," Doctor Price had assured them, pacing the classroom. Young Bill Baronne wondered if Price wanted out of there, to be back to the Student Union, where he could gulp coffee down and eat the buttermilk bars he loved and observe the students flowing in and out until his own mind lost its tensions and it became dreamily creative.

Bill had asked aloud, "What about brainwashing in Korea?"

The other students had groaned, but Price, nearly swearing before the class, glared at Bill for a moment. Most liked him, he was fair, easygoing, generally interesting. But he did like buttermilk bars. "Hogwash."

"You don't believe it?"

"No. Of course not. Drugs maybe, exhaustion, beatings. Some probably gave in quicker than others. But you can't launder minds."

"Then, how come there are so many psychiatrists?" Bill had asked the professor of psychology.

"Money. It's a remunerative business." He'd perched on the edge of his desk. "There are some real nuts out there, but psychiatrists don't make their living off them. They make it from rich people who have allowed themselves to . . ."

"Be brainwashed?" Bill and Doctor Price were consistent in their pattern of entertaining the rest of the classroom.

Price smiled. "To hide, Mr. Baronne. Hide so deep within themselves that it takes someone else to find them and pull them back to reality." He stood away from the desk and glanced at his Rolex. "It's a mechanism that allows people to suffer without pain." He glanced at his watch again. "How about we continue this discussion at the Union?"

"It's fairly easy to own someone else's mind," Bender went on, unaware that his experience caused him to contradict a teacher of psychology. "Beat the holy shit out of it—until it wants you to take over. You make the Marine's life so miserable that he voluntarily hands you his thinking power for a few years, says, 'Here, take it. Tell me what to do.' The average Gyrene doesn't enjoy making decisions on his own anyway. It's basic, Lieutenant. There's no democracy at war. One leader. One commander, one god! Get two, and you've lost the goddamned war."

"One mind, one leader?"

"Exactly."

"What if the leader is screwed up?"

"That, Lieutenant," Bender said firmly, "Is why you got to train just as hard as your men."

For the next few months Baronne worked with Bender. Everyday his troops marched, drilled, hiked to the rhythm of the same cant called out by Bender.

"One," the company of men shouted.

"I can't hear you!" Bender responded.

"Two!"

"A little louder!"

"Three!"

"Get it together!"

"Four!" they bellowed in unison.

"That's better!"

"One! Two! Three! Four!"

The men spent weeks running through a quickly established obstacle course, marching long distances with full field-transport packs, and practicing battle tactics which included fire and maneuver, skirmishers right and left, and relearning their combat signals.

But it was the hastily built barbed wire and machine-gun course that upset Sergeant Bender.

"This kind of training went out with World War II, Lieutenant," Bender complained.

"How else they supposed to know what real combat sounds like without being there?" Baronne remembered the blanks at basic school and smiled at T.C.'s imagination back then.

Bender shook his head. "Colonel's gonna be . . ."

"He's looking the other way."

"You better hope he is, Lieutenant." Bender shook his head gently. "You better hope."

The inexperienced youngsters stood in deep hand-grenade pits. Berry barked instructions. A trainee pulled the pin, cocked his arm, and threw it into the range in front of them. Once Private Dana accidentally dropped his grenade and everybody scattered. Berry coolly picked it up, tossed it into the range, and watched it explode. Then he merely turned to the displaced troops, yelling, "All right you assholes, hucklebuck your tails back here!"

"I thought Berry was stupid. Bravado," T.C. told Bill.

"Yeah? What would you have done?"

"You kidding? Jumped out of the goddamned hole and run. Booked!"

"And if you'd tripped, T.C.?"

T.C. simply grinned and raised one brow. "I never trip. Falling down is injurious to your health."

"You take interesting gambles, old friend."

"This goddamned sub's an interesting gamble."

They'd emerged from the small hatch and worked their

way to the rubber boat in a night that was as black as hell's cellar. The water was rougher than expected, causing the raft to bob more than they liked. Bender reached out and, pulling it toward them, fell into the rubber boat, indicating to the others how it was done. Baronne successfully negotiated the maneuver, followed by Scales and then one of the enlisted men.

"Awww, shit!" Greene had missed and taken a dive headfirst into the ocean.

Bender and Scales looked at each other in frustration. "Christ on a crutch," Bender said. "Fucking beginners."

Next afternoon, the cargo net hung from the side of the AKA *Navarro,* reaching down to the water and the landing craft below.

"Feet on the horizontal rope, hands on the vertical," Sergeant Scales instructed. "You'll move downward as quickly as possible, then step into the landing craft below."

Baronne, dangling from the ladder, looked at Chapman in surprise. "T.C. ! What the hell you doing?" He had a K-BAR in his mouth!

"It's the way John Wayne always does it," T.C. replied, grinning.

But Duke Wayne did not slip like T.C., or fall into the ocean with his heavily loaded backpack, pistol belt, boots, helmet, and utilities.

T.C. sank like a rock.

Instantly Baronne dumped his own gear, but shouted to the boat below, which was nearer. "Sergeant Scales, go after him."

Then Bill dove from high up on the ladder as Scales too followed him into the sea. The ensuing silence was deafening as everyone watched. Men hung on the ladder looking down, motionless. Marines in the landing craft hung over the side, stretching for a look, waiting to help.

Then, just as suddenly as it had happened, three men popped to the surface. T.C. gasped louder than the others for air, but no one minded. The men in the landing craft shouted, reached out, and hauled them aboard—safely, alive, but drenched.

"This is a 3.5 rocket launcher. A bazooka. It fires in this direction." Bender pointed to the front of the weapon, which looked much like the rear of the weapon. "When the rocket comes out this end, a blast exits this end!" He pointed to the rear of the launcher. "If any of you assholes are standing behind this launcher you'll die sooner and quicker than the people you're shooting at."

Everybody seemed to understand.

For a short while, everything seemed to be proceeding smoothly. Then an ear-piercing scream chilled Baronne to the bone at the instant the final rocket smacked into the back of the hillside they had chosen as a target area.

He saw an elderly Japanese man clad in ragged dungarees racing toward them, shouting in terror. "Help him if you can," Baronne commanded a corpsman and other Marines. They trotted out. Watching through his field glasses, he could see that the man was not injured himself. He lowered the binoculars and turned to Bender. "What the hell is he doing over there? This is a closed range."

"Brass pickers, Lieutenant." Bender remained calm.

"It's a kid, Lieutenant!" the radio spat out the bad news. "It's a Jap kid with his whole leg blown off!"

The boy was stretched out on the ground, the aging father over him when Baronne and Bender arrived.

The rocket had shattered the boy's left leg, and the corpsman was applying a tourniquet, trying to halt the copious bleeding.

"Oh, my God!" Bill blurted, shocked and sickened.

"Get a chopper!" Bender ordered the Marine with the PRC-10 radio, who moved quickly to the top of the ridge to call for help.

Baronne looked up blankly at the sergeant.

"They pick up the brass from our shells, then sell it. The buyers make cigarette lighters and other souvenirs." Bender looked down.

"His leg's gone," the corpsman spoke up. "I've

stanched the bleeding, but he has to get to sick bay. Quickly.''

"Taxi past it, son," his father had shouted. The plane in front was burning from its crash landing. *"You're going to take off and fly out of here. You're going to leave that behind!"*

"God!'' His eyes glazed watching the injured Japanese boy. The youth's screams were unnerving. Bill's thoughts were intense, combining facts. *He forced me into the air to keep me thinking, keep me flying.* He looked around at the young Marines in his command, all of whom were motionless, some in apparent shock.

"All right,'' he commanded them. "Back to your positions.'' He'd spoken severely. Now he half smiled. "The corpsman has it under control.''

He saw Sergeant Bender glancing at him, imperceptibly nodding his approval.

T.C. yelled at the Army sergeant: "No fucking way, Sergeant! Not until that Korean colonel is out of there!''

The Asiatic officer in question stood at the end of the jump cable. Each time a South Korean soldier landed, after his jump from the tower, the colonel had beaten him about the head and shoulders for any imperfection in the jump. Then he virtually chased the abused man back to the tower, where he had to do it again.

T.C. had stared expressionlessly at the vicious scenes as he worked his way up the ladder. He was behind Scales, who jumped without any interference from the colonel. But when he stood on the platform, attaching his cable harness, he decided he didn't trust the Korean.

He repeated his demand to the 82nd Airborne sergeant. "No way, Sergeant! If I go, he goes. He stays, I stay!''

For a moment the Army sergeant's eyes and T.C.'s were locked in cold fury and a test of wills.

Then the sergeant shrugged the Korean officer away, looked at T.C. with a taunting smile, and made a low bow. "Now, Loooooo-tenant—if you please!''

T.C. jumped.

On his way down the cable, fast as it was, Chapman's wary eyes were glued to the sadistic Korean. His posture and fiercely watchful stare were quite clear for all to see and brought a round of laughter from Baronne and the others.

It was actually a laugh of appreciation for the way ol' T.C. had lightened an otherwise tense atmosphere.

The very next day they made their first live jump.

And that night they became very drunk, indeed, at the officers club.

"Training," Bill said woozily, "over for a week."

The others cheered him, toasted his health, and Bill promptly passed out.

Colonel Pyne had observed the celebration and understood the purpose for it better than the lieutenants themselves. He'd been there; he recalled how it was and always would. His eyes glided above his glass to Forbes. "You know anything about their jumping?"

"No, sir," Forbes confessed. There had been no official authorization for the Marines to jump with the Army.

Pyne sipped his scotch and nodded. "Well, I knew they were cumshawers from the outset," he said mildly. And Forbes nodded. "However . . ."

"Colonel?"

Pyne shook his head, pressed the glass against his temple. "Nothing," he said, and smiled.

24

Bar California

Gotemba was there because the Marines were there. It would all but vanish later, when President Eisenhower gave the order which transferred the Marines to Okinawa for permanent basing. Gotemba was a conglomeration of bars with names which, with almost American commercial savvy, boasted American states: "Bar America," "Bar Oklahoma," and "Bar California." There were others, of course.

"You don't know what they are?" T.C. exclaimed, staring at Baronne. "Why, friend, they're geisha whorehouses."

Bill scowled, reddened. "Great! What do I want with places like that?"

Don Greene chuckled. Walking energetically through the wildly painted clapboard town, he gestured for Baronne to calm down. "Take a break, Baron," he said lightly. "These places are interesting—and you don't have to fuckee-fuckee."

Baronne just looked at him, making a face. It was just like Greene to pervert the language for his own uses.

"It's like going to buy a ranch," T.C. said, trying to keep his face straight as he glanced at his taller friend. "Or don't you know about that?"

"C'mon, Chapman," Greene injected. "We don't want to stick the Baron with one of the commandant's ranches." He giggled.

"What are you two talking about?" Bill asked. "Ranches? In Japan?"

T.C. shook his head sadly. "You really don't know about the commandant's greatest faux pas, do you?"

"He's got to know," Greene exploded, laughing. "Where have you been, Baronne? I'm talking about Hook—when he visited Iwakuni."

Bill sighed. "I have no idea what you two idiots are talking about."

"The article in *Time*," T.C. said, finally beginning to explain. "It reported Hook told the wives their husbands were doing just fine—that some of them were even living on ranches."

For the first time Baronne smiled. "You mean—?"

Greene's chin bobbed affirmatively. "He'd been told that his men—mostly the pilots—were hanging out at ranches—"

"And our great general didn't know that 'ranch' was a euphemism for shacking up with a whore."

Baronne howled. "It must have made one helluva story."

"Not to mention causing a few marital breakups," T.C. added as they crossed two neatly laned streets and approached the place called the Bar California. "When the American ladies got wind of the real translation."

For an instant Baronne held back, shaking his head. He'd spent his first few months working hard on the base. He hadn't ventured outside the main gate, and going to a house of prostitution wasn't his idea of seeing Japan.

"It's not so bad, Baron," Greene coaxed, opening the door. "They have fabulous food, sake, tatami mats, and our very own room for partying in."

He let himself be dragged inside. And after removing their shoes, in the polite Japanese custom, they were led by a geisha girl to a small but comfortable, exotically decorated room. Tired but alert, they sank to the floor—there were no chairs—around a floor-level round table. A petite girl with alabaster skin trotted toward them, bowing.

"Jo-*san*," T.C. greeted her. "Sake and rice for our friend."

Her tiny black eyes darted from one to the other. "You guys come here alla time?"

"Yep,' Greene replied, grinning. "Sure do."

"Then ware-come home," she replied with a shy smile.

Moments later three geisha girls brought them potent sake, plus fried rice with chopsticks, and sat down easily and amiably with the Marines.

T.C. lifted his sake cup. "To a life that's a little easier," he toasted. Glancing warningly at Bill, he added, "And lay off the constant training, yet."

While they ate and drank, the geisha girls eased behind them and began rubbing their broad shoulders. Each time that any of them drained his cup, the closest girl refilled it. Bill Baronne, all but speechless, listened to a nearly constant flow of feminine chatter in a tongue he could not yet even begin to understand.

Among themselves, with the girls almost serving as mechanical backdrops to the masculine conversation, they talked about the parachute drop and the boy who had been so severely injured by a rocket. They mentioned some of the things they'd learned from Bender and Scales and Berry, while T.C. wondered aloud why they'd spent eight months training at Quantico when a few weeks with pros on the spot would have achieved the same things.

Eventually, as though by a signal none of them could identify, one geisha girl knelt beside T.C. with her earnest young face close to his. "Fuckee-fuckee?"

He paused, nodded, and was gently taken by the hand and led away.

A second geisha bent down to Greene, brightly posing the same question. She received the same response, while Bill Baronne got a broad wink from Don and was left without his male companions.

He braced himself. And the third geisha, appearing on his opposite side so that he had to spin his head around to see her, barely got one "fuckee" out of her small mouth when he'd roared an emphatic no.

Part of it, he ruminated sourly, was that in his whole life he had never heard of any woman who treated the subject of intercourse with such amazing flippancy—a nonchalantly happy attitude as light as the Japanese lanterns dangling and twisting with the slightest gust of air.

To his surprise the girl—could she have been as old as seventeen?—insisted. "You come, boy-*san*," she cried brightly, pretty as porcelain and seemingly as fragile.

"I said, no," he told her, taken aback by her persistence.

"No-no-no," she exclaimed, shaking her bowered black hair. "No fuckee-fuckee, see? No! You come now?"

Bill hesitated, then stood and walked with her through the silently sliding rice-paper door into the adjacent room. He found himself staring at an ornate sunken tub filled with invitingly warm water.

And the geisha girl began removing his clothes.

She only giggled, as if he'd done something amusing, and persisted. She pointed to the steam bath and tub of water, indicated with busy hands that she'd give him a complete rubdown. Dubiously Baronne helped her undress him.

"Skivvies stay on," he barked, stiffly holding tightly to his shorts.

She giggled again and led him to the wooden steam bath. His curiosity overpowered his judgment as he sank into the wooden structure. She closed the contraption and snapped it shut. Only his head protruding from the tank. His large body felt crammed and trapped.

She wrapped a towel around his neck, then poured the boiling water into the small hole at the rear of the wooden box. His mouth opened in a gasp. For a second he wondered if this new generation of Japanese might have found an ingenious way of belatedly winning the war. Then the heat tapered off, and as he relaxed, it felt good. Really good.

Afterward she dragged him out and led him to the sunken tub, where she began washing him tenderly from head to foot. The experience was incredible. Part of his mind waited for his body to respond; all of his body was turning to passive mush. On the tatami mat he closed his eyes and let his mind drift into a valley of nothingness, a soothing nowhere. For a few moments he fell sound alseep.

Greene and T.C. returned to the room they had exited, and found themselves alone. They poured more sake, and waited, beginning to wonder aloud about their friend. Then a geisha entered and brought more sake.

"Where's Baron-*san?*" T.C. asked. The girl simply stood, walked to the sliding door, cracked it a bit, looked quickly into the room. She closed the door and, stepping back, indicated Bill was in good hands. *"Dai jobo."*

"I didn't believe he'd do it," T.C. murmured. There was almost a note of disappointment in his voice.

"What the hell?" Greene said expansively. "It had to happen some time, right?" He laughed approvingly. "Man can't carry a fucking cherry forever."

A voice reached them as from some distant land. It was so hesitant, so soft, neither man looked around for a moment. "It's . . . some kind of . . . fantasy . . .''

The sliding door had opened and Baronne was returning. Crawling.

"I do not believe it" T.C. said, reaching out to haul Bill over to the legless table. "The master has suc-cumbed."

"I don't know about 'suc-cumbed,' " Greene retorted, starting to laugh, "but 'comed' looks pretty accurate."

"All those beautiful cheerleaders at U.S.C., rejected, left broken-hearted," T.C. said wonderingly. "That gorgeous, lovely girl in D.C., turned down flat."

"Twenty-three years of virginity," Greene cried, cackling with amusement, "down the tubes—Jay-pan-eez tubes!"

"And you," T.C. said to Bill, shaking his head in mock displeasure, "you pop your cherry with a Nipponese lady of the night."

Don gave in to uncontrollable laughter. Tom Chapman went on shaking his blond-haired head, a giggle starting somewhere in his broad chest.

"No." Baronne's geisha, finally piecing together the meaning of it all, raised her little hands and shook them from left to right along with her charming little head. "No, boys, he no fuckee-fuckee," she explained. "He

just one whipped Marine from steam and special rubdown.''

And she smiled proudly until a crimson Baronne
hugged her.

25

Last Chance

"It's our job to kill you," Bender announced with professional intensity. "You have seventy-two hours to make it from here"—he pointed on the map in front of them—"to here."

Baronne, Greene, and T.C. looked at him, then back at the map. They listened closely as Bender continued: "You'll jump together." Bender glanced at Berry and Scales. "We'll jump one minute later."

"And if we get lucky and kill you?" Baronne inquired.

"You won't, Lieutenant." Bender rolled up the chart. "You won't."

The Sikorsky-HRS helicopter they sat in continued its flight through the night toward their objective. They fell quiet for a few moments as Bender returned the chart to his map case.

"We have some troops on the ground." He looked at Bill as he spoke over the sound of the chopper's engine and rotor blades. "If you're caught alive, they'll strip you down, paint your body red, and put you in a cage. Then they'll parade you through South Camp." He managed a rare little grin. Bill nodded without speaking.

The pilot of the chopper, sitting above them and forward, his legs showing through the hole in the bulkhead, stamped his foot on the deck.

It was the signal.

"Time!" Bender shouted.

The three lieutenants moved warily to the open hatch. Bill looked back for one last time, then rolled forward into the black night. He trusted fully that he had the altitude required and that the pilot was indeed over the open area they had preselected.

T.C. and Greene followed. After they jumped, Bender leaned over and closed the hatch, banged the deck below the pilot's feet, and yelled, "Put us down where we planned." His mouth formed a half smile. "We ain't that dumb."

"There's nothing blacker than this." Baronne spoke to the night as he floated slowly to earth. With no moon and some clouds on the horizon, the only visible object was the departing helicopter's small navigational lights. He noted the direction of the chopper's flight, looked down, and suddenly wondered when the ground would meet him. He checked for Greene and T.C., couldn't see them. "Jesus! Next time we're carrying flashlights," he told the foreign shadows.

He tilted his head back to check his canopy, and at that instant he met the ground. He rolled his bulk, pulled a little by the whipping breeze. He punched at the T7-A harness release and the canopy collapsed, stopping his movement. He took a grateful breath.

T.C. hit the ground about a hundred and fifty feet away, but he couldn't hear Greene. Bill gathered his chute and placed a few small rocks on the silk to keep it from blowing away.

"Baron?"

"Yeah, here!"

They moved toward each other and then heard Greene's almost accusatory tones, "Hey!"

"Stay there, Don," Bill called. He and T.C. walked to Greene's location. Then they sat and breathed easily for a few moments, marveling they had made a night jump and were neither injured nor dead.

"Which way?" Greene brought them back to reality.

Bill looked at him as well as the night would permit. "The direction the chopper flew."

"What?" T.C. cut him off, surprised.

"We take the offense. We do not run from them."

"That's what they're expecting," Greene chuckled appreciatively.

T.C. sighed. "As much as I love the dark . . ."

They shifted their packs on their backs and quickly began the hike back.

The Sikorsky landed in an open area. The three sergeants promptly jumped out. Bender waved the pilot away, and the chopper disappeared into the night.

Bender led his two men into the direction from which the helicopter had come—in a hurry—back toward the three officers.

"They'll head straight back for South Camp," Bender assured them, and exhorted them on with an expression of evil glee.

Quickly they moved out of the open area and into the woods, seeking a covering that would keep them from being prematurely observed when the first crack of dawn penetrated the area.

"Draw Sanchez on the radio," Bender instructed Berry while they jogged on.

Berry nodded, pulled the prick-six from his pack, and radioed Sanchez.

Sergeant Scales grinned happily. "This shouldn't take too long," he breathed.

Colonel Pyne had breakfasted early, enjoying two poached eggs on toast even before Captain Forbes joined him in the mess tent.

Forbes held back the entrance flap. "They landed safely, Colonel."

Pyne grunted acknowledgment and put jam on his last bite of toast.

"You think this is such a good idea?"

Pyne swallowed the morsel, sipped his coffee, put the cup down, pushed the food tray aside. He glanced through the tent flap and saw it was a nice day. "I dunno, Walt. Maybe so and maybe not. All right?" He retrieved his coffee and peered thoughtfully over the rim of the cup at Forbes. "It was young Baronne's idea. To help him learn

more." Pyne sipped, half shrugged. "Well, I went along
with it."

"I know Bender," Forbes said, pouring himself a coffee. "He can play rough."

"There's some kind of respect and loyalty building
there," Pyne added, a little proud, a little wondrous.
"God knows it's almost an impossible thing for a second
lieutenant to achieve with a noncom."

"From Bender especially." The captain nodded as-
sent.

"In a couple of years we might have a Corps full of
captains and lieutenants who've never been shot at, Walt.
It's gonna take the Benders to train them."

Forbes had had these conversations before. "Every career Marine gets at least two wars, Colonel. Fact of life.
Baronne's no different—he'll see a couple." It was his
way of seconding Pyne's comment.

Pyne nodded and placed his coffee cup atop the tray.
He picked up his hat and slowly pushed away from the
table. "I'd like to believe . . ." He stopped and stared
through the mess-hall tent flap at the barren, reddish-
brown earth that surrounded them, and finished his
thoughts. "I'd like to believe he'll be ready."

Bender turned to Scales, motioned him to crawl alongside, and pointed. "It's Lieutenant Greene. Damn shits
came *at* us." It was as if he'd sought Scales's identifica-
tion so he too could believe the surprise.

"Smart shits, George. College boys." Scales looked
around. "The others?"

Berry pulled up. "I can take him."

"No way, men! This goof-off is mine."

"Hold it!" Bender whispered annoyed. "Make sure
there aren't any others nearby."

Greene stopped walking and dropped to his stomach,
elbows propped up to scan the area. Suddenly he was
shoved beneath Sergeant Scales. He held a bayonet to
Don's throat. "Move a muscle and I'll cut." *This is an
exercise,* Don thought, *why do I believe him?*

Several hundred yards off, Baronne and Chapman were crouched out of sight. They watched through their field glasses. "What now, hero?" T.C. demanded in a low, somewhat sarcastic voice.

"Don't sweat it," Baronne hissed. "We just follow 'em." He looked Chapman in the eyes. "Guarantee ya, T.C., they'll be true to form and take Don back to whatever they have for a camp." His white teeth flashed a smile. "We'll flank 'em while they're doing it. Bender thinks we're still over here." He chuckled low in his throat. "But by the time he leads us to his location, we'll be on the other side. When he leaves camp to find us, we'll have our chance."

T.C. smiled his relief. "Bet that's the last time Greene volunteers."

Colonel Pyne, hounded by curiosity, climbed into his jeep. Although he had given his permission, he still had some reservations, verging on worry. He turned to face Forbes. "I'll be back before sunup tomorrow." His engine started, coughed, and stalled. He used the silence to finish his conversation. "I have to see this for myself."

The bamboo cage they'd built and into which they'd dumped Don Greene, almost with savage joy, resembled something out of a grade-B jungle film. The somewhat plump lieutenant had been stripped to his skivvies. "You'll have company quite soon, Lieutenant," Bender told him with a slight grin.

"This is really a nice touch," Greene quipped, looking down at the red paint they'd applied to his body. "Ever think of going into interior decorating?"

"We thought you'd like it, sir," Scales put in.

He was there with Sanchez, Berry, and one Private Williams, all of whom enjoyed the junior officer's colorful plight. The only black, Scales moved in closer to the cage, looking expectantly at Greene.

"Tell me. You planning to walk me back to the base

this way?'' Don asked, trying to be game but dreading it.

"No, sir, don't think so. Oh, we could, Lieutenant." Suddenly Scales smiled affably. He wasn't, in truth, the tiger he enjoyed playing. "But no, uh-uh. This here is a family matter. All these gentlemen''—he motioned to Williams and fifteen men still standing near the small pup tents in the tiny encampment—"these men are the elite of our outfit. I tell you true, Lieutenant. The elite." He smiled warmly. "And you are an officer. Yes sir, you're sure as hell one of our officers . . ."

"What he's saying, Lieutenant," Sergeant Bender clarified it, "is that there's no way we are going to ridicule you in front of those other pogey-assed outfits." He drifted closer to Greene, becoming confidential. "But if we ever got to go into combat with you," he said quite softly, "we want to make damned sure you do not like being captured."

"That's a pretty nice speech," T.C. chuckled quietly at a distance, reading the sergeant's lips. "It even makes a certain sense, doesn't it, Bear?"

Baronne didn't reply. His gaze was fixed intently on the homemade cage, eager for the moment when Bender and Scales finally departed.

"In the distance, Bill. Someone's coming!"

Baronne looked off to the south and swiftly raised his binoculars. "Can't make it out. Probably a jeep."

"Sanchez?"

"Can't tell!"

"Maybe we can steal the son of a bitch!"

"Hold it, they're moving out," Bill pointed to the camp.

"Back to where they were." T.C. smiled. "Gotta hand it to you, Bear, all those gungie books you read are paying off."

They watched as Berry, Scales, and Bender headed into the brush and woods in the opposite direction. T.C. shifted his binoculars over to the dust trail and finally was able to make out the approaching jeep. He inhaled sharply. "God Almighty, Baronne, it's the colonel."

Instantly Bill shifted his glasses to the scene, saw the old man alone at the wheel, a look of intent curiosity clearly etched in his face.

For a moment Baronne didn't quite dare say what he was thinking. Then, very softly, he asked Chapman: "Old friend, did *you* ever see a Marine colonel . . . painted *red?*"

"You wouldn't. You wouldn't!"

"No?" Baronne chuckled. "Bet your sweet ass, I would."

Unlike others who had attained high rank, Colonel Pyne loved the ruggedness of the field, and emulated the toughness of those men who slept on the ground or in foxholes without complaint.

Thus, when he entered the small encampment in his vehicle, he couldn't keep a smile from creasing his face. It reminded him of many such encampments he had lived in before. Camps he had established, organized. Camps which furnished merely a minuscule target, well hidden in the woods or the brush.

And he recognized the handiwork of George Bender immediately. The camp was a display of the experience he'd sought when he asked for Bender that day at Quantico.

No one was in sight save for the cage and poor Don Greene as Pyne stopped his jeep before the small, pyramidal command tent. He waited. He knew, from his knowledge of Bender and from his own experience, that every rifle in the area was aimed at him. They had allowed him to be like the fly, and land in the middle of their web. It was like coming home. He looked around, took his hat off, and beamed.

Sanchez immediately recognized Pyne. He reached for his radio and used it to whisper to Berry, who answered and confirmed that the colonel was "okay."

At that point, able to relax, the fifteen Marine enlisted stepped from the brush, their rifles at the ready but content to watch Sanchez move to the vehicle to welcome Pyne. Daddy was home from the office as Pyne was escorted into the tent where he was offered steaming coffee and animatedly brought up to date . . .

The sole illumination that night in camp came from the yellowish lantern glowing inside the tent. Private Williams lounged, yawning, beside Don Greene's improvised cage. He was half asleep, scarcely guarding him.

He didn't come close to being alert to the motion behind him.

Baronne was on Williams, knocking the rifle to the earth and, in virtually the same movement, holding a K-BAR to the private's gasping throat.

"If you breathe louder, Private, you'll die. For real."

Williams nodded eagerly. His terrified eyes said clearly, *I believe you, Lieutenant!* as he would inform Baronne later. "I hope p-painting your friend d-didn't piss you off, sir," he whispered stammeringly.

T.C. moved quickly and soundlessly to the cage and released Greene. He retrieved Greene's uniform from the tree nearby and handed it to him. Williams was then stripped and placed inside the cage—with a gag, a can of red paint, and a brush. "Paint yourself," T.C. chuckled. He looked hard at the private, meaning it. "That's an order, Private."

In the pyramidal tent, Sergeant Sanchez and Colonel Pyne were perched on small ammo boxes. Facing each other, they were playing blackjack. The light from the small lantern created fantastic shadows against the green canvas. There was just enough visibility in their corner of the tent.

Pyne's cigar was no longer lit; it had become instead a short, moist stub which he continually rolled around his mouth. His canteen cup with scotch sat to the side.

"Hit me," Pyne ordered, tapping the ammo-box table.

Sanchez dealt him a new card. The two of them, officer and enlisted, were engrossed in the game. The contents of their rude home away from home were quite forgotten.

"Okay, this is the game plan," Bill Baronne said calmly. But his eyes were very bright in the limited moonlight. He held his breath a moment before saying it. "Burn the tent down."

"You insane?" T.C. hissed, gesticulating. "The gee-dee colonel will kill us!"

Baronne had, peeking inside, seen a small stack of firewood near the stove. "I don't think so." He touched T.C.'s arm. "Burn it!"

While T.C. edged toward the tent, shaking his head, Bill and Greene moved with alacrity to capture the other Marines. They pulled most of them from their pup tents, one by one, and locked them into the empty cages. It had been possible to use their rank instead of their weapons to silence them.

When the stack of wood began to smoke, just before the flames burst upward, the card players were startled, staring at it and trying to figure out what had happened. They lost precious time, allowing T.C. to crawl under the flap and in one U.S.C.-style jump, he had his K-BAR held to the colonel's throat. "Don't move, Colonel. Don't. I'll cut you for sure!" *God, I sound great,* T.C. thought, forgetting for a flashing millisecond he was threatening the life of his commanding officer.

Pyne, his face not turned to Chapman, made a snarling sound. It covered a grin of appreciation. "Son of a bitch," the colonel observed.

"Oh, goddamn, goddamn, goddamnit!"

Berry looked helplessly at Sergeant Bender. They were crouched at the edge of the woods, peering at their disheveled and wrecked camp.

"I knew on that fucking bus from Frisco that this guy was different."

"Naw," Berry replied, "he's just a cocky kid officer."

"Yeah? Then why don't he play by the book?"

Berry shrugged, almost smiled. "Why should he, George? Everybody's read the fucking book."

The two of them, joined by Sergeant Scales, had forgotten to keep their cool—and to listen. Bewildered, startled, irate, they stood simply staring at their men in the cages, even failing to realize that the men were not looking back, but instead, past them.

"Your turn, Sergeant." Bill Baronne pressed his rifle against the back of Bender's neck, just above the spine. "Your turn."

And Don Greene, looking more like an embarrassed Indian than anything else, walked up to the sergeant with a broad smile.

Silently, not requiring a word for once, Don handed Bender a red-stained paint brush.

26

Commitment

"It's time."

The air was still, the sun dropping quickly, allowing the last golden light to streak across the short runway, which was surrounded by the small hangars and dairies and the hamburger stand which had become such a favorite.

Bill gazed at his father with surprise. He'd loved flying, but Dad had always been with him in the air.

"Your landing was good," Angelo Baronne continued. Stepping from the plane, he looked up at the darkening sky. "Still enough light. I won't be in the plane," he said, again, looking back affectionately. "But I'll be with you." He smiled at his fourteen-year-old son and gently closed the little airplane's door.

Angelo watched his father's eyes, and the message that beamed back at him was reassuring.

His father waved as he stepped out from under the wing and edged backward toward the lip of the runway. He would wait there. He'd watch Bill all the way.

The boy pushed the small Aeronca's throttle forward, taxied to the end of the runway, swiveling his neck—searching for other airplanes, praying none were flying, lucky that the sky was empty and the runway devoid of others. He guided his little Aeronca to the centerline of the three-thousand-foot strip, and pushed the red-tipped power control forward.

"Keep the plane straight," his father shouted for all he was worth.

Bill squirmed in his seat. "Jesus!" he muttered.

"Bring the tail up now, keep working those rudders," his absent father said in his head.

The small plane shot down the runway, and at the right moment proudly lifted into the air. "It's climbing faster," Bill shouted in awe.

He had forgotten that the loss of this father's weight provided him with a suddenly lighter aircraft. "That's okay, William," his father shouted inside his mind, "just push the nose down a little and you're doing fine." It was spooky—but great!

Bill looked out the plane's side window for the first time. He saw his father standing where he had stood on takeoff. He turned back to stare straight ahead. "Wow, he's been yelling at me so much, I can still hear him," the teenager gulped.

He turned the plane downwind and made an approach for his landing pattern. The plane leveled off with its engine purring smoothly. At that moment Bill Baronne did not want to land at all. Instead he wanted to remain in the air, flying all night. "Once around the pattern Bill. You fly it once around the pattern," his father had stressed.

The plane turned for real. Reluctantly, Bill cut the power. "Tomorrow! I'll fly all day tomorrow!" he shouted.

"Not tomorrow, William," Father said after he had landed. "Sorry. But there's still more to learn . . ."

"What now?" T.C. paused, cupping his eyes and looking straight ahead.

Baronne was marching his company through a training area some thirty miles from base camp. A short distance away, a Kaman-HOK helicopter, fanning up gusts of wind and dirt with its counter-rotating blades, was settling to earth like a condor.

"Oh, shit," Sergeant Bender said softly. Both Bill and T.C. looked at him.

The cloud of dust rising around the whirlybird almost covered the fuselage. Before Bender could explain why he'd sworn, Colonel Pyne and Captain Forbes had emerged and were running—stooped under the chopper's whirling blades—toward them in that strange-seeming silence of human beings in the vicinity of powerful, loud machinery.

"This," Bender said at last, "is how we found ourselves headed for good old Ko-rea!" He shook his head, subtly kicked at the dirt with the toe of one boot. "We took a nice little march and then they'd come after us to ship us out. Just the way we were."

Colonel Pyne strode to the head of the column—Bill— with Forbes following. Bill waited with feet planted while T.C. and Greene edged forward from their platoons to listen.

" 'Morning, Colonel," Baronne greeted him.

Pyne stopped next to him and waited for Forbes. "Let's walk." They turned, going out of earshot of the others. "It's time." Pyne had stopped, turned to look Baronne in the eye. "You're being shipped out, Baron. The trucks are on their way now." He hesitated and peered back hard at the column of troops. His voice was sandpaper. "Are they ready?"

"Yes, sir!" Bill replied. He thought, *What do they need to be ready for?*

Pyne's eyes bore into Bill's, emphasizing with all his command intensity that he was far too serious for this to be merely another training excercise. "Indonesia. That's the word."

"Indonesia?" Baronne glanced at Forbes, then back to Pyne.

"Real bullets, Bill," Forbes added.

"You have to go with whatever you've got with you. The Navy is shorthanded, too." Pyne sighed heavily. He looked to the column of troops again. "How many men you have here?"

"Hundred and eighty."

Pyne shook his head and grimaced: "Let's hope you don't need more."

The sound of the trucks arriving became louder and a track of dust rose for more than a mile down the road. Baronne became aware for the first time that he was about to be sent somewhere, for what he had spent so many months in arduous training. He stood a little straighter, glanced at Bender, and Greene, and T.C., and at Scales and Berry, then back to Pyne. "We don't have any live ammo, Colonel," he said, his voice strained. "Maybe two rounds apiece."

Pyne stepped closer to Bill while Bender, Scales, and Berry ordered the troops toward the trucks. Pyne's breathing was staccato. "You think this is a game, Lieutenant? You think all that goddamned training was for kicks?"

Colonel Pyne, better than anyone, understood he couldn't raise his voice, did not dare strip respect from his young officer before his men. But he also understood that he had better prepare Baronne for his first potentially hazardous mission.

"You get on those trucks. You sail to Indonesia and you make a goddamned landing if that's what the orders are. If you gotta win the"—his voice dropped to a hoarse whisper so that no one else would hear him use language that Baronne and the others had slowly seen disappear from their own vocabulary—"fucking war with two bullets, then that's what you'll by God do."

He walked away with an angry expression, yet with a gut-wrenching feeling for Baronne. Never was there a way to prepare anyone for being shot at, for witnessing the deaths that must occur, for leading and ordering other men into possible suicide.

Captain Forbes stood with Bill for a few moments while Pyne strode back to the Kaman. "He'll cool down on board ship," he began. "Meantime, you better figure out what the hell you're going to do." He smiled the tight smile Baronne had witnessed at basic school. He wasn't laughing. Instead Walter Forbes was saying, "This one's yours."

"I'll be there, too, Baron," he added. "But you'll be making the landing on your own."

The trucks advanced along the same road Bill had traversed on his way to South Camp Fuji from Tokyo.

Somewhere enroute they changed course, finally arriving at Yokosuka Naval Base.

"They can't be serious." He looked in frustration at Bender as they stood on the docks watching the troops board the AKA *Navarro*. "Just pick us up and throw us into some potential damned war with two bullets and—and no briefing?"

" 'Fraid so, Lieutenant." Bender glanced around the docks, then back to Bill. He chewed his toothpick in half and spat it out. "But I'm not sure about the count of men."

"We missing someone?"

Bender chuckled, "No." He motioned around the docks. "I mean, every war I've gone to before had more activity than this."

William Baronne had nothing to relate to. For him it was busy. "Like what?"

"Personnel, Lieutenant. Fighting personnel. You seen any? Other than our own troops?"

Baronne shook his head and, looking up at the *Navarro*, saw T.C. walk down the gangway, step onto the dock, and come bustling toward him.

"Well, sir, like I said," Bender continued, "there's no people. No Marines, no Army, no Navy. Just these dockhands"—he glanced at Bill—"and . . . us."

"Maybe it's not so serious . . ."

"Bullets is plenty serious, Lieutenant. No matter how many or how few. They're always serious." He shrugged and gave Bill his old-timer's smile. "It's a bitch, skipper. Probably means another fifteen cents a month out of my pay for new ribbons." He turned and walked to the ship, saluting T.C. on the way.

"Cruddy ship," T.C. said as he came up to Baronne.

"Yeah?"

"Yeah."

27

I Gotta Pee

Fourteen ships left Yokosuka Naval Base that evening and headed south for Indonesia. They had set sail silently, without news releases or public-relations statements. They weighed anchor, released the lines, and steamed out slowly. It was that simple. Because the press wasn't nervous at all about Eisenhower and Dulles. The press was not following every move made by the military. No members of the fourth estate insisted on being present for assault landings, or training exercises, or equipment tests.

"No big deal" was the unofficial public attitude in a time when most people were exhausted from World War II and the Korean "police action."

It seemed adequate that whenever maneuvers were concluded, the Navy Department would let the news people know why fourteen ships, including the cruiser *Helena,* some destroyers, ammo ships, and troop transports, had ventured south for training maneuvers "with eighteen hundred armed Marines aboard."

The Navy lied well.

Allen Dulles had informed Eisenhower that Indonesian president Sukarno was having problems with communist insurgents. "It is," Dulles urged, "the CIA's opinion that something must be done quickly."

The president studied the information a few moments and called Foster Dulles into the Oval Office. After a short conversation about SEATO, the Philippines, Formosa, and a discussion about the American financial commitments and search for oil in Indonesia, he ordered

Admiral William Duprey, and Marine Corps commandant, General Hook, to visit the White House.

Hook listened, argued briefly, to the astonishment of the admiral, and then passed the orders to General Sharp, who passed them to Colonel Pyne. "Rattle a sword!" was what it boiled down to.

"But for God's sake, Charlie," Sharp stressed, "don't get involved in a goddamned shooting mess."

"That could be suicide."

"Not if you don't land."

"I can't send boats in and not land," Pyne reasoned.

"Yes, you can—if we back down the insurgents." Sharp breathed heavily. "Look, this isn't World War III, Charlie. It's just a threat. America's might and all that—" He sighed, relaxed a bit, and then added. "The Navy will be providing visual backup."

"Well, it's a shitty way to fight a war."

Pyne was sitting in the *Navarro*'s office at a makeshift desk, waiting for Baronne. Forbes sat on the edge of the colonel's bunk, slowly smoking a stale C-ration Lucky Strike.

"Thought you gave those up?" Pyne asked.

Forbes curled a smile, snorted a little, and put the cigarette out. "Tastes terrible." He looked at Pyne. "Sorry, I forgot."

Pyne shrugged. Baronne knocked on the hatchway and Pyne motioned him in. "Sit down, Baronne." Bill took the only chair in the small quarters and nodded to Forbes. Pyne leaned toward him. "Got any scotch in that canteen?"

Baronne handed his canteen across. Pyne took it and poured a little into a small metal glass. "Not allowed on Navy ships, you know," he smiled at Bill. "Bet you carried this stuff on every Middie cruise."

Bill nodded. Pyne handed the canteen to Forbes, who took a drop for himself.

"We're going to put you and your men into the water in peter boats, Baronne." Pyne pulled a chart from his briefcase and spread it on the table. "Here, we have to make it look like the whole goddamned American navy is here.'' He pointed to Jakarta on the map, then looked up. ''And armed to the teeth.''

''Why?''

Pyne jammed his cigar butt into his mouth and leaned back. ''It's a bluff. One of Ike's favorite poker methods of holding down the commies. This time it's insurgents trying to knock off Sukarno.''

''I thought Sukarno was a communist.'' Bill was astonished.

''Certainly a sympathizer,'' Pyne acknowledged.

''He's given speeches about the greatness of Russia and China and their communism and how the West wants to pit one Asian country against the other.'' Bill looked from Forbes to Pyne and back. ''How do we reconcile that?''

''If we back 'em down,'' Forbes answered quietly, ''that may terminate the problems in Indonesia.''

''Back who down?''

Pyne was clearly frustrated by the young officer's persistent questions. ''Apparently, there are people who want to see Sukarno dead. They've already tried . . .''

''They've thrown hand grenades and bombs,'' Forbes broke in. ''Maybe red insurgents with their own brand of communism.''

''Wait,'' Bill said softly, narrowing his gaze. ''We're covering for their problems with the Dutch. Correct? It isn't the communists exclusively, am I right?''

''Perceptive, Lieutenant.'' Pyne was bureaucratically noncommittal. He scowled at no one in particular.

For a few moments they were still. Then Colonel Pyne broke the silence. ''We hope you won't have to use your men''—he continued with a wry smile—''or your two rounds of ammo.'' He paused and rolled up the chart. ''We're going to back up the Sukarno forces. It's not, um, it's not an official, um—frankly, it's not publicly authorized, Baronne. You won't be reading about the assault anywhere. Leastways, not soon.''

Shaking his head, Bill reached for the chart and unrolled it on his lap, accenting the colonel's lack of explanation for an "unauthorized assault" force sailing into foreign waters—possibly into armed conflict. *It's assumed,* he thought, *that they know what they're doing. That's the way it's always been. What other option do I have? And, of course, they know that.*

Baronne glanced up. "Very well. And if we have to really hit the beaches? What then, Colonel?"

"You'll be in serious trouble."

Bill didn't blink. "When will we get there?"

"Four days." Pyne glanced at Forbes. "Do you have any ideas on how to make the rebs think we're stronger than we are?" He chuckled, "Stronger than they are?"

Baronne looked from Forbes to Pyne. "We'll have to paint every helmet the Navy has on board!" He stood. "May I take the chart to show the other officers?"

Pyne nodded his approval. "Baronne, take care when you go in there. The president isn't too thrilled with the idea of actually hitting the beaches. That's not part of his sword diplomacy."

"Mine either." He turned to leave.

"We'll be in constant communication with the Sukarno forces, and we'll be monitoring the rebs. If they put their arms down—" He looked to Forbes, then back to Bill and let his sentence die there, unfinished.

Powers stuck his head through the hatchway. "No available air support, Colonel. Navy kaboshed it."

Pyne removed the cigar from his mouth. "Damn!" he growled.

"You're crazy, Bear!" T.C. laughed later. But Bill wasn't smiling.

"Crazier than shit," Greene echoed. He shook his head.

"Lieutenant, I gotta do what you order me to do, but I don't gotta like it," Berry stated flatly.

"It's out of some goddamned crazy movie he's seen," Scales told Bender, astounded. "Shee-it!"

Bender had ceased wondering about the orders passed down to him by officers years ago. "Just do it, John," he said to Scales, looking resigned. "Paint the god-damned helmets—and nail 'em down!"

Fifth morning out, before the sun peaked, one hundred and eighty men climbed over the gunnel of the paint-chipped gray troop ship, *Navarro*, and lowered themselves into the waiting peter boats below. "Hey, where's your John Wayne pig-stabber?" Bill asked T.C. as they maneuvered their way down the cargo net.

T.C. scarcely laughed. "Heroics only work for the Duke," he muttered.

Each small boat took two of the camouflage-painted Marines loaded down with rifles, backpacks, and shovels. Then it cruised out into the bay to line up for what they prayed would be an aborted assault.

Baron stepped over the green helmets lining the top edge of his peter boat, looked up, and helped his radio-man down into the craft.

"Thanks," Corporal Gomez whispered over the low rumbling of the diesel engine, which throttled them to the demarcation line.

On board the ship, Pyne and Forbes watched from the 0-3 deck level. "This tests all the training we know how to give 'em."

"Without ammo?" Forbes asked half facetiously.

"The real reason they don't have any ammo—"

"I know," Forbes sighed heavily. "Supply people fucked up again. They never have to fight, but they sure know how to kill." He looked at Pyne. "Mostly us."

When the sun finally stroked the beaches around Ja-karta, the communist insurgents found themselves peer-ing in amazement at a formidable representation of the U.S. Seventh Fleet.

A few miles offshore, the battle cruiser *Helena* had its guns aimed at the shoreline. Two destroyers cruised back and forth in front of the fleet of fourteen ships, strafing the bunkers and gun emplacements sporadically strung along the beach with .20-mm cannons.

Sukarno's troops had concurrently launched an attack which had driven the insurgents to the water, pinning them between their army and the scores of U.S. peter boats, capable of carrying more than forty combat troops each, prepared to make their assault.

The insurgent commander would have to make a decision quickly, and he knew it.

Baronne spent the forty-five minutes that the boats had to wait for launch time leaning against the port bulkhead, riding easily with the small craft while it rose, then sank, then rose with the swells that evenly pushed shoreward.

Corporal Gomez was quiet beside him. The static on his radio was steady, unnerving. No one had called or spoken. Even Bill was beginning to feel strangely alone and developing the unsettling vision of being the only Marine who assaulted the beach. His thoughts were interrupted by Gomez.

"Aw, I gotta pee, Lieutenant."

Baronne looked at the corporal and sighed nervously. "Me too," he confessed and was rewarded by a tiny smile.

With the sound of forests being toppled by a spinning chainsaw, the radio Gomez was carrying abruptly crackled. Both men, officer and enlisted, gaped at it as the voice sought to make itself clear over the static.

Then it was clear. "Pull 'em back, Lieutenant," the order came. "There'll be no landing."

Bender, standing braced for action in his own landing craft, swore under his breath. "Quick goddamned war."

28

Chiang Gang

The return trip from Indonesia to Japan, a homecoming of sorts, was to have taken ten days. For Baronne and the others, they'd been close enough to peril for a while and they were glad to return.

Instead the ships were diverted to Formosa.

"Seems we're going to train a bunch of Chiang Kai-shek's men how to fight," Captain Forbes informed Bill.

"Does that mean," Baronne asked sarcastically, "Chou En-Lai is beginning to make Ike nervous?"

Forbes leaned back against the wardroom bulkhead, eyed his protégé, and thought, *Smartassed shit.* He pushed abruptly away from the sterile bulkhead. Crossing to the metal coffeepot, he poured another cup of tasteless Navy coffee. "Okay. Let's talk about it before we go ashore.

They drank coffee awhile and poured Baronne's scotch and talked for more than four hours, addressing themselves solely to the purpose behind the sudden trip to Formosa.

At first they would be assisting some of the civilians from the Tachen Islands who'd missed the Seventh Fleet's mass movement that year before. They would then sail south and assist the Nationalist Army in placing loudspeakers on Quemoy Island, facing mainland China. The speakers would broadcast propaganda to the people of the communist-held mainland, a cozy swimming distance from Quemoy.

After that they were to return to Taipei and teach Chiang's Nationalist Army infantry tactics.

"Those are utterly basic," Baronne argued.

"Not to the Chinese, Baron. They've always fought wars with the theory that you can just throw more warm bodies into battle—because they've always had more where those came from."

Bill shook his head in mild horror. They discussed what chance the Nationalist Chinese might have against the mainland communists.

"Not much, if Chou finally decides he wants to attack," Forbes commented.

"Happily," Bill observed, "he's cautious because of the atomic missile site Ike recently announced. Right?"

Forbes raised his index finger cautioningly. "Remember about their having more where those came from. I'm serious."

"How many more?"

Forbes tented his hands, peered between the thumbs as if sighting. "Our friend Chiang has nearly five hundred thousand men in his army."

Baronne gasped. "Hell, that's—twice, nearly three times more than the Corps! What do they want with us?"

Forbes smiled. "You forget. Chou has millions of troops. Besides, Chiang's people need the training." He paused. "And, I guess, all this equipment." Forbes poured both of them a fresh cup of coffee. "So, we're stuck with them and they're stuck with us. Colonel's job is to teach them what to do with their new M-47s. Twelfth Marines are here to teach 'em artillery." He paused to chuckle. "And Frank Powers is here to guide them through that new air-to-air missile."

"They're gonna stay on their island, right?"

Forbes nodded. "That's what Dulles says."

"Then what the hell are we doing here? They're not going to attack Chou, and I really doubt Chou does anymore than lob a few shells at them." He'd studied recent Chinese military history—had to write a term paper in his senior year at U.S.C. on the subject.

Forbes breathed heavily and lit a cigarette. "Don't tell Pyne about this." He pointed to the smoke and grinned. But he sobered quickly. "If they would just let go of Quemoy and Matsu, things could settle down again."

Baronne paused, then spoke authoritatively. "But that simply won't happen."

Afterward, stretched out on his bunk across from Bill, T.C. asked, "What was that all about?"

Something in Chapman's tone irritated Baronne. He turned to peer at his old friend with new eyes. T.C., it appeared, was content to remain at the level he was now. He was fundamentally fun-loving, indolent, the kind who did what was needed—sometimes, when it suited him, a little more—and then was ready to relax. For the first time Bill intuited that they were beginning to go their separate paths.

"That?" he asked. "Our future," he replied softly.

After picking up one-hundred Chinese civilians on Tachen Island, they sailed back to Quemoy. Thinking over what they had done, Baronne said flatly, "Those goddamned speakers aren't going to do the job Chiang expects."

"They might," T.C. murmured.

"Bullshit. The reds'll sit over there, laughing their asses off."

T.C. glanced curiously at his old friend. "Well, at least they won't be shooting people."

Greene lightened the increasingly tense atmosphere. "How long do you think these people can keep those FJ-3s of ours working?"

"About eight hours," T.C. replied, and they laughed. "Maybe a day if they get lucky."

"Now, hold on," Forbes grumbled, sitting up straight and glaring at the younger officers. "We're here to instruct these people in infantry tactics. What'd you know about it back at the beginning?" His question made Baronne flush. "It'll be basic school for them, gentlemen, and your students will fall asleep just the way you did."

T.L. and Don looked at each other with partial smiles.

"You're going to love it," Forbes declared, spreading his hands as if he'd just given them fine gifts. "Think about it: a war-surplus Quonset for your classroom, a bunch of gooks who can't speak English, and blank-faced officers who won't trust you for five seconds. Welcome to education from the other side.''

"You done this before, Captain?" Bill inquired. "Open a little anything-but-red schoolhouse?"

"Sure, Korea." Forbes shrugged. "It's some civilian's idea of humanitarianism. Or a joke.''

They edged into the tin Quonset hut, not quite knowing what to expect, and stood for several counts to take in their new Chinese pupils. The officers peered back steadily, expressionlessly.

"We'll just sit off here, to the side, Captain," T.C. said in his most obliging tones, and guided Greene and Baronne to empty chairs. Sergeants Berry, Bender, and Scales sat warily at the rear, looking awkward with visual aids which included film strips, rifles, charts, and rocket launchers.

Forbes walked steadily to the head of the classroom, stood at the podium, and, opening his small notebook of completely blank papers, began to speak. As he did, a translator stood, too. Loudly he converted the captain's English to Chinese, obliging Walter Forbes to pause frequently, roll his eyes to his men, understanding from his past experiences the uselessness of his efforts.

"It's not any kind of public knowledge," explained Powers the next afternoon, anxious to explain what he'd learned but almost fearful of bringing it up. Without realizing it, he shook his head from side to side while he spoke, obviously unhappy about his discovery. "What we have here, gentlemen, are heat-seeking missiles." He shrugged, letting it set in. "Simple device. And that amazes me, too, frankly—the simplicity of these killers. And they are cheap to build.''

"Frank . . ." It was Forbes who gently prodded him to get to the point. He knew it was unlike Powers to rattle on; Frank appeared nervous, almost distraught. "Moving right along?''

"Sorry!" Powers frowned. "When the pilot fires the rocket at another jet, a heat-sensitive device inside the rocket guides it to the nearest heat. That's supposed to be the tailpipe of the target plane.''

"You mean, the pilot doesn't really have to aim dead on?" asked Bill.

"Right! Just be within the vicinity. That's progress," he added wryly. He pointed up. "We've got four FJs up there right now." He turned to the radio operator. "Any word yet?"

The operator shook his head, then pointed. Powers looked up and called: "There's the drone now. The target."

Baronne, Forbes, T.C., and Greene peered skyward. They watched while the drone flew overhead in circles, waiting for the fighters to arrive.

"Here they are," Powers yelled. He pointed to four FJ-3 Furies. "We gave them those fuckers, can you believe it?" he demanded. He shielded his eyes from the sun as he watched. "They get to fucking fly and I gotta stay on the ground."

"Do they know what they're doing, Frank?" Forbes asked.

"Search me. And scares me." He glanced down for a second, kicking the dirt. "They seem a little dumb . . ."

The Chinese radio operator spoke with animation to the interpreter, who then translated for the sake of Frank Powers. "Number four pilot says he has drone in sight. And he's ready to fire!"

"No, goddamn it!" Powers shouted angrily. "Jesus! How the fuck do you control this with goddamned translators in your way?" He jumped for the radio, pulled the microphone out of the operator's hand and yelled into it. "No, goddamn it! Do not fire!" He was too late.

Above them they heard the explosion. Tail end Charley had fired his heat-seeking missile and knocked the first plane—his leader—out of the sky.

Powers dropped the microphone. "Awww, for Chrissakes!"

"I'm telling you, Lieutenant, they're stupid animals," Bender argued later.

"They're humans, Sergeant, not animals," Baronne interjected.

"It's just like Korea. They tell Captain Forbes fire and maneuver takes too much time, that they have plenty of men to die. And that damned plane!" He shook his head while they hurried out of their temporary island quarters. "And now you're going to see them attempt a little artillery. Christ!"

The Chinese were standing at the worn-out howitzers, sweating from the afternoon's heat. They appeared a bit confused. The artillery instructors from the twelfth Marines had given their final lesson and were attempting to clear the area, allowing only those who would be operating the weapons to remain near the big guns.

"Over one hundred and fifty howitzers will be shipped to the Chinese on Quemoy later this year, I'm told." A Lieutenant Padderson turned to watch the action near the guns. He shrugged his shoulders. "And these—these—will be the Chinese Army officers and men responsible for training those crews."

"R.O.K. troops were almost as bad," Forbes argued. "Maybe worse."

"I've had some experience with them too," T.C. quipped, remembering his jumps from the parachute-training tower.

"Yeah," Lieutenant Padderson countered, grimacing. "But can you possibly get ready for this? For what must happen?"

Although the infantry officers shrugged, agreeing but not overwrought, Captain Forbes's long face expressed his clear dejection, something Bill Baronne hadn't witnessed before. "Honest to God, I don't know how these people ever survived any war."

It was quiet for the moment. Then Bender, a few feet away, said with deliberation, "Frankly, Captain, I don't know how gooks like these ever killed any of us."

Forbes looked at his sergeant. He answered him in a low, saddened voice. "Wave after wave of people, Sergeant, answers that question." He stretched, feeling indescribably weary. "They always have more."

A crashing sound came from a howitzer as it spat out its deadly payload of destruction. It interrupted them.

Then the huge cannon rolled backward. It careened through a thick crowd of Chinese officers, injuring most of them, knocking them all down, killing two.

"Oh my God!" Padderson screamed. "The shovels, they didn't secure the fucking shovels!"

"Dumb animals," Bender muttered.

"Dumb enough to get us killed."

Bender snapped toward Baronne. "I believe, Lieutenant, you're starting to get the picture."

29

Poker Party

"It's your birthday present," Angelo Baronne announced. He and his son were speeding along San Fernando Boulevard toward the airport, where Big Bear's plane was hangared. He glanced at young Bill with pride.

"I can't wait." The gangly youth couldn't put his excitement into words.

After preflighting the plane, they taxied to the end of the runway, turned, and climbed into a peerless blue sky. The day was gorgeous, visibility was infinite.

The two Baronnes flew toward the Burbank Lockheed Airport, where sixteen-year-old Bill would take his first check-ride on his way to his first pilot's license. With more than seventy hours in the air, the teenager had already doubled the time requirements. When they merged with the Lockheed's airport traffic pattern, Bill contacted the tower through the static-filled radio to alert them, then landed as smoothly as he had done most things in his young life.

"It was easy, Dad," he said smilingly, stating a fact. "It was really easy."

Angelo Baronne looked relieved. He'd prepared his boy for the worst, nagged and warned and rehearsed with him. But when the inspector discovered young William Baronne could fly circles without rising or dropping a foot in two consecutive three-hundred-sixty degree turns, and when he discovered Bill could put the plane on the runway numbers, he ordered the young pilot to return to the Lockheed terminal. "You've earned your wings, feller," he said warmly.

The grown Marine leaned against the gunnel of the

Navarro as it sailed northward to Japan. The water lapped evenly, smoothly against the ship's side. The balance of the Seventh Fleet that had joined them provided him with the most impressive display of power he'd ever seen.

At that instant Bill felt more than before that he'd made the right choices.

"I'm checking in for the night." T.C. stretched. He was exhausted.

"I'll be down in a while," Bill answered in a soft voice. "Greene already crashed?"

"Yeah."

Bill watched T.C. stroll up the gangway, turn into the officer's quarters area, and disappear. The ship was so quiet, the breeze soothing; this air filled his lungs with new life.

He watched the bubbles churned up by the moving ship, the white caps created by the wind. He thought of home, his mother and brothers and sisters, Elizabeth, and the father who had taught him so much. *Lessons that have, for the most part, proven true,* he admitted to himself.

"Evening, Bill," Captain Forbes interrupted his reverie.

Baronne smiled at Forbes and nodded to the sea. "The rest of the fleet seems to have joined us, Captain."

Forbes looked out over the water, saw the silhouettes of the larger ships which now mingled with their Indonesia attack group. "*Bonnie Richard,* the *Thetis Bay,* another cruiser, some supply ships," he stated. He turned and looked at Baronne. 'More ammo ships."

"We'd have been in serious trouble, Captain." He lounged on the rail.

"Yeah. Well, chances are that won't be your last time."

Bill twisted his long body to face inboard eyes averted. "I was a trifle nervous."

"You'd be crazy if you weren't." Forbes turned to lean back against the gunnel alongside Bill. "Most of the time, that apprehension helps keep you alive. Alert."

"Yeah." He turned to face the bulkhead before him, finally relaxing against the gunnel. "My father taught me that with flying.'' Bill peered shyly at the captain. ''How well did you know my father?''

''He joined us just before Bougainville. Third Marine Division. He had just been wounded in the air and re-fused—at first—his rotation to return stateside.'' He chuckled. ''After Bougainville, he accepted that short trip home, but he was back later.'' Forbes waved his cigarette ashes out over the ocean and let the breeze snap them away. ''He was the FAO. I was enlisted then.'' He shifted on the gunnel, turning somewhat sideways to face Bill. ''I was a bad-ass then. Always in trouble.'' Forbes made a face.

Baronne chuckled. ''Go on . . .''

Forbes continued, ''On the way to Bougainville my lieutenant was going to court-martial me.'' He looked at Bill and wrinkled his brow. ''Hell, I can't even remember why! Anyway, your old man stepped in for me. Saved my ass.''

''Sounds like him.''

''It was in battle that I saw what he really was.'' Forbes paused. ''I mean, your father was a pilot, not a ground pounder. But when the shit hit the fan he was about the most heroic Marine out there. He was in the middle of one of the biggest battles I saw up till then, calling down air strikes within a stone's throw of his own position.'' He sucked in on his cigarette and blew the smoke out slowly, allowing some of it to drift from his nose. ''That was new then. We had never used forward air controllers before—never called strikes in so close.''

Baronne leaned against the gunnel with his elbow, hypnotized. These were the first detailed stories he had heard concerning his father's war adventures.

''He came to us wounded and left us wounded,'' Forbes said quietly.

''He was wounded on the ground too?''

''Oh, yes.'' Forbes raised his brow. ''You weren't aware?''

''No. Mom, probably. Not the children. He . . . didn't talk about it with us.''

''Ever see his medals?''

"No."

"Do you remember my dropping by right after the war?"

"No, sir, I don't."

Forbes smiled the smile Bill had come to enjoy. "We didn't talk about the war, but we did shoot the bull about how he got me out of trouble. And how I saved his life."

Baronne drew himself erect, struck. This was entirely new to him. When he looked down, questioningly, he didn't have to ask Forbes to go on. Forbes was deep in his dramatic past, almost remembering aloud.

"It was later—Jesus, it seems like a century ago—on Iwo. Your old man and I hadn't seen each other in more than a year. But fate threw us back into the same outfit." He looked at Bill steadily. "We were attached to the Fourth Marines. Back then, during that war, wc had more than the three divisions we have today." He smiled and nodded. "It was different."

Baronne was mesmerized. Forbes continued.

"It was on Iwo. We were in the first assault wave. And your dad had worked himself into one real hole. He'd climbed forward with a squad of riflemen plus a Navajo code-talker to get a better vantage point. The naval gunfire officer was with them, too. But he was killed right off. Half that squad died on the way to the knoll." A shuddering sigh. "We called the area Death Valley."

Baronne pictured the scene as vividly, he imagined, as if he'd been present. The death, the terror, the hell. He began feeling slightly guilty about his fear in the landing craft a few days before.

"Well," Forbes continued, "your father started calling in the Navy boom-booms at the same time he coordinated the corsairs. All the time the Japs are doing their best to knock him out of there. Everyone else is still pinned on the beach." He slowed his story. "I was in the first wave, Baron, what the press guys called the easy one. That's bullshit, of course. There are no easy assault waves." He sighed and continued. "It wasn't until the second and third waves that the Japs really let loose with their big guns and heavy-caliber machine guns. All of a sudden we were losing men left and right, and we didn't have any cover anywhere.''

"I've seen some of the pictures," Bill grunted.

"Yeah." Forbes's expression said what he thought of pictures. "Well, somewhere in that frigging mess your old man became the only live Marine on the little knoll. And he got himself shot in one of his legs and took a hit in his right shoulder." Forbes's eyelids were half shuttered as he glanced around the empty deck and continued. "But he kept calling in the boom-booms and air power until he was too weak to go on. 'Bout that time, we knew he wasn't going to make it unless someone rescued him."

"You!" Bill gulped.

"Not exactly alone, but yes, I took some men out there." Forbes turned back to the water. "It took us six hours to retrieve him and get back safely." He smiled at his vivid memory. "We had to do it at night."

Bill let some air out through his lips and sagged a bit. "He never mentioned that event. The wounds or even the battle."

"He didn't like the killing." Forbes looked at him. "And I suspect, you won't, either."

They were interrupted by the ship's loudspeaker. "Now this. Now hear this. Marine officers to the wardroom."

Colonel Pyne was alone when Captain Forbes entered the wardroom ahead of the lieutenants. He poured himself a cup of coffee and sidled next to Pyne.

"Rest of the battalion has joined us. They're on the *Johnson,*" Pyne said.

"More poker?"

"Possibly."

Baronne, T.C., and Greene entered the wardroom together and took seats after first grabbing cups of coffee.

"Evening, Colonel," T.C. greeted Pyne. Pyne nodded, grinned, and waited for them to sit.

"Gentlemen," he began, "we're going to the Philippines." He turned to Forbes. "I apologize for not informing you earlier, Walt, but we received this communiqué just a few minutes ago.'' He handed the paper to Forbes.

Forbes quickly glanced down at the note, his head swiveling slightly as he read it. ''Training problem or the real thing?'' He didn't look up.

Pyne was evasive. ''Division landing at Dingalan Bay, Luzon.'' Then he leaned back, crossing his arms. ''It's supposed to be a show of force.''

Baronne, his elbows on the table, took them away when he imagined his mother admonishing him. He sipped his coffee and thought with anticipation: *This has got to be good!*

''Yesterday, Philippine president Ramon Magsaysay died in an airplane accident. Our demonstration is for the benefit of the communist world—to keep them from disrupting a smooth, democratic transition to their vice-president, Garcia.'' He stopped and looked around the room.

''Pretty quick orders, Colonel,'' Greene ventured.

Pyne darted a hard look at the usually quiet Greene. ''When our country reacts this quickly, Lieutenant, they're damned well serious about something.''

''What?'' Baronne asked in his direct fashion.

''The Philippines are important to us,'' Pyne said. ''We have large naval and Air Force bases there. It's our last bastion in this part of the world—''

''So, is this another unauthorized assault, Colonel?'' Bill asked gently.

Pyne leaned forward. ''Yes, and no, Lieutenant. The code name for the overall operation is Beacon Hill, but your operations within that authorized adventure will not be . . .'' he said, evading the question. ''The entire division's here. We'll be landing with the Philippine Army on our right flank.''

''They were screwups in operation Firmlink . . .'' Forbes muttered.

''Firmlink?'' Baronne asked.

''Thailand. A year ago. This division—before our time—made a demonstration assault with other services and the Filipinos.''

"A demonstration for the commies?"

Pyne was agitated. "No, SEATO. Lieutenant Baronne, you're pushing me."

Bill rubbed his chin hard with his right hand, fighting off a terrible itch that seemed to suddenly possess him. Before he could say anything, Captain Forbes spoke.

"No one will read about our mission . . . unless we screw up." He watched his lieutenants for a reaction.

But the quickest response came instead from Pyne. Obviously he was working at controlling himself and not saying things he'd be sorry for later. "This time, gentlemen, you will have plenty of ammunition. Plus, should you find yourselves in too deep, the rest of the division to help."

Baronne curled his mouth into a tight smile and spasmodically nodded his head. He brought his cold cup of coffee to his lips.

"Will that be good enough for you, Lieutenant?" Pyne pushed.

T.C. didn't wait for Bill to reply. "Is there any known anti-government activity taking place there?"

Magsaysay dies and suddenly we're making a landing, Baronne thought in response to T.C.'s question. *Why else, other than some anti-government—*

"No. Huks were put down effectively a few years back."

"Well, not all of them." Forbes gave the colonel an apologetic lift of one brow and leaned forward to answer Chapman. "The Filipinos still do report some slight activity from Huks. Now and then." He rose and strolled to the coffeepot, refilling his cup.

"He's right," Pyne said shortly, "they could pop up. Magsaysay was the man who forced the Huk defeat."

"Commie sponsored." Forbes turned around, sipping thick, black bilge the Navy called "joe." He looked directly at the lieutenants, then Pyne. "With Magsaysay dead, they could try something."

"Ah. And that's why we're here," Baronne pushed, "isn't it?"

"Coincidence," Pyne muttered.

"I doubt you'll see any," Forbes brushed it off.

"And if we do?"

"Then, well, um, capture them," Pyne snapped. He squinted his eyes, then blinked as if he'd seen something unpleasant. "But don't kill 'em."

"I understand," T.C. murmured.

"I'm not sure I do." Baronne got up to pour coffee for himself. "If we aren't supposed to shoot anybody, why the live ammo?"

30

Hill 491

Tom Chapman stood at the cargo net awaiting the order to climb over the side and step down the Jacobs ladder again. He watched his men tightening their belts and adjusting their backpacks. He looked around for Bill and, finding him, walked over.

"You feel like something's happening?"

"What?"

"I mean all this." He motioned to the scene in front of them. "We seem to be making it a routine to crawl over the side of this tub, like roaches or something. And hell, Bear, I'm starting to be comfortable about that damned ladder!" He shook his head. "Now, that's bad."

Bill grinned and quietly replied, "You're probably right." He gazed uncomfortably at his friend for several seconds, feeling the past tug at him but also wondering about the future. "But honestly, man, I doubt that anything big's going on. Just another show of force, the way it has been before."

"And what did your daddy do in the war? Well, he climbed rope ladders a lot," T.C. joked, "And went around scaring piss out of everybody."

He chuckled at his own good-humored mockery, failing to see that Baronne remained strangely quiet. T.C. ordered his men over the side. Baronne waited. He caught the concern in Don Green's eyes before he stepped over the gunnel. Greene was confused, looking to him for some explanations, but there were none. Bill shrugged and clapped Greene's shoulder. Together they disappeared in stealth from the ship and slipped down to the waiting landing craft.

More than one hundred LCMs pushed toward shore, carrying more than four thousand Marines. Once ashore, Sergeant Bender called I Company to formation, and in a battalion-point column of two abreast, they began their march inland.

"Jesus," Baronne cursed. "It's a hot son of a bitch."

"Everyone's carrying two canteens." Bender was hot, too.

"Mocatbong," Bill answered Chapman when T.C. came to the head of the column. "It's another ten miles by the chart."

"This jungle crud is for the birds," Greene complained.

"Not all that bad." He trudged ahead uncomplainingly. "Map shows we'll be in the open area just a few miles up ahead."

"What about the darkness?" T.C. still reflected his own fears first.

"We just keep pushing," Bill grunted without glancing at Chapman, "till we get there."

"What about the battalion?"

Baronne froze, frowning. "Oh, Jesus!" He'd forgotten. He had turned to call for Sergeant Bender, when two shots rang out. There was the sensation of swift wind whizzing close by.

Baronne wheeled around, surprised by the mildness of the death that had almost claimed him, but he saw nothing: no enemy, no Marines. Everybody else was out of sight.

"Better get your ass down here, Lieutenant," Bender's voice called gruffly, "before you lose it or your head!"

He headed straight for the ground, landed next to the sergeant. "What in the hell was that? And where in the hell is the rest of the company?"

"Those were real bullets, Lieutenant. And the company's doing what we been training them to do." He laughed shortly. "Skipper, you been so busy training everyone, you forgot to take cover and set up."

Baronne saw the humor, but he wasn't laughing. Not yet. "Our bullets or theirs?"

"Theirs. Whoever they are."

Two Marines emerged from the thick brush, pulling a Filipino with them. Private Janson and Corporal Wilkens pushed the man to the ground and knelt over him with their rifles aimed at his head. "He fired the shots, Lieutenant. But he wasn't alone," Wilkens said.

"Want me to kill him?" Janson was entirely serious.

Bill shook his head.

"The others got away, sir. 'Bout ten of 'em," Wilkens added.

Bender stood, the others following. He motioned the rest of the company up. They approached carefully.

"Take him to the rear of the column." Bill turned to the radio operator. "Call S-2. Tell 'em we need a prisoner pick-up." He was suddenly fully aware of his surroundings. As the two Marines dragged the Hukbalahap away, Bill turned back to Bender. "This was supposed to be a show of force," he snorted. "A goddamned training exercise."

"It's okay, Lieutenant. Korea was just a police action, too." Bender's voice dropped an octave. "Now, that was some exercise."

Mocatbong proved to be a disappointment. What had been a large dot on the chart was, in fact, a village of a few huts and a dirt road. Baronne spread his troops in a wide perimeter for the night, leaving security in Sergeant Bender's capable hands.

Bill joined T.C. and Greene over a small camp fire. They drank scotch and coffee and ate biscuits from C-rations, and drank more scotch, and talked little.

When he wakened at 0500, the sky was a hot and searing blue, and the air was stifling. "Jesus, it's going to be a bitch," he muttered.

Rolling over, he pushed at T.C.'s unzipped sleeping bag. Chapman grumbled, opened his eyes, and instantly moaned. "God, Baron."

Bill simply sat up and looked around. He pushed away from his bag, pulled his boots on, and walked over to the bugler's bag. He gave it the toe of his boot, just enough to jar and to awaken. "You're late."

"Oh, kuh-rappp," exclaimed the bugler, coming to consciousness and leaping to his feet. He looked as if someone had turned a hose into his sleeping bag.

Baronne, glancing both ways, walked to the side of the road. Unbuttoning, acutely aware of the need to look for cobras, he urinated, then returned to get his backpack. Sighing, he took his toothbrush and raced it across his teeth—Mom had called such things "a lick and a promise"—then returned it quickly to the pack. "Dammit, T.C.," he exclaimed, "get your lazy ass out of there." Unceremoniously he kicked Chapman in the rump.

Bender heard the order and rolled out of his own bag quickly as the bugler played reveille, breaking up dreams and calling men into the hot, humid day.

T.C. rolled his bag, then kicked Greene, who hadn't budged. He stacked his gear and sat down to make a cup of coffee. "Want some?" he asked Baronne.

"Yeah, thanks." Bill glanced around. "I'll be right back." As he walked away, he called to T.C., "Gonna check the area. See if there are any signs of activity."

"Right, *kemo sabe*," T.C. answered with a grin, resorting to Tonto's language. He stared after Baronne, watching him walk down the dirt road away from the company. Then he returned to his Sterno, in urgent need of a morning caffeine fix.

Bender observed Baronne while he strode along the dirt road, then turned to Sergeant Scales, who was probing warm fruit cocktail in a green can. "He's gonna be all right, John," Bender said. Scales just grunted. "He's a smart sort of s.o.b., you know. He doesn't have everything down pat yet, but he doesn't forget it once he's learned it."

"As long as I'm not one of his lessons." John Scales slammed a piece of pineapple back into the can.

That was when the isolated shot sounded.

It dropped Bill Baronne first to his knees and then his left side. The horrified sergeants saw him clutch his chest in approximately the location of his heart.

"Jesus, mother, holy shit!" Scales yelled.

Berry had already grabbed his rifle and a squad of men,

and they were running in the direction of the rifle fire. The rest of the company was diving for cover, loading their rifles, kicking sleeping bags and canteens and C-rations aside.

Scales, Bender, and Bill's old friends had already taken off, reaching his side and finding a pale, torpid form collapsed on the earth. Anguished, T.C. simultaneously grabbed his friend's wrist and covered his prone body with his own. Checking his pulse, Chapman looked up at the others eagerly. "It's still beating! I found his pulse!"

"Mommy, Mommy, look what I found!" Tiny Bill was running through the front door, excitedly waving something over his head. "Look it!" He placed a small, smudged King James Bible on the kitchen table, and pointed at the bullet hole shot straight through it. "It was in Mr. Drake's trash!"

His mother immediately telephoned their neighbor, and told him what her Billy had found. "Your name is written in it, Mr. Drake . . . ?"

Her implication was that surely Mr. Drake had accidentally lost the Bible in the trash. He replied slowly, "That was a Jap bullet. I used to carry it in my shirt pocket, and when I was shot at, the Bible stopped the slug, saved my life." He'd added, "I've been cleaning out the house. Must have thrown it out by mistake." When he dropped by to retrieve the small Bible and repeated the story again, young Bill whispered hoarsely to his mother, with childish awe and wonder, "If I ever fight Japs, I'll do the same thing."

T.C. and Greene watched Bill Baronne open his eyes to slits, foggily trying to identify their familiar faces. He mumbled something and Chapman, his hair glinting golden in the flash of hot sunlight, lowered one ear to hear what his friend had to say. "Your what did how much?" he asked.

Bill fumbled in his jacket pocket, pulled something

out, and stared wonderingly at it. "My pocket missal," exclaimed the Catholic Baronne. "Look."

All of them stared at the fresh bullet hole as Bill, handing it to T.C. whispered, "You remember old man Drake?"

Sergeant Berry trotted back to them, a bit breathless, staring hard at Bender. If he noticed that his lieutenant was not seriously injured, he didn't let it show in his face. "Nobody out there, George," he said angrily. "Goddamned lucky little shits must be hiding in fucking holes or something."

They walked back to the center of their bivouac, assisting Baronne until he waved them off and continued on faintly wobbly legs. Scales, despite the way he phrased his remark, displayed some traits that were out of character. "I guess maybe we should all carry Bibles in our pockets now, huh?" Bender, merely shaking his skeptical head, quietly told his sergeants to prepare their men for departure.

The corpsman closely checked Bill Baronne's chest, clucking and shaking his head. "That bruise is going to be the champion of bruises!" he said. "Maybe we should wear Bibles in both pockets?" Bill smiled, walked to the Sterno stove, accepted coffee from T.C., and then motioned Bender, Greene, and T.C. to a meeting. They angled away from the main body and sat on rocks, stumps, and grass, falling quiet for several moments.

"They must have been out there all night, skipper."

Bill remarked sardonically, "I imagine so. Whoever it was sure scared the life out of me!"

Bender glanced up the road and then back to Baronne. "How many do you suppose are out there?"

"I'm not an Indian scout, Sergeant," Bill snapped. Then he reddened and was instantly apologetic. "Sorry, sorry. Guess I'm a bit unnerved."

"Jesus Christ, Bear," T.C. defended him, "you could have been killed."

"I'll write Mr. Drake when I can," Bill added. "If he's still around."

"It's happened more than once, skipper," Bender contributed. It was as far as he could go toward religion. He crossed over to Sergeant Berry and sent him off with a squad of Marines. "I'm having them check out the entire area," he said in response to their questioning gazes.

Baronne leaned forward to spread his long legs. He covered the ground at his feet with the chart and gathered his nerves. "We are moving out soon to this location." He indicated a hill on the chart. "Hill 491. We're to secure the top, then wait for further orders."

"That's twenty miles from here," Greene remonstrated.

"Should take us the better part of the day." Bender moved his finger along the line they would march. "If we're not shot at again, that is . . ."

"Fresh water en route?" Baronne quizzed him.

"Due here in fifteen minutes," Bender said, pointing.

"Make it fast. Put the men on water discipline. I don't want to see anyone drinking while we're marching."

"Who's point?"

"Lieutenant Chapman's platoon."

"We'll water them first," Bender sighed.

Berry caught up ten minutes later. "Looks like about a dozen of 'em," he said, panting.

Baronne nodded and turned to Chapman. "T.C., keep your eyes peeled." He looked up and down the long, dusty road, off into the brush. "Someone's got their sights on us."

To ease the fear, T.C. looked over at his friend and quipped, "Have an extra Bible on you?"

The first break on their way to Hill 491 came an hour after departing Mocatbong. Baronne walked the length of the company to ascertain the condition of his men, then jogged back to the head of the column. "Next break in two hours."

"Sir?"

He looked at the questioning Bender. "While the air's only *this* hot . . ."

The column left the low lands, entering the hilly area around noon. When they crested a small mountain, they found themselves in an open meadow surrounded by tree-lined hills. Bill ordered a break in the long march, giving his troops an hour for lunch.

When the column separated and moved off the dirt road, four large, empty troop trucks passed through and headed up the hill at the close end of the field. Halfway up, they halted. Bender and Baronne and T.C. and Greene and the others watched as the drivers exited, pulled their packs with them, and gathered alongside the last truck for their lunch break.

"Monkey see," Bender began.

"Monkey do," Baronne agreed. "They like our reasoning or taste, I guess."

They sat down, the new officers and sergeants, quickly digging into their C-rations. Baronne thoughtfully passed scotch around for those who cared for any.

As T.C. idly watched the trucks, one of the drivers went to the fourth vehicle and climbed up on the front bumper. He opened the hood and jumped down just as the truck in front of his began rolling backward.

Tom Chapman saw everything, to his horror. At the instant the truck began clipping, rolling, he promptly yelled, "Aw, man, get out of the way!" But it was too late. T.C. turned to Baronne, sickened. "Christ, Bear," he managed.

The heavy truck had rolled back and pinned the driver. Far worse, it had amputated his legs with the terrible weight of crushing, bumper-to-bumper contact, and his hideous scream could be heard throughout the small, outwardly peaceful valley. Sergeant Bender was quick to react, grabbing the company corpsman by the arm. Together they dashed past Baronne to the young Marine's aid.

"Let's see if we can help," Greene prompted T.C.

"I can't," T.C. said softly. He looked incredibly at Greene. "Did you hear that scream? Christ, Don!" He sat down and stared at his untasted food.

Greene, running up the hill where Bill, Scales, Berry, and Bender, with the corpsman, were already tenderly placing the tragically wounded Marine driver in a truck, stopped just to stare at Chapman, a man he'd known—thought he'd known—for years. Up the hill, Baronne—

Don hadn't even heard the Bear leave his side—was sending the corpsman with the injured man to the division hospital. Then they were gone, heading back through I Company.

Tom Chapman, ol' T.C., had never again looked up.

Hill 491 was barren. A few trees, but mostly without shade or cover or relief from the humidity and the blistering heat. I Company arrived in the late afternoon and set their foxholes and defenses before finally collapsing.

A group comprising Baronne, T.C., Greene, and Bender talked quietly adjacent to two of the trucks which had remained after the accident that noon. Don Greene noticed the Navy AD attack bomber first as it swooped over them, low, fast, and noisily. He wondered at its behavior. It pulled almost vertically up, winged over, and disappeared beyond the ridge line.

Greene shrugged and made no comment to the others. Baronne had given it a glance, but was too engrossed in conversation with the others to do much more.

But then Greene became aware of a C-54 troop carrier crossing over them in the same general direction. The noise level had picked up, and Baronne, shading his eyes from the ferocious afternoon sun, responded to Don Greene's's nudge by peering up.

T.C. glanced first from one man to the other. "What's all that about?"

Bill merely shook his head. Everything seemed wrong that instant. It was bizarre, even eerie in a way, but he had a premonition of impending doom. His heartbeat accelerated as he followed Don's pointing finger. "The AD is coming back," Greene cried.

Baronne, seeing the positioning of the two planes, could scarcely believe his eyes. "Sweet Jesus!" he exclaimed. "They're going to collide!"

Coming together seemingly in slow motion fashion, the AD and the C-54 converged—and when the fighter bomber crashed into the left wing of the C-54, a tremendous explosion destroyed the silence of the valley. Bill, helpless to stop it, saw separate parts of the planes flying from the apex of the terrible encounter—saw human bodies, already burning, twisting, plummeting from the sky.

With the others, Baronne darted from foxhole to foxhole, hauling the Marines on Hill 491 out of their dugouts or gun emplacements to run for the protective cover that only a reasonable distance from the accident above them could provide. For an instant the sky was a fireworks display of airplane and human parts. T.C. shouted at two truck drivers to get the vehicles moving as he saw the flaming remnants of the planes falling to the ground.

He had spun about to jump into a truck to move it himself when something careening from the sky struck one of the other trucks and bounced before his face. Glancing up, flaming metal hit T.C. and knocked him to the ground, unconscious.

"Corpsman!" It was a driver who'd seen what transpired. At once he'd jumped from his truck and yelled for help.

Bill and Don Greene heard the cry, turned, and saw what had happened. Weaving and vaulting over other bodies between them and T.C., they sped to their friend's aid. Other Marines were rushing to the bodies which had fallen from the skies, and, only fleetingly, Bill noticed several Filipinos who, appearing from nowhere, were apparently trying to assist with the dead and dying.

"Who the hell are they?" he shouted as they ran toward T.C.

"Beats the shit out of me!" Greene answered, just glancing at them. "Maybe they're Huks!"

"If they are," Bill panted, "they make a helluva enemy!"

The corpsman who'd returned from Division was first to reach T.C. Immediately he'd bent down, removed Chapman's helmet and rested his head on a quickly folded poncho. As Bill and Don rushed up, the corpsman was checking for Chapman's carotid artery.

"Is he all right?" Baronne blurted. "Will he be okay?" He wasn't quite sure he could deal with the answer.

The corpsman paused. Finally satisfied, he nodded.

"Yes sir, I think so. But he's hurt and he's gonna hurt for quite a while."

Bender arrived, knelt down next to Baronne to ask, "You want me to round up these Filipinos?"

Bill looked around, then back to this sergeant. "They Huks?"

"Dunno, sir. But they're probably the people who've been following us, whether they're Huks or not."

"But they don't look any different than the Filipinos who've been trading us beer for rations," Greene observed.

Sergeant Bender got to his feet, looking disgusted; the two officers also stood. "Lieu-tenant!" Bender muttered, wrinkling his forehead. "Gooks is gooks. The friendlies and the foe all look alike. It's best you never trust any of 'em."

Baronne started to answer, then saw what the Filipinos were doing. He was shocked to see that some of them were stripping the mangled, badly burned, steaming bodies to take their boots, jackets, or whatever recoverable items were available.

Baronne forced his hand to his thigh, flattening his fingers out to keep from drawing his piece. "Sergeant, just stop the little bastards from doing—*that!*" he said, before he was nearly overcome by a wave of nausea.

31

A Few Good Men

"Such injuries occur so often," Captain Forbes said with a sigh.

They sat around a small camp fire. Despite the presence of canteen mugs with coffee and scotch and the occasional "John Wayne biscuits" purloined from their rations, it reminded Baronne of earlier camping-out times. He and Greene had been listening both to Forbes and the badly bruised T.C.

"Sometimes," Forbes was saying, "it seems that we lose more men in training than in actual combat. But when the training is as serious as this exercise, we're almost bound to lose an abnormal number of good men." He glanced toward his lieutenants. "Fact is, gentlemen, we lose one hell of a lot of men by accident. Can't always blame the enemy."

T.C. squinted his eyes tightly, trying to see straight and reduce his pain. His head was swathed in gauze, his eye blackened, his nose cut deeply. "Why are we here? Here in the Philippines?" He didn't so much lower his voice as let it reflect the horror of what he'd seen close up when the planes collided. "All those bodies . . ."

"It's because we signed up to be anywhere the commandant sends us." With a long, charred stick he stoked the fire and looked up sharply at T.C. "And . . . without questioning it."

T.C. put his canteen mug down. He looked unsteady. "Didn't you ever question it?"

"Not out loud, But I wondered after the Chosin reservoir . . ."

Greene asked, "Do you know why you were in Korea?"

"No. No, not that." Forbes paused. For a moment it was as if he were answering Don's question. Instead he added "I don't want to go over it again—because that's what we did: went over the same ground again and again and again." An unfamiliar note showed in the captain's voice. "The same damned ground. Over and over . . ."

The road back was dry, the dust choking. The lieutenants rode jeeps while the troops traveled in large trucks following them. As they crossed the island toward the bay where the Navy awaited them, the rising dust virtually overwhelmed them. Many wore cloth masks to aid their breathing.

At a small junction surrounded by grass-thatched huts on stilts, where red-and-white metal Coca-Cola signs leaned incongruously against each structure, Baronne stopped his jeep to count the trucks. He needed to make sure no one had become lost in the cloud of dirt which had hidden them from each other.

T.C. stopped and waited alongside, coughing rackingly, hoarsely, as the dust penetrated his cloth shield. While Bill counted, another vehicle pulled from the column and drove up to T.C. The driver handed Chapman a note. "The colonel wants to see you two right away, Lieutenant." He pointed down the road. " 'Bout half a mile. Take the small road to the right. He's parked in there with some other men."

After the column passed, Bill and T.C. drove to the colonel's temporary post and met him in a pyramidal tent.

When they entered, Pyne was ordering a sergeant to locate Captain Forbes, pronto. Turning, he gave them a particularly grim smile. "Tell me, Baron, got any of that scotch with you?"

"It's yours, sir," Bill said with a grin. He handed it over. "Couple of decent swigs left."

Other superiors were present in the tent, he saw. Pyne, accepting the scotch, poured it into his own canteen cup and saw where Baronne's gaze had wandered. Bill knew none of them and shuffled uneasily. "You sure didn't call us in here to drink scotch, Colonel," he observed.

"You're getting smarter, Baron." He moved from his chair to a field desk at the edge of the tent and picked up a message packet. "I'm pulling you and your officers"—he looked through the packet, then continued—"some sergeants and a few men out of the Philippines. Ahead of the others." He walked back to his chair and handed Bill a piece of tattered brown paper. "They're calling that Operation Dragonfly."

Bill glanced at the paper quickly. "A small strike force?"

"The balance of your orders will be given to you on board ship, Lieutenant."

T.C. reached over to take the scrap from Bill and read it as Pyne continued talking.

"I won't be going along with you on this one, Baron. Captain Forbes will be, but—well, once ashore, you'll be entirely on your own." He finished the scotch in a gulp. "Both the captain and I believe you can handle it."

Captain Forbes stepped into the tent quietly, stopped, and peered almost incuriously at the many officers gathered inside. Pyne returned his glance and motioned affably. "Come in, Walt."

"Welcome to Wonderland," T.C. whispered to Baronne.

"Welcome to flying, son, and happy birthday!" Angelo Baronne positively beamed as the plane leveled off for its return from Burbank. "This is great—you're a full-fledged pilot!"

Together they flew until the small airport young Bill had spent so many hours flying into and out of hove into view. Angelo leaned down, pulled the magneto key from its hole—and threw it promptly out the window.

The engine stopped.

"What are you doing?" Bill yelled against the sudden silence. "Dad, what—?"

"A major test coming up, son," Angelo Baronne shouted back. "Let's just find out how committed you are to flying. Remember, William, you know everything you need in order to survive this. It's time to put it to use, son—now!''

Startled but understanding, young Bill had watched his father smile and peer lazily out the windshield of the plane. Dad had full confidence in him—and he'd taken him every step of the way.

Angelo had been right: Bill had the training, the ability, the heart. And after they'd landed safely, his father congratulated him warmly. "Do you see, Bill?" he'd asked then. "This is why you have spent so many arduous hours in practice, in training. For survival. To learn how to survive . . .''

32

Help Me, God, I'm A Marine

"Titty Bay?"

"Yes, sir. That's what she's called." The Navy chief was happy about it, too.

"Great name," T.C. muttered appreciatively.

"Strange boat," Greene observed.

"You guys'll be the first Marines ever to make a helicopter landing from a Navy ship." He looked around doubtfully. "I guess it'll work."

"You're encouraging," Chapman said sarcastically. "Why are you dubious?"

"Because it'll be at night," the chief said with a laugh. "And hell's bells, we ain't ever done it in daylight." Flipping a salty salute, he added, "It's really terrific to be the first, right?"

T.C., Bill Baronne, and Don Greene made worried faces as the chief strode off and the *Thetis Bay* sailed on toward Indochina. The sun had set, the air cooled, and the breeze created by the ship's motion provided a respite from the previous week's efforts in the Philippines.

They turned without speaking further and continued their exercises along the aft starboard gunnel, near the last davit. As Baronne straightened, Captain Forbes joined them.

"In Korea," Forbes began when they stopped to listen, "we just landed and kicked the piss out of them." He threw his half-smoked cigarette overboard and spit a piece of tobacco after it. "Until the civvies took over, that is. Pushed their asses right up to the Yalu, we did." He paused, moved to the gunnel, and leaned against it, looking back at the three officers. "But this! This is kinda like back in the old China, Shanghai days."

"The orders said we're advisers."

"Yeah, sure," Forbes said. "Baby sitters. Battle guides."

"We're actually combatants?" Baronne asked.

"Well, if you'd like to stay alive." He allowed a low, throaty rumble to escape. "Later they'll tell us we aren't to ever look the enemy in the eye, never get ourselves in that position."

"It's not a real war, correct?" T.C. began. "I mean, if they—"

Forbes was on him in a snarling flash. They'd all heard it: the sound of an unsure, hesitant Marine Corps officer. It was a sound Forbes had to snuff. Now. "What'd I teach you in basic, Chapman? Eh? Anytime you're fired upon, it's war." With some difficulty he curbed his anger. "Look, anytime we go somewhere to help with somebody else's damn problem, there will usually be some shooting—and death."

"I think that's kind of sick, Captain." As T.C. spoke his piece, Bill looked at him in astonishment. T.C. shook his head, seeking the right words. "I mean, sir, shooting blanks in training, that's one thing. But getting involved dangerously in someone else's war—"

He was cut off by the ship's loudspeaker. "Now this. Now hear this. Strike-force officers to the wardroom."

It had been well over a month since Baronne, his fellow lieutenants, and Forbes had left Japan. They had become detached from world news, even letters from home. They had expected on two different occasions to be back in camp by now, not sitting with Admiral King in the wardroom of the U.S.S. *Thetis Bay.*

King was Seventh Fleet Commander. He was in charge of everything. "Everything west of California," Greene clarified as they entered the wardroom.

They took seats around the large table, accepting coffee from the steward. Another naval officer, Captain Easterbrook, who'd come aboard with King, was taping a large chart to the bulkhead behind the admiral.

"Gentlemen!" King began in an imperious tone, "as you know, your outfit is going ashore in three days." He turned to the chart behind him. "The exact beach for your landing is still secret, but the area is not a secret. Indochina. And because of communist aggression from the north. A chap named Ho Chi Minh." He turned back to them, scanned their faces, and then continued: "Probably using troops from China itself." He lowered his voice and in a magnificently bureaucratic manner mumbled, "We believe." More distinctly: "You will be part of the American military assistance advisory group."

T.C. listened intently, as did the others. He darted glances to Baronne and then Greene. He didn't like what he was hearing one bit.

"President Ngo Dinh Diem has asked Ike for help." He pointed to the chart. "This country—South Vietnam—has successfully rebuilt itself into a thriving nation. They are a democracy and we are heavily involved here." He stopped and inhaled deeply, his raspy voice creating the sound of lungs suffering from emphysema. "Not to mention the fact that we have a treaty to help the country defend against aggression."

The admiral paused, a not-quite-closed fist raised to his mouth to cough. Looking out at them steadily but unwilling to proceed just yet, he wondered at how they had accepted the lie. Ho had announced his intention immediately after the Geneva Conference, in '54. King was additionally aware that Diem had refused to participate in the election of the prior year, and that the United States had backed him with both millions of dollars and tons of material—even though, by all counts, Diem would surely have won without the assistance.

Forbes winced and mentally rubbed his eyes. What the admiral was stating, whether it was quite true or quite false or something in between, was like déjà vu to the captain. *It's like returning to Korea,* Forbes thought. *The politicians have fucked up royally, so they're calling on us again. It's unbelievable!*

"These people, a gentle sort, have cut their untrained army back by twenty thousand fighting men." *Untrained isn't even the word*, King thought. He absolutely could not tell these fine Marines that the north had increased its army by thirteen complete divisions during the same period. "They are a country of some twelve millions, gentlemen, mostly poor people. Mostly farmers." He edged closer to the table, looked down at the three lieutenants and the solitary captain. "Why the goddamned, godforsaken commies want to rule them, I don't know." *Oil*, he yelled within his own shell for an answer. "But they're blowing up villages, roads, and buildings."

"Why do we want them, then, Admiral—or it? Admiral, sir?" T.C.'s throat was so dry it nearly matched the rasp of the aging naval officer.

"We don't want it, Lieutenant. We have a treaty. A pact to assist, to protect—"

"Is this another unauthorized venture, Admiral?" Baronne interrupted.

No wardroom had ever been quieter. Admiral King shot a look at Baronne which should have melted his new silver bars. As though counting to ten, he straightened and stepped back. "Diem's army is not well trained. You will work closely with them. Show them how to combat the insurgents from the north."

"Admiral?" King's head spun to face Captain Forbes. "Sir, is this unauthorized? Because we did not hear your answer. Sir."

Bill stared at the older Marine with undisguised admiration. At that instant, for the first time since reporting to Quantico, Baronne felt that he had become a one-hundred-percent U.S. Marine. Captain Forbes had joined him—or he had joined Forbes; that didn't really matter. They were, simply, unequivocally together.

Answering the question now was as unavoidable as the grave. King, steely-eyed, hands locked behind his back, nodded slowly. "Yes. Yes, it is not authorized, not by Congress. But it is the will of the president. Our commander-in-chief has ordered it. And you will not fire upon the north, either!" He yanked the chart from the bulkhead with a ripping sound. "Gentlemen, it's not that different from the orders sending your peers in the Atlantic Fleet to Lebanon recently. They did as they were told.''

''That was a rescue mission,'' Bill remarked.

''So's this.''

''We can't shoot?'' T.C. asked.

''No. You may not.''

''Can they?'' Forbes demanded, half rising.

Admiral King recoiled at the flurry of questions. Captain Easterbrook stepped beside him. ''Yes, Captain, lieutenants—they probably will.''

''Sir?'' Bill responded. ''I'm telling you now: If I'm shot at, I'm sure as hell shooting back.''

Forbes glanced at Baronne and inwardly smiled. He looked at King. ''Begging the admiral's pardon, sir, but I trained these men. They will shoot, sir. Neither you nor I can take that out of them now.''

''Then by God, don't report it, Captain!'' the admiral exclaimed.

The Marines were rocked back in their chairs by the remark, which was, in point of fact, more than a remark: It was an order. Baronne paled. He saw that second that there was little question about the immediate future for all of them. They were being dumped into an armed foreign country and left to fend for themselves.

Forbes's steady, unflappable gaze met Bill's with a measure of reassurance.

And when Admiral King continued, it was in a voice Baronne would hear in nightmares so vivid the words came to mean nothing.

''You will be operating in and around the Mekong Delta.'' He nodded to Easterbrook, who dimmed the wardroom lights and projected a slide onto the bare bulkhead at the end of the room. ''This area.'' King pointed to the slide. ''The Mekong is heavily populated. About half to three-quarters of the country's people . . .''

King droned on, knowing but not telling them that they were, in effect, becoming refugees—running, hiding, helpless refugees with uniforms that turned them into targets. And that the real refugees in Nam were thousands of bewildered people from the north, running from the oppressive, totalitarian Ho to where no one wanted them.

He spoke of Bien Hoa, the American advisory headquarters, Saigon, and both the U.S. compound and U.S. authorities. He told shocking lies about the French losses and the projected future of the area, failed to inform the Marines that the French had won the war in Vietnam, but that the French press had slaughtered the will to follow through, helping to cause the unnecessary loss at Dien Bien Phu—later utilizing that loss to subdue and subvert military morale.

And while the admiral rasped his way through his all but rehearsed recital of falsehood, T.C., not caring a fig for how it looked, slipped from his chair and quietly left the wardroom. He walked to the aft end of the ship, where he stood at the gunnel for a while. Watching the ocean pass, he listened to the water lap at the ship's side like some monstrous spaniel. His mind had gone blank.

"Any questions?" King was finishing, immensely relieved.

"Yes sir, I think so," Greene murmured. "Who are we fighting? I mean, what does the enemy look like, Admiral?"

The admiral puffed out his cheeks, allowing air to escape between his teeth. "You aren't fighting anyone. You are advisers. The South Viets will be fighting. Not you."

Forbes came back to life. "The enemy, whoever they are, Admiral—Chinese or North Vietnamese—aren't going to be selective about who they kill."

"Captain Forbes, you are here to train, to assist a developing nation. No one, Captain, will ever know whether you kill anybody or not—nor, Captain, whether or not you are killed. Or by whom." He stepped to the table and with all his gold braid, stars and bars, and buttons clearly in evidence, leaned nearly into Forbes's face. "Is that understood, Captain—gentlemen?"

But Forbes remained staunchly unimpressed. "Okay, Admiral. How long are we gonna be in there, anyway?"

"End it soon, Captain. Soon!"

33

To Die
For A Friend

Baronne went up to the main deck where he found Chapman still at the gunnel, still staring out at the eternal, uncaring ocean below. Neither man felt a need to speak. They stood together for some five minutes, watching the shifting waters, listening to the motion of the big ship, waiting—for what, neither man knew.

Finally, when T.C. hadn't moved or spoken, Bill said softly: "You want to tell me?"

T.C. stayed motionless, except for the way his broad chest heaved slightly. It was hard to be sure, but Baronne believed his friend might have been crying.

Baronne turned back to the ocean. "My pop used to tell me that almost everyone was scared shitless." He glanced sideways at T.C. "That heroes were nuts." He chuckled softly, something he hadn't done for a long time. "I guess that made him a little nuts."

T.C. shook his head, looking at his old friend from the corners of his eyes. "It's no good, Bear. See, I can't do it. For God's sake, man, they're talking about a real war!" He turned round to face Bill squarely. "Other circumstances, an enemy of ours, one we all hate, that'd be different. But I can't go in there for bullshit, and—die!"

Baronne saw T.C.'s head slump on his chest in a mixture of determination and embarrassment. He yearned to reach out, to touch his friend, but held back. Times were changing; everything was starting to get out of hand. "You won't die, T.C. You're too lucky for that."

T.C. snorted. "Lucky? Now, you're the crazy one, Bill. In less than two years I've almost drowned—twice. I've broken my leg once and damned near got killed by those stupid fucking falling airplanes! Yeah, Baron, I'm so lucky I might just wind up a vegetable instead of getting killed!''

Bill cut him off briskly. "Damn it, T.C. !" He took a deep breath. "Are you or aren't you going to be there? When we go ashore, will you be by my side?"

T.C. provided no verbal answer. Bill sensed a shudder of shock running through his old friend from head to foot. When he had to look straight into Bill's eyes, his own eyes glazed and finally shut. Moving back with palms up, as if he'd nearly touched something hot, T.C. shook his head and walked away. With salty tears smarting, Bill saw him disappear into the night.

Forbes, who'd been standing only a few feet away in the dark shadows of the *Thetis Bay*'s flight-deck overhang, lit up again, and hid the glow in his cupped, practiced hands. When T.C. departed, the captain drifted up to Baronne as quiet as a wraith. Bill saw him approach but did not move, or speak. He saw Forbes lean back, relaxing his shoulders and sighing. "I thought your father never talked about this?"

Bill silently shook his head. His thoughts were focused entirely on T.C.

"Don't worry," Forbes said. He nodded. "He'll be there."

Restless hours later, the flight deck appeared to be consumed by HRS helicopters. The sun had yet to provide any illumination and would not until the Marines were on the beach.

Baronne stood at his assigned helicopter, observing his men as they put the last cautious touches to their gear. Sergeant Bender stood with him, checking the flight manifesto for each plane.

"Lieutenant Chapman is assigned to the second chopper, skipper." Bender said it lightly, informatively.

Bill's jaw moved, shifted, before he spoke. "Has he arrived?"

"Ah, no, sir." Sergeant Bender carefully kept from looking into his lieutenant's eyes. "Lieutenant Greene will be with Sergeant Berry; they have five men with them." He was so conversational this morning!

"And Captain Forbes?"

"He'll be with us."

Sergeant Scales walked from his helicopter to Baronne's. Scales was never shy about asking bold questions. "Will Lieutenant Chapman be here, Lieutenant?"

"Yes, Sergeant." Bill raised himself to his full height. "Of course, he will be."

As the engines of the choppers were fired up, the whirring blades crackled. They spun faster and faster, then began to smooth out. Captain Forbes moved onto the flight deck, and without a word to anyone went directly to his plane, where he stood beside Baronne. Hands lightly clasped at the small of his back, he inspected the scene with every attitude of professional interest—still without uttering a word. Once his glance flicked to Lieutenant Baronne, as if attempting to obtain some sort of reading about Lieutenant Chapman, but then he was, again, merely observing preparations.

And knowing, Bill realized, that the decision would be made for T.C.—one that would certainly wreck his career, quite possibly his reputation, if he did not appear—when they could no longer wait.

His helicopter blades had reached full warm-up. Something very important to him, although buried deep inside, was turning to liquid, when Bill caught his first glimpse of his oldest friend in the hatchway leading to the flight deck. Chapman had kept his pledge. Pausing there, fully battle-dressed, he cast a seemingly idle, professional glance at the scene.

Baronne caught Forbes' eye and Bender's. Then he strode toward T.C. at what he hoped was a casual pace.

Once there, however, beside the towheaded Marine, Bill rested his arm across T.C.'s shoulders for an instant, smiled, and spoke a few words while Walter Forbes, the sergeants, and Don Greene averted their moist eyes. And one instant later, as if nothing at all had gone wrong, the two young lieutenants were jogging to their respective helicopters.

Bender, his voice hoarse, hesitated under the cacophony of the blades. "Hell of an officer, Captain," he muttered.

"Yeah?" Forbes looked around. "Which one?"

The HRS group lifted moments later from the *Thetis Bay,* and under cover of night flew the first United States of America Marine advisors to Vietnam—flew them ashore just east of Bien Hoa.

PART FOUR

34

The Crossing

"We got ourselves two rivers to cross, Colonel."

The wounded Baronne scanned the chart carefully, making his eyes focus. "They should be low."

"Maybe, but they aren't. They're wide and pretty darn deep in spots. But Bertram has found a way across." Private Jordan, it was proving, was young, wary, and smart. Maybe it was the heady business of saving his colonel and of having been the one to find him.

Baronne's glance trailed to the three men who were finishing the burying of Sequoya. Perhaps there was something, however psychic it sounded, about being a survivor that let you take in part of the vitality of the deceased. Certainly poor Sequoya had no further use for it. Colonel Baronne looked back at a chart and placed a neat mark on it, identifying the location for the later body snatchers. If there was a "later."

"The rest of the battalion will meet us right here." Young Jordan indicated a topographical line that demonstrated they'd have some hills to climb as well. "It's Hill 479."

Baronne nodded and sought to straighten out the kinks in his back.

"How's that shoulder, Colonel?"

"Medicine burns. But I feel sure it'll be okay by the time we get back." And it was true, because, amazingly, some of his energy had returned. Now the colonel was sure they would find their way out of their mess.

And his outlook, as he sometimes realized, tended to infect his men with a similar mood. "Suppose we better go," Bertram said almost lazily, and yawned. He shoved his small shovel back into its pouch. Like Jordan, Bertram was very young, but a corporal; he was a wary individual, too, Baronne noted. As he observed the youths taking the point, he wondered if they were merely cautious about their current situation or his recuperative powers. In any case, Corporal Bertram was becoming a leader since Scales's death and his own separation from the company's remnant.

Following the youngsters, Baronne picked up his own gear and headed south, assisted by a black Marine, Private Jefferson. Jefferson carried his equipment as if it were weightless. "You're a strong son of a bitch," Bill said amiably.

"Fought in the ring as a kid." He paused to see how relaxed his colonel wanted this conversation, and added, "Worked out a lot."

"See any sight of Charley on the way back here?"

"No sir." Jefferson opened his eyes widely, winked. "Didn't care to do so, either."

Baronne chuckled. They continued on, walking as quickly as they dared, putting aside care for their noise and trying instead to put a huge gap between themselves and any enemy from behind.

Ahead at the point, Bertram suddenly raised his hand in the air. Darkness had come on and he was scarcely discernible in the illumination furnished by a faint half-moon. Jordan, Jefferson—who'd darted forward—and the other Marine, D'Antonio, set themselves promptly in a small circle, bringing their rifles up in readiness.

The colonel sidled next to Bertram. "What?"

"Movement," the corporal said just as tersely, and pointed.

All waited. Again a sound: draggingly slow, deliberate. But it seemed to break branches, seemed to step on leaves and mulch. Bertram aimed his rifle in the direction of the stealthy sounds. Jordan looked at him, back toward the noise source, again to Bertram. "I don't think it's human . . ."

Bertram snapped an irritated glance to Jordan, and saw he was serious but not, in all likelihood, talking about the supernatural. A long, slender shadow moved out before them, then stopped.

The immense tiger cat's nose had caught the odor of human being; now it was frozen, silhouetted. A momentary standoff existed. The sleek animal certainly was not afraid, simply wary, like the men. It edged a slight bit forward, again stopped, beautiful but menacing in the evening shadows.

Bertram, glancing at Jordan, nodded his head toward his rifle.

Jordan hesitated. "Not yet?"

For another instant the cat stayed put, an uninvited guest who'd arrived too early for services. Then it slowly backed off, finally turned, and bounded away in another direction.

"Whew." Bertram mopped his forehead, grinned his relief. All of them stood again, prepared to move forward once more but quietly, with renewed care.

Nam has aged them so, Baronne thought, joined by Jefferson and falling in next to him as they moved out. *They're so young, but their bodies cooperate with their maturing minds, add stoop to their shoulders, worry lines to their cheeks.* He thought of the Nam youth, glimpses of child gangs; at a distance, they were exotic, clustering flowers too rare to be taken into any house.

"Jesus, how could any kid understand all this?" Baronne asked aloud. Groggy, he saw that Bertram had stopped walking and, holding up his hand, was shouting back to him. Something about reaching the river.

Bill took several more steps forward, paused, and tried to see across the water. "I think we'd better wait until we can see."

"Maybe." Bertram and Jordan moved up the river, searching for an entry spot they had marked earlier. They returned and motioned the others to follow.

"We can get across here. We marked it earlier, because it doesn't get over our waists."

Bill nodded, searched the river again, and found only blackness. "Cong?"

"We saw nothing earlier."

Rivers were dangerous. Not the water or the snakes especially, but because they were helpless, stranded, easily killed on the water.

"Okay, let's do it, then."

Baronne shivered. The night blackness of the river might have been eternity itself as he waded in. "Water's fast, though," he responded to Sergeant Jefferson, who was helping him across. "My arm's lost its strength."

"Bullets don't help arms, Colonel. That's an old Jefferson family saying." The private grinned his encouragement.

They made it to the other side of the river finally and sat on the ground to rest, swatting mosquitoes and eating rations from green cans. Baronne was tired but feeling better. Jefferson applied more medication to his shoulder and rebandaged it before they stood and began their inland trek again, Bertram leading the way.

They were talking too much, making a racket. Baronne saw that with the river separating them from the enemy, they'd let their guard down. "Better slow down a bit and cut off the noise," he ordered.

The men obeyed, realizing they had become sloppy again. "You think we still got slopes around?" Jordan asked.

"Absolutely." Bill, looking around, saw no sign of the enemy or, as the moon was swallowed by clouds, much of anything. "They're like germs. Protect your ass . . ."

Charley was waiting for them.

The colonel lugged his exhausted body to an erect position, trying to clear his head for the next mortal combat. He'd seen the V.C. through the nocturnal blackness at the same instant as most of his small band of Marines, and he moved from man to man, quietly encouraging them to fire under control, not to panic.

"Horseshit, Colonel," Jefferson blurted, "there must be more'n a hundred of them."

Bill patted the man on the back. "We can handle 'em. Bank on that."

Without warning, young Bertram darted—low, to his right—ten yards, and began firing into one pocket of enemy troops. Again Baronne saw men spinning, dying, others running, moving out of range but not soon enough. "We got 'em now," he shouted, encouraging his men. "Jordan, the grenades." He aimed his own M-16 into the same pocket of V.C., squeezed off rounds methodically.

"Colonel. Look!"

Baronne turned quickly. It was Jefferson, incredulous. He was holding his right cheek, which paunched forward now; his right eye was closed, clotted with blood; a new hole had appeared in his helmet. Not quite believing what had happened to him, he stared wide but one-eyed at the colonel and fell over, dead.

"We got to move, Colonel, or they'll be on top of us."

Bill saw that only the river offered a way out. "We get into the water," he said to his men, "and we're goners."

Bertram peered down the midnight riverbank. "We could try that way."

"No." He said it in his smallest voice and shook his head. He understood now. He accepted that their only answer was to stand and fight. To stay, do their heroic best, and die probably. "No, dammit." Baronne fired into the Cong repeatedly. "We win this one, gentlemen, or we lose it. But here we stay, and here we're going to fight it out!"

That was okay with Charlie, too. They'd doggedly chased this split-off remnant of a former Marine battalion through the dark jungle, separating them an even farther distance from their own outfit. They marveled at the Americans' physical endurance, not fully understanding how so few men could put up such a helluva fight. But it would be a coup, they knew, if they could kill these Marines. They were the best they'd ever fought, and killing them would earn a week's rest behind the lines from their commanders.

"Bertram!" Baronne shouted, looking at the other Marine. Dizzy now, he was trying to think above the thundering gunfire of the AK-47s and SKZ carbines. He saw Bertram spin to face him and jump down from the riverbank over which he'd been shooting. "You, get out of here. We'll cover. Get back to the regiment if you can find them. Tell them what's happening." *Find T.C. if you can, damn it. He'll help us.*

"Aw, Christ, Colonel. They'll run all over you, sir!"

"Go, Bertram. That's an order."

After another look at Jordan, D'Antonio, and finally Baronne, Bertram grimaced and then ducked down. Falling back into the river, he quickly swam downstream with the flow. Baronne turned back to the enemy and began firing heavily along with the other two men. They were dipping into their last clips of ammo. He looked back once to see Bertram disappearing downriver. "At least one of us might make it."

Charlie was moving toward them. *Damn,* Baronne thought to himself. Aloud he shouted, "Jordan, to your right. Watch 'em."

Jordan spun around, but his clip had emptied. He reached down to his belt and felt for another, but there was none. He spun back to D'Antonio. "Clip," he shouted.

D'Antonio could only shake his head.

Baronne reached back to Jefferson's belt, pulled his last single clip of twenty out, and threw it to Jordan. His own rifle had emptied by now, and Jordan had the end of the ammo. "Make them good," he shouted.

Charlie was ceaseless. They could feel the Marines' absence of fire. Like a shadow of silhouetted wraiths, they rose from their cover and, lining up shoulder to shoulder, began to move steadily toward Baronne and his men, still firing their weapons.

D'Antonio made a mistake. Turning to Baronne, he stood in order to point to Jefferson's body for more ammo, and caught a fusillade of Charlie's hot copper. The bullets tore through his helmet and neck, and burst out through his face, splattering blood on Baronne's front.

Jordan whipped around and threw his useless M-16 aside. Jumping down from the riverbank, he grabbed Baronne's right arm and strongly tugged him into the river "We gotta bug, Colonel. Ain't no time for hero shit."

But Jordan's strong right arm went limp. Baronne,

searching the corporal's eyes, knew that he'd been hit. "I'm okay," Jordan yelled, knowing he wasn't. "Keep going."

Together they swam downstream, Jordan trying like hell to dog-paddle with one good arm. Baronne too felt the onset of exhaustion, and wondered, *How will we ever make it?*

35

Second Battalion

He was twenty miles away but not aware of it. The latest report from Baronne's surviving stragglers had stated so flatly that Lieutenant Colonel William Baronne had died with his men that he'd finally accepted it. But not without crying deeply inside, T.C. admitted. *God, it hurts so much.*

They'd been split up at the beginning of the massive counteroffensive the VC had unexpectedly thrown at them. Much of Bill's Third Battalion had found itself in the heart of the battle before they'd even realized they'd allowed themselves to be separated from the rest of the regiment. But by then there was nothing T.C. or the others could do about it.

That Bill had placed himself in the thick of the fight was unusual for his rank, but not for him. Rather than asking the commanders of his two rifle companies to hike back to the CP with their platoon commanders and leaving their men behind for a few hours, he'd done the thing that had helped make him so popular with his troops. He went the distance to them under the cover of night.

And, of course, Charlie struck at that very moment.

It had been a helluva battle. T.C.'s own battalion, hell, the whole regiment, had taken tremendous losses, the largest of any Marine unit up to that time.

But for now his fight was over. They'd knocked the Cong back into the jungles, knowing they'd regroup and return in a day or a week or whenever they could pull themselves together again. The Marines were licking their wounds, too. They were redigging their protective cover and restocking with mortar shells, M18A1 Claymores, rifle ammo, RPGs, launchers, hand grenades, and food. Only this time, they would have more on hand. *We damned near ran out*, T.C. marveled. *It could have been a lot closer.*

He stood quietly at his CP and listened to the night. He'd learned to do that well in Nam. He could hear things better now than during his previous tours. Well, he wouldn't really call that time in 1960 when they were advisers a real tour. But what the hell, despite his initial fears, he'd spent his time here.

It was when he returned to this godforsaken land in '65 for his second tour that he'd finally understood the usefulness of the night's many sounds. At first, some of them were pretty damned eerie, but eventually each became a telltale friend. He could smell them, he thought. The enemy. A click here, a twig there, the sound of rifles thumping against trees and ground, depending upon whether Charlie was walking or crawling.

But on this night, nothing. Just the sound of Marines moving in the dark, stacking ammo boxes, lifting out bandoleers for themselves, clicking rounds of ammo into their clips.

"Patrol coming," someone shouted.

He smiled. He'd heard them already from a hundred meters out, he guessed. They'd had to climb over the concertina wire that Fox Company had placed around the perimeter, and nobody in Nam made quite the same noise as a Marine patrol returning from a midnight search. He chuckled to himself. Night patrols were kind of like the stable horses at Griffith Park, where he and Bill had ridden as children. Couldn't force the stubborn animals away from the stable with fire, it seemed, but once you turned them for home, they were all gallop.

"Hey, they got somebody with them," the same voice shouted.

T.C. looked over at Fox Company's area. He would learn for himself what kind of Cong the patrol had captured this time. Otherwise, he mused, it'll be hours before the info gets through the chain.

"Bertram," the disheveled, exhausted Marine was

saying. "Corporal Bertram, I Company, Third Battalion, Ninth Marines. Man, my colonel needs help. Now."

The chill that swept through T.C.'s body unleashed tears he couldn't prevent.

Bertram ate five cans of rations, downed cups full of coffee, and smoked half a pack of Marlboros before he felt human again. He'd explained the battles, the losses and Bill's predicament to everyone in the pyramidal. And now they were discussing among themselves if it was feasible for a patrol to make it at night to the wounded colonel.

"We could lose the whole patrol if it's as bad there as he says," Captain McDowell said. "Then again, the colonel may be dead by now."

T.C. shook his head. "Not Baronne."

Every man gazed steadily on their colonel. They understood his relationship with the Third Battalion's CO, and were nervous that it might cloud his decision-making process.

"Regimental commander thinks we should try," Major Banner stated flatly. "S-2 thinks Charlie's pulled back for regrouping. They could have some light patrols out, but that's about it."

T.C. nodded his head. "Can we get choppers?"

The airedale, a paunchy, fighting Captain Onorato, told him it might be possible at daybreak. "But VMO-2's stretched to the max."

T.C. glanced at his watch. "Three hours." He ran his finger along the map where Bertram had drawn his trail from Baronne's last known position. "Most we can do is make it this far before then," he said.

"There's some good LZs through there," Onorato said. "I could get a chopper in here. They're mostly bombed-out rice paddies." He pointed to an area about twenty meters from where Bertram thought Baronne to be.

"Could you pick us up here?" T.C. stabbed at an area he thought they might be able to hike to in four hours.

"Then fly us to here." He moved his finger to a spot downstream of Baronne's last battlefield.

"Why not just fly straight there at first light?" McDowell asked.

"He might be trying to get here right now. If we can intercept him, stop Charlie from getting him, then it's worth a try."

Onorato nodded. Looking up into T.C.'s eyes, he saw the fire of intensity he'd seen in his colonel in the heat of battle. "We'll get him out, sir. If he's alive."

The radio crackled when they spoke, but T.C. could understand his regimental commander well enough. "You don't belong out there, Colonel. You damned well know that. You send someone else to find Baronne."

"Sorry, sir. Baronne's my friend."

Colonel John Bartles had done his job. He'd reminded T.C. of his role and commanded him by the book. Now it was time to show compassion. Time to throw the damned book away. "Good luck, Tom. Give them hell."

Fourteen men joined him, each a volunteer. The first to jump in was Bertram, who would not accept T.C.'s order to remain behind. Next was the five-man patrol that had just returned. They'd explained to their colonel that they had already scouted the area and were confident Charlie was not out there.

"But just in case," Corporal Arkin from Little Rock said, "I got us some big-time backup here." He tugged on his homemade string of grenades that were wrapped around his midsection. "Twenty-five of them," he proudly boasted. His back too was loaded with spare weaponry.

T.C. grimaced. The man was as dangerous to himself as he was to Charlie, but he was a big son of a bitch'n farmboy and nobody ever argued with him. But they did joke with him, hoping it would help ease the tension they felt. True, they were all volunteers, but that wasn't enough by itself to mask their fears.

The balance of the rescue team—that's what they were calling themselves—was comprised of men from Fox

Company who'd heard about the mission and come forward on their own. It was a proud unit, T.C. thought. It made him want to get going all the more. "Let's move out," the lieutenant colonel who didn't belong on a night patrol softly commanded.

He had no way of knowing that his friend was on the way to rescue him. Baronne's thoughts centered only on survival for himself and for Jordan. And they were in a lot of trouble. Jordan's wound was worse than they'd realized at first. Two bullets had hit him instead of just one. The first had torn his right shoulder and apparently lodged at the rotator cup, immobilizing his arm. The pain had become so severe that Jordan involuntarily cried out more than once with a whelp that would tell anyone within a hundred meters they were there.

The second bullet had hit him in the left buttocks and torn away a handful of meat, which hung on by flesh only. The combination of the two wounds, and the loss of blood from both, had weakened Jordan so much that Baronne, even with his own wounds, was now carrying him and praying they'd reach safety soon, whether it was a cave or embankment or the remainder of his battalion. Bertram was their only hope.

"Colonel, you can't make it with me."

Jordan was straddled over Baronne's shoulders and still in terrible pain, but acting like a Marine.

"Just shut up." Baronne went on fording the river, pushing against water with his powerful legs. The darkness made his splashes sound louder than they probably were, he hoped. His wounded shoulder was screaming, his broken rib was ripping at his insides. He wondered if he was stabbing himself to death. There was another involuntary, sharp moan from Jordan when the colonel reached the opposite shoreline, eased them up the embankment, and fell to his knees. Walking on them, he continued on a few yards.

"Oh God it hurts."

"We're gonna make it, Jordan. We will beat those bastards."

He summoned all his strength. Resting Jordan across his broad shoulders, forcing his body upright to his feet again, he began striding downriver along the left bank. It was grueling, pain-wracking progress.

"I'm so sorry, Colonel. I'm so terribly sorry." Jordan's voice was starting to have a delirious edge.

"Shuddup, Jordan! Save your energy."

"Colonel?"

"Yeah?" Talking was grinding words out.

"Slopes, sir. I can hear them. Straight ahead." Then he whispered. "Put me down, Colonel."

Baronne knelt down and lowered his man to the ground. Then he flattened himself out. He'd been right. Jordan was out of it. They would need to rest. But Baronne straightened up a little, raised his head up with agony, and began scouring the shadows ahead of them. "Dear Jesus." He stopped, staring. He didn't know if he'd spoken aloud. Chances were, it didn't matter.

Eight V.C., their rifles held at the ready, were walking slowly, soundlessly toward them. The colonel let the air seep out of his lungs and grasped Jordan tightly on his good leg. "Hang on, son," he muttered. "It is not over yet."

36

Rescue One

"Bravo Delta One, this is Fox Two." Onorato had contacted a Navy UH1-B helicopter gunship. Exactly what he needed, he thought.

"Go ahead, Fox Two."

Onorato explained his mission and asked for assistance.

"Roger, Fox Two. Understand your coordinates are—" The radio clipped off with only the squelch making any noise. Onorato looked around the tent with concern in his eyes. Then the radio barked again. "Mayday. Mayday. This is Bravo Delta One. We've taken a hit." Again the radio clipped off.

"Baby Jesus," Onorato muttered. Wherever BD1 was, they had probably just been victims of ground fire.

"What now?" the major from regimental S-2 asked. He had a stone-cold voice.

Onorato shook his head. "Still can't get VMO-2 on the horn, sir. They got big problems, too." But he knew a guy, he remembered, who might be able to help.

"Well, keep trying." The major left him there with his radioman and two riflemen. It could prove to be a goddamned tough day, Onorato thought.

They'd pushed hard for three hours, until the initial light from the sun cast new shadows ahead of them, producing the dancing trees that more often looked like gun-toting V.C. The men had held up well, but it was past time to give them a break. Much more of this and he'd probably lose them.

Gunny Sergeant Tyler Triplett, otherwise known to his

men as the Tripper, sidled up to Chapman after he'd rested them. "Where are we, sir?"

T.C. pulled the folded chart from his map case, scanned it, and pointed to one of the green areas. "Here. I think." He looked skyward, then back to his chart. "Stars are gone now, so it's hard to get a good fix. But from what I can see in this light, the contours match up all right."

"Funny we ain't seen or heard a single slope. I mean, after a full week of fighting them bastards and all."

T.C. hoped Tripper's words wouldn't turn out to be a bad omen. "Keep your ears open for a chopper, Gunny. Captain Onorato should be here within the hour."

"Goddamn, where'd you get that?" Onorato asked the crew chief he'd called earlier for help. He was standing fifty feet from an old Sikorsky that had arrived in Nam probably five or six years before. "An antique auction, maybe?"

"You don't want it, Captain?" Staff Sergeant Brandon Guiles teased. He was proud of his HUS. It had taken some real talent and a lot of make-do to keep it going.

"If that's all you got, we gladly accept."

Guiles smiled. "HMM 362 left a half dozen of these babies behind in '62. They were flown up to Da Nang when the squadron left Nam. We've been cannabalizing four of them to keep two flying. Staff officers have been using them to get into the field for recon. We get them there and back pretty safely, too." He laughed lightly. "I always figure the V.C. don't waste groundfire on them 'cause they figure they're gonna fall out of the air anyhow."

Onorato squinted appreciatively. "By God, Guiles, you ain't changed one damned bit. Let's go for it." He was followed into the chopper by four riflemen, who carried enough firepower with them to chop down a good-sized forest, he thought.

* * *

They were in a lot of trouble and things were not getting better, Baronne knew. *Damn, if I just had a radio,* he decided. *Yeah, Mr. Colonel, what then?* He shook his head to clear his mind of the wandering thoughts. They did him no good at all. They'd been fortunate earlier when the eight V.C. had stopped short of their position and turned into the river to cross it at that point. *To be that close and survive—or was it to be that close and not be able to kill that made me so itchy when they passed through?* he wondered.

Who cared? Jordan had passed out from his wounds, a blessing of sorts, he thought. At least he can't feel the pain now. But they would have to move downstream from there, and soon, he told himself. If they were to survive, both men would have to be attended to by the medics pretty damned quickly. He couldn't see his backside, but wouldn't have been surprised to learn that the first stages of gangrene had begun.

He leaned over Jordan and gingerly tugged his jacket, trying to pull it back to see his wound, but it had dried to the blood-soaked skin. It would have to wait. The matter of how he was going to pick the corporal up again also crossed his mind. It was a question he wasn't yet prepared to answer.

He fell back to the ground, still exhausted, wondered if it was safe enough to grab a few winks. It wasn't a decision he would have to make. His eyes had already closed, his mind already shut down.

Lieutenant Colonel William Baronne finally passed out.

Tripper stopped the short column of Marines. He'd heard something. T.C. asked with his eyes only, since they'd agreed to remain as quiet as possible. They were alongside one of the thousands of miles of South Vietnam's waterways, but hadn't yet gotten close. On the chart, the river was too open at the banks, increasing the possibility of exposure to the V.C.

Tripper's gaze was glassy, but his ears were tuned to what could be a threat. All of the riflemen had already spread out in a circle around Tripper and their colonel. Tripper raised his right arm and pointed in the direction of the river. T.C. determined before any of them that it was one of the heavily armed V.C. amphibious tanks that had been so prolific around Khe Sanh but nowhere else. If that damned machine found them, they'd be in a whole lot of trouble.

Tripper wanted to get to the river and take on the enemy. T.C. shook his head almost wildly. "No," he croaked. "Not our mission."

At least the sound was moving upriver and not in their direction. They knelt down until it passed, wondering just how many meters through the thick foliage they had been from the amphib.

Then another sound. "Oh my God, not now," T.C. moaned. It was Onorato and he was damned close to them.

Tripper's head whirled around at the sound of the chopper, and then swung back to the river. The tank was returning. He'd seen only one of them, but remembered that the firepower on it was enough to blast any chopper out of the sky. Three machine guns were mounted above what was at least a 57mm recoiless boom-boom. He'd assumed the ChiCom machine guns were modified .30- and .50-caliber guns, used for antiaircraft. They'd wreak terrible hell on the chopper.

T.C. jumped to their radioman. "Can you get the chopper?"

Corporal Dearborn, a kid from Boston, punched in the AIRTAC line and called out. "Marine helicopter, can you read this?"

"Christ, who's that?" the pilot asked Onorato.

"Our guys. They have us in sight."

They were flying at treetop level, a tactic the HUS pilot had learned was safer than cruising at higher altitudes. He hadn't yet seen the V.C. amphib.

Onorato punched his mike button. "This is Rescue One. Go ahead, Fox."

In the back of the chopper, four riflemen sat at the ready, all nervously keyed for anything to happen. As ground-pounders, they preferred flying in the swifter, newer Chinooks, but not when they were over enemy territory. Falling out of the sky, they believed, left them small odds for survival. They would prefer to take their chances on the ground.

"We've got you in sight. Turn back now. Turn back now. Enemy tank on ground at the river."

That's all the pilot needed to hear. Having flown staff officers for the past six months, with his primary mission to keep them alive, his reactions to such messages had been tuned to function even before his brain could give him the command. Before Dearborn had uttered the second turn-back command, the HUS was headed 180 degrees in the opposite direction and damned near down into the trees. In the back, the riflemen had cocked their weapons, released their safeties, ready for the battle that would have to wait.

"Thanks, Rescue. Let us know when he's gone."

"Christ," Tripper blurted. "Now we got problems." The tank wasn't going to stop at the river's edge. It had left the water and was pushing through the jungle straight at them.

"I brought this," Corporal Arkin announced. He held up one RPG 40mm antitank rocket-propelled grenade.

"How do you carry all that shit?" Tripper asked.

Arkin smiled broadly. "Piggyback, Gunny. Kinda like bales of hay. Want me to get him or not?"

Tripper looked to T.C., who nodded. They'd have to if they were to continue their mission. He turned back to Arkin. "Two men need to go with you," he said quietly, hoping for volunteers he figured to never see alive again.

Pfc. Blackstone from Grants Pass, Oregon, and Pfc. Jacobsen from Brooklyn, New York, stepped up. "Let's go," they said.

"Rescue One, Fox One, over," Dearborn radioed as they slunk away.

"Go ahead."

"Can you hover, wait for us a few minutes?"

"Roger, but be snappy."

Arkin and his two men edged slowly through the foliage. They could feel the light of the more open waterway ahead of them and hear the tank, which seemed to be idling at the moment. "There." Jacobsen pointed. "It's stuck."

"Hung up on a tree or something," Blackstone said.

Arkin knelt down, placed the collapsible launcher on his shoulder, and aimed at the amphib. This would be a great chapter for his war stories and he wanted it. But before he could fire, Blackstone grabbed his arm. "Hold it," he whispered hoarsely. "They're getting out of it."

They watched while four V.C. climbed up through the hatch at the back of the tank, just behind the gun turret. The first of them reached up and armed the ChiCom machine guns. But then he turned and jumped off the tank along with the others.

"Jesus, they're gonna piss," Jacobsen said.

"Just like us," Blackstone chuckled. The Marines looked at each other, grabbed up their M-16s, and zeroed in on the V.C.

"Now," Arkin commanded. He too had taken up his rifle. They fired full clips, releasing their pent-up anxieties as well as sixty rounds of ammo.

The four V.C. fell dead to the ground.

Jacobsen stood, but Blackstone pulled him back down. "Hold it. There may be more of them in the tank." But nothing moved.

Arkin patted Jacobsen on the shoulder. "We'll cover you."

"Aw, Christ," Tripper moaned. "They've bought it. Jesus damned Christ."

T.C. shook his head. "No, they haven't. Not unless the V.C. have M-16s."

Then they heard the sound of the tank cranking up and

backing away from them. "They're leaving," Corporal Dearborn volunteered, but he was wrong.

Blackstone burst out of the trees. "We got the damned tank, Colonel. I mean, we own it, sir." It felt good to win one.

"C'mon back," Dearborn radioed Rescue One.

37

A Promise Kept

He wasn't sure if it was the heat or the light from the intense sun, but it wasn't important. He would have to get his butt out of there, he knew, or lose it forever.

He looked at his arm for the watch that had been stripped from him by passing V.C. a century or more ago. He shook his head to remind himself of where he was and what he had to do.

Jordan was awake, too. *Not very alive, but awake*, he thought.

"We've gotta go," he muttered through parched, cracked lips. He was worried that they may have been spotted or would be anyway. They were in an open part of the river now, with the jungle behind them. They hadn't noticed that in the darkness of the previous night or they would have moved on, wouldn't they? *Probably not*, he answered himself, remembering how exhausted they'd been.

"Can't move," Jordan moaned. "I've tried, but I can't move. Hurts to talk," he added.

"Got to." Baronne tried to stand, but his stiff, angry legs complained. His back too wasn't cooperating, and he'd lost movement of his right arm. *Dammit, William, move it*. But his muscles wouldn't obey his command. The wound had finally taken its toll. Bill Baronne, you're in a helluva lot of trouble, he admitted.

He fell off his knees backward to his butt and stared at the water that moved slowly in front of him. "What now?" he asked aloud. *Is this what I was saved for? Did all those men die so that I could just end up here and be some goddamned Charlie's target?*

"Colonel?"

He turned to Jordan. "Yeah."

"I hear them again. V.C., sir."

Baronne swiveled his head around painfully to the left and right, up and down the river. He couldn't see anything, couldn't hear anything. "What do you hear?"

"A tank, sir. Upriver."

Bill craned his neck. His hearing wasn't the same as it was a decade ago. Too much shooting, he thought. One too many gun blasts.

"Another one, sir. Downriver. Headed this way."

"Oh, my God." He struggled to move his body next to Jordan. They'd have to pull themselves into the brush and duck out of sight. He looked over at the woody area. It was fifty meters, he judged. "C'mon, Jordan. We can't let them kill us now. Not this way."

Together they crawled, tugged, painfully headed for the thicker foliage, and used up the last of their remaining energy.

The tank worked better than they thought it would. With Blackstone alongside him, Jacobsen was driving, trying to figure out with one of the other men how to operate the 57mm cannon. Arkin sat outside on the tank's flattop, his RPG and launcher resting against the turret. Tripper had elected to ride inside the tank with his head sticking out the hatch. T.C. had joined Onorato in the chopper, taking four of their men with him. The balance of the team sat on the tank with underbrush stuck into their helmets and belts, a weak effort at camouflage. They were happy to be off their feet, but nervous about being so exposed.

Rescue One zigzagged with large sweeping *s* turns toward their selected target area in an effort to spot Bill Baronne and his men if they'd made it this far on foot. They kept the captured tank in sight at all times.

"Hey, Sarge, tank coming. In the water." Downstream they could see another V.C. amphib moving toward them, fording the water as they were.

Tripper thought the tank was at about one thousand

meters away. "Shit, they must be patrolling this river all the time."

"What'll we do?"

Tripper let the ideas race through his mind. *They won't know we're Marines. That's good. If we fire this thing and miss, we're dead asses, that's not good.* "Move this thing closer to the water's edge," he commanded. They might have to bug out into the trees.

"Sarge," Blackstone interrupted. "We got this thing figured out."

Arkin also contributed his idea. "I can jump off here and when they pass by, I'll blast them."

Tripper made his decision and leaned down through the hatch. "Load this sonuvabitch and figure out your shot." He turned to Arkin. "How far can you shoot that thing?"

"Hell, from here if you want."

"No. Wait until we're real close." He glanced at the balance of men on the tank. They looked too much like Americans, he decided. "Everyone else off, now. Hucklebuck Gyrenes, we got work to do here."

Dearborn was one of the men who left the tank. As soon as he hit the ground, he was calling Rescue One.

"Damn it," T.C. muttered. He was regretting their capture of the tank.

Onorato pointed downstream, and then motioned they could fly around the area and come up behind the second tank. He was aware that the V.C. amphibs were not capable of covering their backside while firing forward. Either they would end up being aerial decoys while Tripper's men fired at the tank, or the men in the back would be able to fire from the helicopter and maybe inflict some damage to the infantry that always seemed to be with tanks. It's a long shot, he thought, but they would have to try it.

"Men on the ground," the crew chief shouted. He was pointing to the second tank, the one downstream.

T.C. could see them now, too. About a dozen of them walking alongside the tank, probably tired of riding on the cumbersome vehicle.

"Men on the ground," the pilot called to Dearborn. "Charlie's walking with that tank."

Dearborn shouted to Tripper, but he couldn't hear over the sound of the lumbering amphib. The two tanks were drawing closer together.

"Go!" Tripper shouted to Arkin.

Arkin leaped from the tank to the hard ground along the water's edge, twisting his right ankle when he landed. But the sprain didn't slow him down. He immediately knelt into his firing position. The V.C. tank was only two hundred meters away and he could worry about his damned foot later. "Easy shot," he said, his eye glued to the sight.

But the tank had spotted him, too, and someone aboard had finally figured out that these were not brothers in arms.

The barrel of the cannon on the V.C. tank came down and aimed. Tripper pulled his .50-caliber around and began firing the first shots.

The twelve V.C. soldiers ran to the water's edge and began firing at Arkin, but he got off his RPG before diving to the ground and flattening himself.

Arkin's rocket sailed quickly through the air and smacked the tank between the turret and the hull, a perfect shot. The penetrating nose burst through the metal and separated the turret from the body of the tank.

Then Tripper's men fired their 57mms and watched while the shell hit the V.C.'s hull, impacting it hard enough to push it over into the water and causing it to explode at the midsection.

Rescue One entered from behind the tank with eight Marines firing at the V.C. infantry, but his effort was useless. The firepower from the helicopter had cut them down just as quickly as Onorato had suspected they might.

"Colonel," Jordan began but stopped, it hurt so to talk.

"Yeah?" Baronne too could hardly speak. His throat,

lips, and tongue had swollen so badly he wondered if he'd ever be able to open his mouth again.

"That's a helluva battle out there," Jordan squeaked.

"Yeah, it sure as hell is." If he could only figure out through his blurred vision who it was and why two V.C. tanks were fighting each other, he might be happier about it all. *At least,* he told himself, *V.C. are dying and not us.*

When the smoke cleared, Tripper and T.C. were happy to find that none of the Marines had been injured except for Arkin, who'd sprained his right ankle when he jumped from the amphib. Onorato had directed the pilot to land the chopper alongside the shore, where the enemy tank lay on its side, and was standing at the water's edge wondering when the damned war would ever end.

"No sign of Colonel Baronne," Tripper told him. "We popped out at the river upstream and not a sign of anybody from there to here."

T.C. hadn't seen anything from the air either.

Onorato joined them. "Maybe, Colonel Baronne's—"

T.C. darted a hard look at him. "I don't want to hear it," he said. "He's alive and I'm gonna find him."

"Yessir."

"How's the chopper's fuel supply?"

"Not much left. About a half hour's worth before we gotta head back."

"Then let's search some more."

When he realized it was T.C. talking out there, Baronne started to crawl to them. But no matter what his will screamed at him to move, he simply couldn't inch out more than a few feet and that wasn't enough to get him out of the brush. His hands clawed the dirt while he willed his toes to push him. It just wasn't working and he couldn't understand why not. Hell, hadn't he done this same thing playing football with T.C. ? *Oh, damn it,* he screamed inside. *Damn it to hell.* Had he become delirious?

Jordan was out of it, too. His strength had left him altogether and he'd fainted in the Nam heat, possibly forever, Baronne thought. *And I'm next.* It was hard to accept. To have fought so hard to survive, to have gotten this far, and to have seen T.C. without being able to get to him, yell at him even.

And when he saw the chopper lift off the ground and fly away, his heart gave up and his head crashed to the hot, firm Vietnam soil.

Tripper turned Charlie's tank around and headed back upstream. They'd take one last check upriver before hitting the surface as ground-pounders again. They'd probably give up the search, he'd heard someone say, and return to the Second Battalion's CP.

Since Tripper had a radio in the tank that worked fairly well, once they figured it out, Dearborn remained near the destroyed V.C. tank, which was pretty near the site where they'd thought Colonel Baronne had been. He cautioned them to stay out of sight for fear another amphib might cruise by. Two of the riflemen and Arkin, who could hardly walk on his sprained ankle by now, also remained. The men understood they could end up bivouacing for the night, so Arkin assigned the Pfc. with the thick glasses to secure them a safe spot.

"Rescue One," Dearborn called to Onorato. "This is Fox Rescue."

"Go ahead." Onorato's eyes were glued to the fuel gauge. They had to head back in another five minutes.

"We have the fox. Repeat, we have the fox. And, Colonel, he needs a vet pretty badly."

Again the pilot had the plane flying in the opposite direction before the radio message had ended. He could feel the tension in his ship. It was the kind that came with the excitement comrades felt when victory was theirs, when the world seemed so, so right.

When the chopper hovered close to the ground alongside the river, T.C. jumped out, nearly flying the distance to earth. He ran to the brush where Dearborn and the others were pointing. When he got there he couldn't believe his eyes.

William Baronne was a mess. And his back was in serious trouble. *But he's alive*, he yelled to himself. "Get a stretcher," he called out. "Now!"

It was already on the way.

T.C. bent down over Jordan, opened his right eye with his fingers. He could see life in there. "Take this man first," he commanded. It was the Marine way, and by God he wasn't going to change that. He'd carry his friend himself if he had to.

The men with the stretcher carefully placed Jordan on the canvas and dashed back to the chopper. Then they returned for Baronne.

When they arrived, T.C. was already on his knees, brushing the grit from his friend's face. Baronne's nose and eyes were clouded with Nam soil. His lips cracked so badly T.C. thought they'd never heal.

It was the absence of strength in his friend that frightened him the most, though, a sign that his body and his fighting soul had finally given in.

Baronne was carefully moved to the stretcher and lifted gently, the men understanding T.C.'s love for his friend. Off to the side, Tripper, the veteran with too many years of war in his makeup, surprised himself with a tear.

"T.C. ?" Baronne croaked. He couldn't believe it, but there he was. Or was it just an apparition for him before he died?

"We've got you now, Bear. Hang in there." He grasped Bill's hand while they walked him to the chopper, its blades still turning, ready to lift them to safety, and felt Baronne's weak squeeze. It was a signal that things were going to be okay. T.C. glanced down, saw Bill close his eyes, and allow his parched lips to crease the weakest of smiles. Then he remembered what Baronne had told him so many years before.

. . . *The* Thetis Bay *rolled smoothly, quietly in the early morning swells. Bill's arm was around T.C.'s shoulders. He looked his best friend in the eye, smiled quickly, and spoke softly. "C'mon, T.C. Stick with me . . ."*